A Labor of
Love

Leah Omar

Fulton Books, Inc.
Meadville, PA

Published by Fulton Books 2021

ISBN 978-1-64952-472-0 (paperback)
ISBN 978-1-64952-473-7 (digital)

Printed in the United States of America

To my husband and kids, who had to listen to me say, "Just one more chapter" a million times last year, and who claim to still love me.

To all those brave enough to love who they love.

And to my mom, whose support got me to this point. (And who will make sure Dad skips the sex scenes)

CHAPTER 1

In the moment of crisis, the wise build bridges and the foolish build dams.

—Nigerian Proverb

PETER

My mom told me you're leaving. Do you have time to see me first? We need to talk.

"You've got to be kidding me." I look up from my phone and wipe at my eyes.

How did my life get this messed up? Peter hasn't answered a text or reached out in nearly a month. Now he wants to talk? And today of all days. It's a day I've been dreading since agreeing to my dad's half-brained idea—a hospital volunteer position in Tanzania. I want to run downstairs and beg my parents to let me stay. I know I said I would go, but I'm in full-on panic attack mode, and I don't think I can.

"Kate, if you aren't down here in five minutes, we're not going to get to the airport on time!" my mom's voice screeches from downstairs.

I'm frozen in front of the mirror, staring at my reflection. I'm not sure I know who I am anymore. I don't trust my decisions. Honestly, I haven't trusted my gut for too long as it's betrayed me one too many times. I resist the urge to run down the stairs and tell my parents that I'm backing out of this entire endeavor.

"I'll be right down, Mom. I want to throw on a sweater."

I'm a dreadful packer. What do people even wear in Tanzania? I know one Tanzanian—my sister, Maria. She isn't actually my sister, but she did live with my family for an entire year during my senior year of high school, and she's the closest person to a sibling I've ever known. She dressed like me, though, in fact, she mostly wore my clothes, so maybe she isn't a good reference point for Tanzanian attire.

"Just remember, it gets chilly at night!" my mom yells from downstairs.

By everything I'm hearing, I'll need clothes that span all temperatures. To complicate matters even more, even though it's summer in Minnesota, Tanzania is in the southern hemisphere, and it's winter there. However, Maria tells me it never really gets that cold.

"Hey, sweetie, I'm going to start loading your bags in the car." The low-pitched creak of my bedroom door reverberates, as my dad walks in and grabs my lone suitcase. I'm glad I packed light, as I'll mostly be wearing scrubs all day. Plus, I already know I will have zero social life while there and will have little purpose for excess clothes.

I look at my dad, and in a moment of panic, I lose all control and allow the words to pour out of me. "I don't want to go. Please don't make me go."

As I breathe in, a sob escapes without my permission. I've never been one to embrace change. That's one of the reasons I stayed with my high school boyfriend and chose a university in my hometown. Taking risks has never been one of my personality traits, and this all feels like a significant risk.

"Kate"—my dad lowers the suitcase to the floor and places his hands on his hips. His intense gaze is too much for me, and I drop my eyes to my feet. He lowers his voice as he turns his head to the side—"I know this is a change, and I know you're scared, but you have to move on with your life at some point. You can't hide in this bedroom for the rest of your life."

I close my eyes and tap the bridge of my nose, hoping it will prevent the tears from falling.

"Please, Dad. I'll get over it. I'll be happier. I'll come out of my room more. Please don't make me go. Please I am begging you." My words drip with desperation.

I open my eyes, and Dad walks toward me. The wood floor groans under his weight. He rests his hands on my shoulders. "Kate, going to Tanzania will be good for you. Maria and Noor are expecting you, as is the hospital staff. More importantly, if you aren't downstairs in two minutes, you're going to have to deal with your mother." My dad's strong hands squeeze my shoulders, and my teeth scrape against my bottom lip.

The reality of his words hit me in the chest like a bolt of lightning. I know he's right. I nuzzle my head into my dad's neck and breathe in the Old Spice aftershave that lingers on his skin. The dam of tears opens. For the past month, I've been numb, but now the tears pour out of my eyes. I pat at my dad's shirt, where I left a wet mark from my tears the size of a quarter.

He puts his hand under my chin and tilts my head up to look at him. "Kate, Mom and I love you. You're going to be fine. Tanzania will be good for you, you'll see. If it's miserable, you can always come home. Give it a chance."

My dad picks up my suitcase, and his blue eyes pierce into mine. "Now I'm going to take your suitcase downstairs, so please clean up your face and come down." Dad's firm but tender hand pulls my chin up to look at him, once again. He wipes away my tears and gently pats my wet cheek with his hand.

I take one more glance in the mirror, and my eyes are puffy, and my ordinarily vibrant blue eyes look dull and tired. I pull my long blond locks into a messy bun on top of my head. I put my hand up to my cheek and pinch it, trying to add some color as my skin has become pale. I pull on the waist of my jeans that now hang on me. I inhale sharply, wishing the tight ball that lives in my stomach would dissipate. I like feeling numb better than facing the pain of the past few weeks. But now the pain sits in my stomach, weighing me down, causing me to feel everything I've tried to ignore before.

I'm a planner by nature, and going to Tanzania for four months after graduating from my master's in science in nursing and midwifery is not part of the plan. I can barely catch my breath, and I want to throw my yellow and blue comforter over my head and live in my childhood bedroom for the rest of my life. I know I agreed to this, but now I want to hide.

I yell through my open door, trying to sound more put together than I feel. "I'm ready to go. I just need to throw a couple more things into my bag."

I take one more look around my room and remind myself that I'm coming back and that this is only for a few months. I have many emotions tied up with this house; in fact, it's the only house I've ever known. As I walk down the stairs, the wood floors beneath me scream out rhythmically in protest, with each step I take. I feel much younger than my twenty-four years. I want to put on my pajamas and sit between my mom and dad, drink grape soda with a bag of popcorn, and never face the realities of life.

"Are you sure you have everything? Passport, visa paperwork, phone?"

"Mom, I have triple-checked everything." I avoid looking at her, as I know my eyes are still puffy, and my mom has never been a fan of public displays of emotion.

"Oh, honey, we're going to miss you." Her hand rests firmly on my lower back as I bend over to throw in some last-minute travel items.

"Let's go, you two. It's rush hour, and the news is saying security lines have been terrible. Let's get Kate on that airplane."

I should be offended at how eager my dad seems to want to get rid of me, but I know he is doing this because he thinks it's best for me. I'm going to miss my parents. It's only ever been the three of us. I guess doing what's best for me means facing the outside world and leaving my parent's house. I haven't lived at home for the past six years, but I stayed in the same city to go to university and graduate school, so I have only ever been a short car ride away. Tanzania is on the other side of the world. And from everything I've been reading about where I'll be living, it will no doubt feel like another world.

We take the parkway to the airport, and I'm happy my dad has chosen the scenic route, even though the highway would be faster. I lean my elbow against the car window and place my face in the palm of my hand. We put up with six months of winter in Minnesota because of beautiful and warm June days like today. The trees that cover the parkway are entirely in bloom, and I can smell the fresh-cut grass from my open window as a city worker mows around the trails.

As a child, I spent my summers in Minneapolis with my best friend, Jane, going on raft rides down the creek. Once we were old enough, our parents let us haul the raft the few blocks on our own, and if we were lucky, some of our classmates would also be at the creek, and we'd ride our rafts down the small rapids in a large group. We would bring a few dollars and stop at the ice cream shop at the end of the creek before the water fell abruptly into the falls and then drained into the Mississippi River. I have many happy memories growing up here. I place my hand on my stomach as the heaviness returns, and I realize I didn't even tell Jane I was leaving.

"Be sure to call or text when you get to Amsterdam. You only have a two-hour layover there. I would work your way to the gate right away. You'll need to clear customs there before your next flight." My dad glances at me through the rearview mirror.

"It will be the middle of the night in Minneapolis, so I'll just shoot you and Mom a text."

"Fine. Also, I set up your phone with an international plan, so call or text whenever you want. You won't have internet, though, kiddo."

"Got it, Dad."

We arrive at the airport after a twenty-minute drive. The drive goes by too fast, and I take deliberate slow breaths, vowing that I can make it through the next few minutes without crying again.

"Maria and Noor will be at the gate once you get to Dar es Salaam. Also, do you have that piece of paper with their address? You may need that once you land."

I grab my bag. "I have everything."

"Okay, good. Do you—"

"John, Kate has everything. We need to let her go." Mom chuckles and puts her hand on his.

9

"Kate, we love you. We know this will be a culture shock for you, but Maria will take excellent care of you. This trip will be life-changing, and you'll finally get to meet Maria's fiancé, Noor." My dad holds my shoulders as he looks at me.

My mom pulls me into an embrace. "You are going to come back with more midwifery experience than you ever could have gained from staying here." She then lowers her voice into almost a whisper. "And it will be good for you to be somewhere else on *that* day." She gives me a knowing wink, and it feels like a laser beam directly to my heart, as I pick up on her not so subtle reference.

My dad reaches in for one last hug. "We're proud of you, kid. We hope this experience will be everything you hope it will be. You're going to be fine, Kate. You'll be better than fine."

My mind flashes back to one of my first memories. I was five years old, and my dad sat me down to tell me that the baby sister my family was planning for and anxiously awaiting died during childbirth. Maybe I always would have been a homebody, but that moment in my family's life seemed to have changed the trajectory of everything. I spent the next several years, unwilling to leave my parent's side. My mom was always embarrassed by how much I struggled with branching out into the world. My baby sister dying during childbirth is also what fueled my eventual interest in midwifery.

"I love you, guys. I'll text as soon as I'm in Amsterdam."

I grab my suitcase from my dad, give them both a reassuring nod of my head, and turn my back to walk inside the Minneapolis— St. Paul International Airport. I enter the airport, where my parents can't see me, before hot tears once again fall down my face. I almost get trampled several times as travelers hurry by me in every direction, and I try to keep my head down so as not to draw attention to how big of a mess I am. I maneuver around people as I check in and send my bags to my final location, Dar es Salaam, Tanzania. I have a total of three flights, and this will be the farthest I've ever been, and my only time ever traveling alone.

I find my gate and pull out my phone, yet it's only a prop because I'm much more interested in the movement around me—of the people coming and going. I've always loved people-watching at an airport. Where are these people going? What is their story? Are they happy? Are they running away from heartache? I wonder if anyone would glance at me and accurately guess my story.

I start scrolling through my phone and open up my social media apps. I realize that most of my friends here don't even know I am leaving the country. I am no longer friends with Jane or Peter on social media, but we have mutual friends. As I scroll, I am sometimes faced with pictures of them and immediately know more about their lives than I prefer. I have no desire to keep up with them. I delete all my apps and vow to start over and live in the present and quit stalking Peter and Jane online.

"Now boarding flight 1251 to Amsterdam. We are going to start with those needing extra assistance or those traveling with young children." Just like that, all three hundred people who are on this flight stand up and get in line. I look at my ticket—sky priority, seat 11A. Having two doctors as parents has its advantages.

I board the plane and put my backpack on the floor under the seat in front of me. My phone buzzes, and I glance down to see Maria's face.

MARIA

Noor and I can't wait to see you, Kate! Text me when you land in Dar. Noor will circle the airport, and I'll meet you at baggage claim. You'll clear customs in Kilimanjaro. Dr. Andrew (who you are going to absolutely love) said he'll reach out as well.

As if on command, a new email displays on my phone, and it's from Dr. Andrew.

DR. ANDREW

Kate, I wanted to wish you safe travels on your journey to Tanzania. I am especially excited to have your expertise and partnership while you are here.

Building a hospital in rural Tanzania has been my dream since being a young boy, and I hope you find your accommodations and the hospital up to your standards. Do not hesitate to reach out to me as you journey to this side of the world.

I force myself to smile at the messages from Maria and Dr. Andrew. Maria has told me so much about him that I feel like I already know him. Everything I know, however, is through Maria's eyes, and this was the first contact I've had directly with him. I lean against the window, shut my eyes, and the tears trickle out of them. The bright lights from the tarmac shine on my face, and as I feel the wheels lift off the runway, I let out a sob that sounds so foreign that it takes a moment for me to realize it came from me. I open my eyes as the downtown skyline disappears below. It feels like a bowling ball sits on my chest as my mind wanders to Peter and then Jane.

For some reason, I think back to my favorite high school literature teacher. I don't remember what book we were discussing, but he told the class that hate and love are nearly the same emotion. He said that it's indifference that we should fear. I remember rolling my eyes, thinking that hate and love are nothing alike. Now I think I understand what he meant. Hate and love take up the same amount of energy, and I hate Peter and Jane with every fiber of my being.

I feel the worst kind of lonely. I look to my right, and the plane is full. There are couples happily chatting, kids crying, and flight attendants starting to serve beverages. Yet even though people surround me, I've never felt more alone.

Chapter 2

Chance all; see what destiny yields.

—Angolan Proverb

I don't know if sleep deprivation can kill a person, but when I arrived in the village, I was sure I was going to die from it. It took over twenty-four hours to get to Tanzania, and when I finally arrived in Dar, it was a ten-hour drive to get to this remote village. I'm not talking about smooth blacktop, with bright-yellow lines in the center of the road either. Instead, the roads were bumpy, with some pavement, a lot of dirt, and at times, we'd get stuck behind donkeys carrying a wagon. I have an overwhelming sense of being out of control of the situation, and the farther I travel from home, the more I realize how alone I am.

After a full day where all I did was sleep, Maria sits at the table in my bungalow, waiting for me to get ready so she can show me around the hospital. I pull on a pair of jeans and my favorite Prince T-shirt, as I know I'll change into hospital scrubs when I get there. I peek out and smile as Maria bops her head to imaginary music, as she sits at the table and scrolls through her phone.

My chest feels less hollow, almost like there is a working organ in it again, being this near Maria. She makes being far from home a lot easier to bear, and although I have my own bungalow while I'm here, she and Noor are next door, less than five feet away. My mind goes back and forth a few times daily on whether I should be here. At least once a day, I consider calling my dad and telling him I need to come home. I probably would have already done that if going home didn't involve Noor and Maria driving me ten hours back to Dar. I want to be brave, but inside, my stomach is in knots, and I feel very unsure of myself.

"Thanks for waiting, Maria. Do I look okay?" I put my arms out and shrug my shoulders.

Maria looks up from her phone and wrinkles her face. "Is that your shirt from high school?" Her chest shakes as she laughs, and her long braids hit the back of the chair.

"The one and only. It's my favorite." I look down and admire my shirt, although the material is wearing a bit thin. "Seriously, though, do I look, I don't know, professional enough?"

"Kate, you look perfect. The years have been good to you."

I smile. The years have been good for both of us. Maria has always been stunning, but now, six years after the last time we saw each other in person, she's absolutely radiant. She's a tiny thing, with solid muscles and curves and the biggest and most beautiful eyes I've ever seen. Her hair is much longer than it was before and hangs mid-way down her back in tight, meticulous braids. And me, well, when I said goodbye to Maria as an eighteen-year-old, I was tall and thin, and my body refused to develop. I finally grew much needed curves and am no longer mistaken for a teenage boy.

"Well, this is the best I have for today, so it will have to do." I glance down at my outfit again and chuckle that I'm paying homage to one of Minnesota's finest.

As we step outside, the wind comes up, and loose hairs fly out of my top bun. The hospital bungalows all sit in a line directly in front of the hospital, and I realize it creates a wind tunnel effect. I look up at the hospital and to the staff bungalows that surround us, and it's the only part of the entire village that looks like it hasn't been around for thousands of years.

Even though I'm several inches taller than Maria, I can barely keep up with her and her quick steps. Maria speaks almost as quickly as she walks.

"I'm sorry that you didn't have more time to get settled in before bringing you here. But the hospital has been busy, and our staff can't keep up. You are a welcome addition."

Maria speaks almost too fast for comprehension as she points out things in the hospital. I look around, and everything looks and smells brand-new. The walls are white and bare, and I can smell the fresh paint that still lingers in the air. The space is small but welcoming, with a long hallway and doors on each side. People rush by me, mainly in scrubs. Maria wears her smart clothes as she's the hospital's administrator and does all the financial work.

"In this corner of the hospital, Dr. Eric performs orthopedic and general surgeries. He's with us for a few months and is from South Africa. This wing is only a year old." Maria's arms flail about as she points to different sections of the hospital. "Originally, Dr. Andrew's vision was only to be labor and delivery, but with some extra funding, the hospital was expanded. Dr. Eric and Dr. Andrew are the only physicians on staff. There are a couple of office staff like me, and then Noor and a few others are nurses, and the rest are learning on the job." Maria leans toward me and whispers, "We've recently identified additional funding opportunities, and I'll be working on proposals that will help with the hospital's sustainability."

We climb a set of stairs that lead us to the top floor, and I laugh as Maria runs up the stairs, skipping every other step. I have forgotten how much energy she has and that she never stops moving.

"The second floor is dedicated to prenatal care and labor and delivery. We have one operating room, and the rest of the rooms are exam or delivery rooms. We have one nurse anesthetist, who spends a week a month at the hospital, but Dr. Andrew and Dr. Eric also need to step in occasionally. As I told you in my emails, this entire hospital is Dr. Andrew's vision. His family and my family are lifelong friends, and I've known him since we were both young children back in Dar. Over there is the waiting room." Maria points to an open room with a desk out front and a few women sitting and waiting. The woman behind the counter waves us over.

Maria slows down her words. "Editha, I would like you to meet Kate."

The woman smiles but stares ahead at one of the exam room doors. "It is very nice to meet you, Kate."

Editha then looks at Maria. "If Kate is able, can she go to exam room 3? Bupe and Alvin have been waiting, and Dr. Andrew is delivering a baby in exam room 5 and will be a while."

Maria places her hand on my elbow. "Kate, are you ready to suit up and see a patient?"

I look at Editha, whose large brown eyes stare at me intently and then look to Maria. I fake confidence because beneath the surface, my insides are a puddle. "Sure. Show me to the scrub room."

I attempt to calm my breathing as I put my clothes in the locker and pull on scrubs. The ink on my degree is still dripping wet, and I've never seen a patient alone before, let alone, in a foreign country where language and culture will be a barrier. I thought today would be nothing more than meeting the staff and learning the layout of the hospital, but I now see I'm going to be thrown into patient care right away. I look around the hallway as I slowly walk to exam room 3. I knock lightly on the door and wait a few seconds and then walk in. A beautiful woman sits on the exam table, and her smile nearly reaches both of her ears as she sees me.

I try to match her smile. "Hi, my name is Kate, and I'll be examining you today." I step closer, and deep dimples appear in her cheeks, as her smile continues to widen. I nearly reach my hand out to shake hers, but quickly pull back, as I'm not sure what a proper greeting is for a patient in Tanzania.

"I am honored to meet you. I am Bupe." She motions to the man in the corner. "This is my husband, Alvin."

Alvin walks over to me and looks more skeptical than his wife. He stops several feet short of me. "It is nice to meet you," Alvin says monotonously as he barely looks up.

"My husband hasn't seen many white people, Ms. Kate." Bupe's laugh vibrates through the small exam room. "He will get used to you in no time at all."

Bupe reaches for my hand, and I take hers. My skin flushes as our hands touch. The coarseness of her hand tickles the inside of my palm. "I look forward to getting to know you and your husband, Bupe. Thank you."

Bupe's bright-green headdress provides a beautiful contrast to her rich dark skin. Her large eyes follow me as I look around and realize I don't see a chart. In fact, I don't know if the hospital uses charts like I'm used to back home.

"Bupe, as I said, my name is Kate, and I'm here to help out with labor and delivery. What can I do for you today?" My voice shakes with nervousness as I speak.

"I usually see Dr. Andrew. Is he around?" Bupe looks toward the door.

"He is with another patient. Let's start by getting your history."

Alvin walks closer to the exam bed and puts his hand on Bupe's shoulders. She looks down solemnly and then our eyes meet.

"My mom died while delivering my younger sister, and then I lost my first baby over a year ago. Dr. Andrew says I'm not a typical pregnancy case, so Alvin and I try to drive from our village to this village every two weeks or so."

"I see." I smile, and Bupe's shoulders relax. "Why don't you lie back, and I'll begin your examination."

Bupe lies back in the bed, and I lift the sheet that covers her. I take measurements and listen to the baby's perfect heartbeat. I smile when the beating drum sounds through my stethoscope. No matter how many times I hear the sound, I continue to be amazed at the miracle of it. I motion for Bupe to sit back up, and then I listen to her heart and lungs. Both Bupe and Alvin turn to the door as if they see something, so I look toward the door as well. A larger-than-life man watches me as he quietly shuts the door behind him. I continue to hold the stethoscope to Bupe's chest.

Bupe claps her hands together and smiles. "Dr. Andrew, there you are."

Dr. Andrew walks over and shakes Alvin's hand and then puts his hand on Bupe's shoulder. I can barely catch my breath as he looks at me and smiles. He is a very tall man, maybe the tallest man I've seen in real life. His features are striking. His cheekbones are enviable, and his skin is a golden brown that shines when the light hits it. For being so tall, he isn't too thin. Instead, he has a muscular build, and his scrubs hug his body with every movement. I watch as he continues to close the space between us. I quickly look down when I feel heat spread across my face and chest, and my skin turns a fiery red as Dr. Andrew catches me staring at him.

I finally remove the stethoscope, and Dr. Andrew smiles at me. "Bupe, Alvin, it looks like you're both meeting Ms. Malone at the same time I am. She is with us for a few months, all the way from the United States. She comes highly recommended from our hospital administrator, Maria."

Bupe smiles at Andrew and then at me. "Yes, we met Ms. Kate."

"Good." Dr. Andrew looks at me. "I apologize that I wasn't here to greet you, but welcome to the hospital and our village."

Dr. Andrew then looks down at Bupe. "I'm going to go put in an order for blood work, and if you don't mind, I'd like to examine you as well."

Bupe lies back down, and I watch as Dr. Andrew performs the same examination I just conducted. I quickly deduce that Dr. Andrew doesn't trust my abilities to conduct an examination, and my own self-doubt starts to creep in. I observe Dr. Andrew as he gently asks Bupe questions about how she is feeling, how Alvin is doing with the pregnancy, and how the clinic can support her. His voice is like honey coming out of his mouth. A perfect British accent falls from his voluptuous lips with precision and a deep richness. Each syllable is spoken with deliverance and perfection.

After his questioning, Dr. Andrew pats Bupe's knee, and she sits back up. "Alvin, everything with Bupe and your baby looks great. She measures where she should be at this point in the pregnancy. I do want to give you vitamins, and you can make sure Bupe takes one a day. If anything comes back abnormal with your blood work, I'll visit you. Do you have any questions for us?"

Alvin puts his hand to his chin as if he were in deep thought. "Is there any reason to come back here? Everything is going great."

Andrew's hand looks commanding as he places it on Alvin's shoulder. "I want you to continue to come back every couple of weeks. I know it's hard to get here, but it's important."

Alvin shakes his head as if he doesn't agree with this. After some silence and a long sigh, he says, "I suppose we could come back."

Bupe's voice interrupts the conversation. "Alvin, you and Dr. Andrew wait outside, and I'll speak to Ms. Kate as I get dressed."

Andrew looks at me, seeking permission with his eyes, and I nod in his direction. Andrew puts his hand on Alvin's back and ushers him out of the room.

"I don't need grown men watching me change out of this gown," Bupe says with a deep laugh. Her face turns serious as she looks down at her hands and then back up at me. "Do you think I have anything to be concerned about?"

My heart palpitates, and my self-doubt exits as confidence takes over. "Everything looks great. I do agree that you should come back regularly, even if it's a long journey."

Bupe looks down again and nods her head. "The history of hard pregnancies in my family scares me."

"Even more reason for you to continue seeing Dr. Andrew."

Bupe purses her lips, and concern spreads across her face. "You're right. And he's been great. He always goes out of his way to make sure I'm okay."

"I just met him today Bupe, but he does seem great, and he knows what he's talking about."

Bupe looks at me thoughtfully. "Do you have a husband, Ms. Kate?"

I laugh, although it sounds more like I am choking. My mind goes to the fact that I'm supposed to be getting married this summer.

"No," I say with a pained smile.

"I believe Dr. Andrew also doesn't have a wife."

"Thank you for letting me know that." I look at Bupe, and she gives me a mischievous wink, and I laugh.

Bupe pulls on a long skirt that matches her bright-green headdress. She takes both my hands and places them on her face. My skin looks pale in comparison to her deep brown skin.

"Dr. Andrew has been great, but I'm happy to have a woman in my company." Bupe smiles. It's the type of smile that lights up a room and instantly changes a mood—the sort of smile that could end a war. I know immediately that she is going to be one of my favorite people in Tanzania.

I pull my scrubs off and put my clothes back on. I walk into the hallway and see Dr. Andrew leaning over the front desk, talking to Editha. His attractiveness surprises me, as does my reaction to him. Maria has mentioned Dr. Andrew to me repeatedly, especially since moving to the village with Noor to assist at the hospital. She wrote in detail about growing up with him and how he moved away to attend school in England and stayed there for university and medical school. Maria told me how convincing he was to get Noor and her to work here. She wrote me letters about how excited Dr. Andrew was to have Noor come with, as Noor had just finished his nursing degree in Dar.

I struggle to reconcile the Dr. Andrew whom Maria has described in meticulous detail and the one before me. I did not picture a gorgeous man who dropped all his plans to help out a rural Tanzanian population. I imagined an old man, the male equivalent of a spinster, and short. Yes, I definitely pictured Dr. Andrew as a short man. My phone vibrates, and I look down at the screen.

Peter

I'm hoping we can find time to chat soon. I have a few things I want to say to you.

I look up from my phone, and Dr. Andrew stands at his desk, watching me. Peter continues to force me to live in the past, even though I have moments in the past couple of days where I am present, finally. He didn't text or call me once after we called off our wedding in early May. Yet now that I'm on the other side of the world, he wants to talk. Part of me wants to talk to him too, but I can't imagine what he could say to me that would change things between us.

CHAPTER 3

There is no better mirror than a best friend.

—African Proverb

After a quick shower, I stand in front of the mirror in my bathroom and apply makeup. I like my bungalow more than I was expecting. It's small, but it's mine, at least for now. As I look around at the space, it occurs to me that I've never lived alone. The bungalow feels like a blank slate, just like my life, and we can together become whatever we choose from this point forward. My bungalow overlooks the hospital, as all the hospital workers' bungalows do. The hospital is the largest structure in this one-thousand-person village, and I'm looking forward to venturing out and seeing what the village has to offer.

Maria and Noor's bungalow is directly next to mine, so I walk over there, as I promised I would help Maria prepare tonight's dinner. I knock and walk through the door. Maria hurries over and wraps her strong arms around me and bounces me up and down, never letting go. Maria is the only one I know who hugs with every inch of her body. When she pulls me in, the energy of her soul presses into me.

"Kate, you look much better than this morning. I can no longer see through your skin, so that's a good sign." Maria gently strokes my cheek with her hand, and I turn my face to her and enjoy the touch. "Noor will be here soon. He is finishing up a case with Dr. Eric. Are you sleeping well so far?"

I follow Maria to the kitchen. "I don't remember ever sleeping so well in my life."

"It's because you don't have the noise of the city. I'll never forget how hard it was to fall asleep when I lived with you. The ambulances and airplanes kept me up all night." Maria's laugh fills her small bungalow as she reaches in the fridge and pulls out a bottle of wine.

"You may be on to something. I've been sleeping like a baby for the last couple of nights." Despite how well I slept, I still put both arms up in the air and let out an exaggerated yawn.

Maria takes my face in both of her hands and then puts her forehead against mine. "I've never seen you look more tired. I have a feeling you haven't been sleeping well for a while."

I look down but nod, and I know Maria is right. She is only seven months older than me but has always felt like my spiritual advisor. She has a gift for reading people, and I'm convinced she knows me even better than I know myself.

I'll always remember the summer before my senior year of high school when my parents told me that we would be hosting a foreign exchange student for the year. One of my dad's classmates in medical school was from Tanzania, and his daughter was going to spend a year with us. I was skeptical and against the idea of having a girl my age come and live with us for the year. I was afraid I would have to spend my senior year babysitting her.

In mid-August of that year, Maria walked through the front door with my parents. She had a camping duffel bag that was as large as she was and straddled her back. She was tiny and couldn't have been much taller than five feet, but she seemed fierce. She walked through the door, and the entire room got brighter. The air felt purer. The lights shone with more brilliance, and I realized it was futile to continue acting like I didn't want her here. I could see every one of her pearly white teeth, and when she saw me, she dropped her bag and ran over and threw her arms around me and started bouncing. I threw my head back and laughed, and I fell in love with her instantly. My love for Maria has only grown.

"Earth to Kate, are you still here?" I'm brought back to reality by Maria as she continues to rummage through the fridge.

"I'm sorry, what did you say?"

Maria pulls out vegetables. "Will you help me by cutting up these vegetables?"

"Yes, of course."

Maria takes my hand and holds it. "Noor and I are very happy you came. We have loved being here and helping Dr. Andrew, and I think you are going to love it too."

"I'm sure you're right. And I got my first patient out of the way, so that's good." I'm happy to be with Maria, but I recognize the melancholy in my voice.

Maria stands next to me at the counter and starts cutting up chicken. "Do you want to talk about it, Kate? I know how much you loved him. It's okay not to be okay."

"Ugh, I feel embarrassed and ashamed. I mean, my mom had to call two hundred people to tell them the wedding was off." My heart nearly pierces out of my chest at the memory of my mom on the phone all day long, calling person after person to tell them the same made-up story. Peter and Kate are just too busy to get married at this time.

No one was more surprised than me when Peter asked me out during our junior year of high school. My best friend, Jane, was the popular one. I was nothing more than her shy best friend, who spent most of my time studying for college entrance exams. Peter and I grew up together because our moms were and still are best friends. Not only that, but our dads were in medical school together with Maria's dad. But no one expected us to be together. Peter was the star athlete; my best friend, Jane, was the outgoing and beautiful type. Everyone thought they'd end up together. But Peter asked me out, and we were inseparable through the remainder of high school, college, and then my master's in nursing and his law school.

"Forget Peter." Maria puts a hand on her hip and shakes her head, bringing me back to reality.

"Forget Peter." I turn to face her and smile.

Maria pops a piece of cheese in her mouth and chews slowly and deliberately. She dramatically swallows. "Can I ask you something, Kate?"

I put my arms out, knowing Maria will ask anyway. "You met Peter when you were sixteen. He's the only man you've ever been in a relationship with."

"That's not a question." I playfully swat at Maria's shoulder, and we both laugh.

"Part of me wonders if you are only sad because this is a huge change in your life. Or are you still madly in love with Peter and want him back?"

I look down at my feet; a light coat of dust covers them. I firmly rub my temples with the palm of my hands. "That's what I'm trying to figure out. Peter has started texting me in the past couple of days. It's like he has radar and knows I'm starting to move on, and now he won't quit contacting me."

Maria shakes her head disapprovingly. "I'm sure your parents told his parents you were going to Tanzania."

"And that's when Peter decided it would be a good time to be in touch again?"

I look up at Maria and can't read her expression, but she slowly nods at my admission.

"Do you think this has something to do with control?" she asks.

I've never spoken a bad word about Peter, and I won't do it now, but Maria's words linger in the air, and I can't stop myself from pulling them in and pondering whether there is truth to what she said. The heaviness and ball of stress still live in my stomach, but being with Maria feels good. I've always been terrible at letting people get close to me. Besides Peter and Jane, Maria has always been my closest friend and confidant. When things fell apart with Peter, Maria was my first call. We hadn't physically seen each other in six years, but we video-messaged a couple of times a week, and I will forever consider her my sister. I never want to give my parents the satisfaction of being right, but it feels good to be out of my childhood bedroom, where I have spent the last month hiding from the world and avoiding reality.

"Maria, Kate, we're here." Noor's voice echoes through the bungalow, and he walks into the room with Dr. Andrew and a man I don't recognize.

I smile as Noor pulls Maria into a warm embrace. I've spent the past two years hearing about this man who has made Maria so happy, and although we sometimes chatted during our video calls, I love witnessing their love firsthand, in person.

Noor turns to me and takes my hands in his and smiles. "Kate, it is so wonderful to have you here. I believe you met Dr. Andrew today, but I would also like to introduce you to Dr. Eric."

A man with sandy blond hair and tan skin puts his hand out and shakes mine. "It's nice to meet you, Kate. Please call me Eric."

I smile at Eric and recognize that he must be the South African doctor that Maria told me is here temporarily. "It's great to meet you, Eric."

Dr. Andrew puts his hand out to greet me. "I apologize that I wasn't able to introduce myself properly earlier, but it's great to have you here, and please call me Andrew."

His hand is soft and warm as it envelopes mine. Andrew's smile is warm, but his presence makes my heart beat fast. "Thank you. I'm happy to be here."

Noor turns on soft music as Maria grabs everyone a glass of wine. Noor finishes my job of cutting up the vegetables, and I stand near Eric and Andrew. Eric puts his glass down on the table and smiles at me. "Kate, I hope your first day was good."

"It was. Thank you, Eric. It was busy when I arrived, so I got thrown in with a patient faster than I was expecting, but I think it went okay."

"Which patient?" Eric looks at Andrew and then to me.

Andrew speaks before I have a chance to answer. "Bupe. I've told you all about her."

Eric affirms this. "You see, Kate. You're going to realize quickly there isn't a lot to do here, so Andrew and I spend a lot of time enjoying a beer while talking about clinical matters. Consider this your warning."

Eric and Andrew look at each other and laugh, and I know I've walked into an inside joke. I laugh with them because what they don't know is that I live for that type of thing. My mom is a cardiologist, and my dad is a radiologist. I used to love coming home from a day of rounds and discussing the clinical aspects of what I saw. My dad would sometimes bring home x-rays, and he would quiz me on different disease states of the de-identified patients.

"We also spend a lot of time talking about the fundraiser in September. Hopefully, you'll still be here," Eric says.

"I should be."

Maria yells through the dining room to the four of us, "Everything is ready. Let's all have a seat."

My stomach continues to gurgle as the food is passed around. Everything looks and smells so good.

Eric leans into me and points at what I put on my plate. "That there is *ugali*. It's maize, flour porridge, and common in Tanzania. It's quite good."

I smile at Eric, thankful that he's explained it to me because I wasn't sure what I was eating.

"Before we eat, I would like to make a toast." Noor raises his glass, quickly followed by the rest of us. "We are happy and honored to have you in our village, Kate. We hope being here provides you happiness and fulfillment."

I can feel everyone's eyes on me, and we all clink glasses. I look down for a moment and quickly dart my eyes back up as I know it's polite to look people in the eye during a toast.

"Thank you, Noor. And thank you too, Maria, for telling me about this place, and for all of you for welcoming me."

I look at Maria, and she doesn't hide the tears that streak her face. "Now let's eat this food before it gets cold."

Everything tastes good, and I surprise myself with how much I eat. The *ugali* is an interesting texture, and I watch how the others eat it and imitate them by grabbing pieces of it and eating it with my hands. The chicken is flavorful, and I can taste cardamom. My body relaxes as I continue to eat after depriving myself of food for too long. I think of my mom, who would be happy that I'm eating so much; she more than anyone was scared for how thin I was getting.

Eric turns to me as I have the glass up to my lips, which are now warm from the wine. "How long will you be here, Kate?"

I put my glass down and can feel all eyes once again on me. "I plan to stay until October." Out of the corner of my eye, I feel Andrew's eyes on me. I turn to him, and he quickly looks down as our eyes meet.

"I think I have told you all this, but I lived with Kate and her parents for an entire year a few years ago. Her father and my father went to medical school together and have remained friends. It was my gap year, and I decided to be a senior in America for a year." Maria looks at me and winks.

Andrew looks up at me again. "Do your parents host many foreign exchange students?"

I laugh, thinking back to how upset I was when I found out Maria would be living with us. "Maria is the first and only. After her, no one else would have lived up to the high expectations she set." Maria grabs my hand and laughs, and I give her a little wink back.

Andrew sets his glass of wine on the table and looks at me thoughtfully. "You two must have gotten along well then?" Andrew has a quality that when he asks me questions, I feel like he is genuinely interested in getting to know me.

Maria continues to hold my hand and squeeze it. "I believe Kate was adamant that she wasn't going to like me. But the moment I walked into the house, I won her over." Maria laughs loudly, and everyone joins in.

I confided in Maria at some point during the year how upset I was when I found out she was coming. I remember Maria laughing for a long time after that. She and I became close so quickly, and most nights, even though she had her own room at our house, we would share the queen bed in my room. We were inseparable, and I will never forget the day she left. We both made a massive scene at the airport as we hugged and sobbed into each other's shoulders. I was sure this is what it felt like to have a broken heart.

Eric breaks my concentration as he leans into me. "We are all happy to have you here. Me especially, as it's nice to have another foreigner at the hospital." Eric laughs as I smile over at him.

My stomach is full, and I can't imagine eating another bite, yet I manage to have some dessert. Maria stands up to start clearing the dishes. Andrew quickly stands up after her and starts taking plates off the table.

"Maria, let me help you," Andrew says.

Maria puts her hand on Andrew's arm. "Thank you, dear. That would be lovely."

Maria and Andrew walk to the kitchen, but there are still a few dishes on the table, so I gather them up and follow them. Their backs are turned to me as they fill the sink, and I can't help but notice the difference in their sizes. Maria barely reaches above Andrew's elbow. The two speak in Swahili and talk in a loud whisper.

Even though I can't understand what they're saying, I feel like I'm eavesdropping on something I shouldn't be. I clear my throat loudly, and they both turn to look at me. "Maria, is there something I can help with?"

Maria looks up at Andrew and then back to me. "Actually, can you finish drying while Andrew washes? I want to clear the table and see if anyone could use another glass of wine."

"Of course." I walk over to Maria, and she hands me the drying towel. My arm brushes against Andrew's as I stand next to him, and my skin immediately feels like electric shocks are pelting it. I look down as I feel my face redden, and I'm confused about why I'm having this reaction to him. Andrew hands me a dish as our fingers lightly brush up against each other. I want to break the silence but feel unable to catch my breath. For some reason, being alone with Andrew makes me nervous.

I stare up at him. "I hear you and Maria go way back?"

Andrew looks down at me and smiles, and it looks like he's thinking back to a memory. "I'm pretty sure we used to run around our yard together in just nappies."

I laugh as I picture it. "That is very far back."

"But then I left for England as a young boy, and only came back for a couple of months a year, so we lost touch. Imagine my happiness when she said she and Noor would come here and help me run the clinic."

"Why did you decide to build a hospital here?" I look around the space.

Andrew hands me a plate without looking at me. "There are many villages about this size and the closest city is much too far for people to travel. I thought the hospital would help this village economically and be a central point to the surrounding villages."

Everything Andrew says makes sense. When I landed in Dar a few days back, we drove at least ten hours west to get to this village, and the last large town before arriving here was four hours away.

"Thank you for having me to your hospital. I can already tell I'm going to learn so much from being here."

"No, Kate. Thank you for coming here." Andrew turns the faucet off and dries his hands. "I'm sorry you were thrown into things today. Bupe is a patient I've been following closely. What did you learn from seeing her?"

I dry the last dish and look up at Andrew. "She gave me her history, about her mom dying during the birth of her younger sister and of her losing a baby. But from everything I saw today, she seems healthy."

"How far along did she appear to you?"

Instead of getting to know each other, Andrew starts quizzing me on my midwifery skills. "I measured twenty-eight weeks. The baby's heartbeat sounded strong and healthy, as did Bupe's."

Andrew nods his head. "I measured twenty-eight weeks also, and am hoping for a mid to late August delivery. I've been doing regular blood tests, and those have all been normal so far."

Andrew rubs his temples as he wrinkles his face. "I can't figure out if her mom dying during childbirth and her losing a child have anything to do with each other. Both happened in her village, so all I have to go on is what Bupe has told me."

I cross my arms over my chest and turn my head to the side. "Is there an ultrasound machine at the hospital?"

"Yes, and Bupe's ultrasounds have been normal. The placenta is developing properly, and the baby looks great."

Self-doubt flows through my body. "Andrew, I don't know if Maria shared this with you, but I'm a recent graduate in midwifery studies. I haven't seen patients on my own yet. Today was actually my first time. I'm a quick study, but I thought you should know that."

Andrew laughs softly. "You are a nurse practitioner who special-izes in midwifery. You are officially the most experienced staff I've ever had. The best thing you can do is believe in yourself and your ability to make the best clinical decisions."

How does Andrew know about what plagues me so soon after meeting me? So many of my problems come down to a lack of con-fidence, and being here, I won't always have someone to fall back on, so I'll have to find a way to gain the confidence I'll need to be successful.

I hear my phone vibrate on the counter, and walk over to it.

JANE

*I know you don't owe me anything, but I still want
to talk. I'm not with Peter. I'll never be with Peter.
Please can we talk?*

My skin immediately feels clammy, and I feel like I have a weight sitting on my chest. I close my eyes for a second and focus on my breathing. I forget for a moment that I'm not alone in the kitchen.

"Is everything okay?"

I open my eyes quickly and look over at Andrew, who is still standing at the sink, watching me, and looking concerned.

"Please excuse me, Andrew." I smile and nod and walk back to the dining room to say goodbye to the others and head home for the night.

CHAPTER 4

The sun does not forget a village just because it is small.

—African Proverb

The meaning of days is vastly different here. Sunrises turn into sunsets, and the time between is spent at the hospital. Delivering babies is where I feel at home. It's what I'm good at, and focusing on others gives me very little time to think about my life. I welcome the distraction, and my favorite days are the ones where I'm too tired at the end of it to lie awake in bed and process or read my text messages and think about the what-ifs. There is never a slow day at the hospital. There are always patients to see, and when there aren't, there are always projects to work on. My life feels small and isolated to this hospital, and on days I do venture out, I'm still isolated to this small village. I appreciate the simplicity of it all and feel more relaxed than I have in ages, perhaps ever.

I turn the corner and can hear several voices from the waiting room, alerting me to the fact that it will be a busy day in labor and delivery. Editha sits at the front desk, and I take a moment to glance at her, and then I observe the women who have ventured here today, trying to determine who to see first. There must be about eight women sitting, waiting to be seen. I'm not sure I'll ever get used to the lack of processes, but it's only my second week here, so perhaps with time, I'll adapt.

I approach a woman who looks the most pregnant. "Hello, my name is Kate. Can you understand me?"

In very broken English, the woman responds, "I am Firyali. I hope you look at me today."

I smile at Firyali and lead her back to an exam room. In the past few days, I have become very accustomed to young patients, but Firyali looks aged more than many of the women I have seen. She wears a long brown skirt and has a brown and red ribbon wrapped on her head. Her face looks weathered like she has experienced a lot of life.

"Are you from here, Firyali?"

"Yes, I live in the village, and I hear being checked is free?"

I reassure her, "That's correct. If you are comfortable, I will have you put this gown on and undress from the waist down." I turn around to give her privacy.

"Are you feeling any pain today?"

"No pain. I feel many kicks."

From the look of her belly, I am guessing Firyali must be seven or eight months pregnant, but I know looks can be deceiving. I measure her and am surprised that the baby feels full-term. I grab my stethoscope and smile when I hear a perfectly normal baby's heartbeat. Because she feels full-term, I want to see if there is any dilation.

"Firyali, is it okay if I check inside of you to see if the baby is ready to come soon?" She nods her head but looks at me, panicked.

"I'm going to put these gloves on. I then need to check you on the inside, but you don't need to worry. There should be no pain."

As I put gloves on and spread her legs gently, Firyali inhales sharply and her legs tense. I smile and try to put her at ease. Her cervix is soft and open. I tell her I would also like Dr. Andrew to see her. I hide all concern and walk out of the room, then quickly walk down the hall to his office, which is empty.

Editha is back at the desk. "Editha, have you seen Dr. Andrew?"

"I believe he's in room number 3, Ms. Malone."

Without even thanking her, I walk quickly to exam room 3 and knock before entering. My heart feels like it's beating through my chest. Dr. Andrew appears to be finishing with a patient and looks startled to see me.

"Dr. Andrew, would you be able to assist me with a patient?" My eyes go wide as I motion toward the hall.

He says something to his patient, who nods, and then he walks out of the room with me.

"I have a patient in exam room 6. Her name is Firyali. She says she is in no pain, but when I examined her, she is dilated ten centimeters, and the baby is breech, and we're either going to need to deliver this baby breech or prep the operating room."

"Thanks for getting me." Andrew puts his hand on my back and follows me into Firyali's room. She looks tense as she lies there on the bed, legs wide open, but covered with a blanket.

"I hear you are Firyali. My name is Dr. Andrew, and I'm going to be helping Ms. Malone today."

He puts on his gloves, and before he starts his examination, he asks for her permission. Firyali nods slowly, and then Andrew checks her. He quickly stops and pats Firyali on the knee and smiles at her.

"Firyali, it looks like you are going to have a baby today. Is there someone we can reach who should be here?"

She stares at us, eyes wide open. "It is just me."

"Okay. You should know that your baby is breech. Have you had children before?"

"This is my first child."

Andrew continues, "When babies are born, it is best they come out head first, and I don't think we'll be able to deliver vaginally. I think it's best if you go into surgery immediately." Andrew looks at me and then back to Firyali, who looks confused. He switches to Swahili, and many words are exchanged between the two of them.

"Kate." Andrew's eyes cut to mine as he catches me staring at the interaction between the two of them. "Please go have the staff prepare the operating room."

I nod and grab Editha from the hallway, who calls a couple of the staff. I don't even know who all should be involved in this as I haven't stepped foot in the operating room since arriving here. Eric rushes up the stairs and hurries toward me.

"Editha called. Things are slow downstairs, so I'm here to help."

"Okay. We're supposed to prepare the operating room."

Eric takes my shoulder, and we walk in. There are a couple of people setting up equipment. Shortly after, Andrew wheels in Firyali.

"Good, Eric, you're here." Andrew starts getting Firyali situated. "I'm hoping you'll do a spinal block."

Everything happens quickly. Andrew, Eric, and I scrub in for the surgery, and Andrew gives me instructions on the tools. I have no idea Eric gives spinal blocks, but he performs it effortlessly. Andrew makes sure Firyali is entirely numb and then makes his first incision. I watch Andrew move around the muscle until the uterus is visible, and another small incision is made. With some maneuvering and a tug, the baby is out. I've witnessed cesarean sections before, and I'm always impressed at the skill of doctors who perform them. Andrew turns to me where I wait with blankets and a bassinet and hands me the baby.

"Here, you take him."

I take hold of Firyali's baby and get him cleaned up and perform a quick Apgar test.

"Congratulations on your son, Firyali. He is a healthy boy."

Firyali cries out as Andrew works to stitch her up, and Eric fiddles with her IV. Everything happened so quickly with this birth, and I'm amazed at how well we all came together, with limited equipment and no anesthesiologist, to perform a successful cesarean section. Professionals back home would be shocked by the resourcefulness required here.

Andrew works quickly and has excellent precision with every stitch, and almost as quickly as it began, Firyali is out of surgery. I get her situated in the room where she'll spend a few nights with her newborn baby boy and she speaks to a nurse I hadn't met before, Adimu. I think of what would have happened if this hospital didn't exist. The baby was so lodged in there; I think the results would have been quite different.

I glance at the clock, and it's already 5:30 p.m. I smell and have blood on me and, most definitely, need to shower. I walk into the women's scrub room and peel off my scrubs and throw them in the hamper. I throw on my favorite Prince T-shirt and pull on my jeans, which I realize are beginning to fit me better and are not as loose as they were. I pull up the center of my shirt to sniff it, which confirms my need to do laundry.

My phone vibrates in my back pocket, and I pull it out to look at my screen.

PETER

Kate, I need to talk to you. Please quit shutting me out like this.

My hand hovers over my phone, and I consider whether I should respond. I close my eyes and focus on filling my lungs with air, before slowly releasing. I feel eyes on me, and my eyes quickly dart up.

"Hi, Kate. I didn't mean to interrupt. I'm hoping you'll walk out with me to discuss a business proposition." Andrew looks down at me with eagerness in his eyes.

"Yes, I was just leaving. Are you ready?"

Andrew smiles as we both turn to walk down the stairs. We walk in silence for several moments, and when we reach outside, there is a crispness yet warmth in the air. The sun hangs lower in the sky, and my skin pebbles with goose bumps. Andrew and I stroll slowly, and I need to take two steps for every one step he takes.

"Kate, I need to travel to the countryside for a couple of days to visit the surrounding villages. I have two patients I want to visit, and Bupe is about due for her next appointment, so I'm thinking we can save her a trip and visit her as well. I'm hoping you'll accompany me?" Andrew stares straight ahead at my bungalow.

When Maria told me about this opportunity, she mentioned there would be an occasion for me to travel to the countryside to see patients.

"Who will cover the hospital while we're gone?"

"Nyla is also trained in labor and delivery, so she'll move from the first floor to the second. We do the best we can to see everyone, but unfortunately, not everyone may get seen while we're gone. I thought the experience of seeing other villages would benefit your learning."

I pull open the door to my bungalow. "When would we leave?"

Andrew smiles down at me. "Tomorrow morning, if you can make that work? I would pick you up at seven in the morning. I've asked Maria to accompany us, but she's not sure if she'll be able to attend. If you would feel uncomfortable without her present, I understand."

My mind wanders as to what purpose Maria would serve on a trip to the countryside to see patients. "Do you have fundraising work in these villages?"

Andrew covers his mouth with his hand and hides his smile. "No, there is no fundraising that will happen in these villages." Andrew moves his hand from his lips and tucks them into his pockets. He looks at me like he knows a secret that I'm not in the loop on.

"If you'd rather go with Maria, Andrew, I understand. I can hang back and see patients here." As the words leave my lips, I think about how not ready I am to not have Andrew to fall back on while seeing patients.

"It's fine, Kate. I thought it made sense for Maria to come because—"

My skin flushes as I look at him, wondering why he quit talking.

"I'm fine attending with or without Maria."

"Perfect. I wanted to make sure you were comfortable, and if you are, it's all settled."

Confusion extends across my face. "If you think the area we are traveling to is safe, of course, I'm comfortable."

Andrew looks at me, and I can't help but think I'm missing the point entirely. Andrew's mouth turns up in a smile, and his chest expands as he exhales a breath he seemed to be holding.

"Pack enough for a couple of days, and I'll be here bright and early in the morning."

I smile as Andrew turns on his heels and walks toward his bungalow. I open up my refrigerator and pull out an already opened bottle of wine and pour myself a glass. I open my back door and sit in a chair out back. The sun nearly disappears below the horizon of my fence, and the stars start to appear over the African sky. My hair blows in the wind, and the fresh air strokes my neck. I pull out my phone and look at Peter's text message. I take a long and slow sip of my sweet wine, and my stomach immediately feels warm and tingly, my lips full of sugar. My finger once again hovers over my phone as it moves between delete and reply. I haven't responded to any of Peter's texts.

ME

What do you want to say that hasn't already been said? I'm listening.

I sit back and think about the decisions I have made in life, big and small. Sometimes the decision is as small as responding to a text message. Yet all these decisions can change the course of what happens next.

CHAPTER 5

We should talk while we are still alive.

—Kenyan Proverb

I wake up before the sun, and the first thing I do is glance at my phone. I have several text messages from Peter that he wrote while I was sleeping soundly. The time difference can make real-time communication difficult. I sit down at the kitchen table and scroll through my messages.

PETER

Kate, I think we made a mistake calling the wedding off. I made a mistake. I should never have kissed Jane. It's not like that with her, I promise. I was confused for a moment, but us being separated has made me rethink everything.

PETER

I know it was mostly my idea to call off the wedding. I was confused about my feelings. It's you I love. It's always been you.

Peter

*Looking back, I think I panicked. Our wedding was
coming up, and I got scared. If you let me, I'll spend
the rest of my life making this up to you.*

I throw my phone down on the bed and force myself into the
shower. The only temperature available this early morning is frigid.
For some reason, when the cold pelts of water hit my body, it makes
me feel alive. I punish myself and stand underneath, and the cold
water feels like hail hitting my head, causing my scalp to tingle and
burn. I throw clothes on and put my hair into a side braid and grab
a straw hat to protect myself from the fierce sun.

I'm having a hard time formulating a cohesive thought. Peter's
text messages have sucked all the oxygen out of my body and left my
brain in a fog. I had given up all hope. I have started to mentally and
emotionally move on, and now I get these text messages, which leave
me confused. I hear a vehicle pull up and a door shut and, a moment
later, a light knock at my door.

"Hi, Kate. I hope I'm not too early." Andrew looks down at me,
ready to go.

"Hi, you're not early at all. Your timing is perfect." I smile up at
him and am thankful for the distraction from the messages that will
remain unanswered, at least for a while longer.

"Is everything okay?"

I hand Andrew my bag, and he puts it in the back of his jeep.
"Yes, everything is fine. I'm still waking up, I think." I'm lying, but
my boss at the hospital is the last person I'm going to discuss my
failed engagement with.

I sit down in his jeep, which is open on the top, and he hands
me a hot cup of coffee. "I made you a strong cup of coffee if you're
interested."

"I'm very interested. Thank you." I smile as I take the cup from
Andrew's hands, thankful for his thoughtfulness, especially because
I don't like to start days without caffeine, and reading my messages
prevented me from making my own coffee this morning. I glance

in Andrew's direction, and whether he's wearing scrubs or regular clothes, he always manages to look breathtakingly beautiful. Today he wears fitted khaki shorts that end right above his knees, a light-pink polo shirt, and white tennis shoes. He is cleanly shaven, and I wish I could lean over and breathe him in. His skin looks like he just put on a layer of lotion, and when the sun hits it, it looks golden. His legs look muscular in his khaki shorts, and I look at both of our legs, just inches from each other, but not touching. He has on aviator sunglasses that hide his eyes from me. I rest my right elbow on the fully open window and find myself in another world. I realize I've been staring at him for several minutes.

"Kate, you are very quiet. Are you sure everything is okay?" Andrew says as he glances at me.

"I'm sorry. I was thinking of back home." I chuckle as I feel my face redden with embarrassment. I look over at Andrew as our eyes meet. "Andrew, your name doesn't sound Tanzanian." I would have said anything at that moment to divert the attention off me.

"You're very perceptive, Kate." He laughs.

"My given name is Andwele. When I moved to London to attend boarding school, many of my classmates couldn't pronounce my name and were always saying it wrong. Some of the boys started calling me Andrew, and it stuck. Then when I went back to England for university, I started introducing myself as Andrew. It felt easier."

"So no one calls you Andwele?"

"My family does. And my close friends who knew me from before. But those from the village all call me Andrew."

"Andwele," I say slowly, "Andwele." I look at Andrew, seeking feedback on how I did. "Am I saying it right?"

Andrew's shoulders shake as he laughs. "That's perfect. It means 'God brought me.' My parents found it appropriate as I was their first and only son."

I nod, saying his name in my head. "I like it. I'm sorry you had to lose your name because people couldn't pronounce it though."

Andrew smiles but never looks at me. "Thank you, Kate. It did surprise me as a young teenager that the people in England struggled with Andwele while I had no problem learning names like Chandler or William, but such is life I suppose." Andrew turns to me and winks, and that one action of his takes my breath away.

We sit quietly, for I don't know how long. Oddly, I don't feel nervous or uncomfortable with the silence between us. I mostly look at the scenery, which has turned barren, without a lot of civilization. The land outside has grown flat, with an occasional tree off in the distance. Sporadically I steal glances Andrew's way. At one point, I find myself staring at his hands on the steering wheel and can't get over how large they are and how much skill is in those hands.

I enjoy the simplicity of being in this jeep with Andrew in the middle of nowhere. I purposely put my phone in my bag so I wouldn't be tempted to check it. I'm not ready to deal with Peter yet. The breeze circles me as it enters the jeep from the open top. We turn down a road, and the wind hits Andrew perfectly, and the aroma of vanilla and fresh linens hits my face at the same time as the whipping wind. I close my eyes and inhale this most exuberating scent of him.

"Bupe's village happens to be on our way to our destination, so I thought we'd stop there first."

My eyes pop open, and I haven't even realized I closed them, and I bring my hands together in a clap. Up ahead, Bupe waddles toward the jeep.

"Ms. Kate Malone, hello! You are in my village, and I am so honored." Bupe embraces me, and her excitement is suffocating.

Andrew walks over to us, laughing. "I see how I rank with you now, Bupe." She laughs as they greet each other, and Bupe playfully smacks Andrew in the arm.

"Where is Alvin today?" Andrew looks around.

"He ran to town today to pick up a few things. He will be sorry he missed you. Unless you can stay longer?" She looks at us, hopefully.

"Oh, Bupe, as much as we would like to, we have a very long drive today. But since we were passing so near, I thought it would be good to give you a checkup and save you a trip to the hospital."

"That would be great. And reassure me so much."

Bupe leads Andrew and me into the hut. It is modest, but bigger inside than it looks from the outside. The floor is dirt, and a broom sits against the closest wall. My nose is overwhelmed by the burst of spices in the air. I'm not sure what it is, but the spiciness tickles my nose. As I walk, I kick up dirt from the floor. The only furniture in the room is two wooden rocking chairs and a cot-like structure that must be the bed. Rusted pans hang from the ceiling in the kitchen by a rope. Bupe pulls open a couple of curtains, and the sun bursts through the window and lights every surface of the hut.

"Bupe, I will step outside. If you could, please undress from your waist down, and I'll examine you on your bed."

"No worry, Dr. Andrew. I will have Ms. Kate assist me."

Andrew turns away from us and steps outside. "He is a very good man, Ms. Kate," Bupe says, as I look at a wall to give her a sense of privacy.

"Yes, you are in great hands. He's a great doctor."

Bupe laughs so loud I must shush her. "Ms. Kate, that is not what I mean. I mean, he is a good man. Do you have a good man in your life?"

"No, remember, I told you I have no good man in my life." I playfully roll my eyes but can't help smiling.

"You are wrong, Ms. Kate. You told me you have no husband."

"You have too good of a memory, Bupe. But I am quite content without a man right now." I laugh as my eyes meet hers, wondering if she senses this unexplainable attraction I have to Andrew.

"That can't be true, Ms. Kate. No one is happy without a good man."

I turn around as she places a blanket over her waist. I imagine that our lives and culture are vastly different, which is what holds me back from giving her my feminist speech on the fact that women don't need men. I looked at Bupe's chart after the first time I met her, and she recently turned twenty years old. I've read about the different tribes and cultures within Tanzania, and it's quite common for people, especially in the country, to marry and start families at a young age. I'd be a hypocrite anyway if I started preaching to Bupe. After all, I was tied down to someone from the age of sixteen.

I attempt to redirect the conversation. "If I had a good man back home, I wouldn't have been able to come to Tanzania, and I wouldn't have been able to meet you." I raise my eyebrows.

"Perhaps God's plan in coming here was for you to meet a good man." I laugh at her relentlessness. I have a feeling Bupe is never going to drop this. And I know she is wrong about why I am in Tanzania.

"Dr. Andrew, you can come in," I yell through the hut, knowing it's the only way I can think to end this conversation. Bupe is on to me and smiles and shakes her head.

"Ms. Kate," Andrew says, "would you like to do the initial exam?"

"Sure."

I take out my stethoscope and smile at the sound of the beating heart of Bupe and Alvin's child. I then do my measurements, and she measures right on track, and if everything goes according to plan, she will be delivering her baby in mid-August.

"Bupe," I say, "I would like to examine you on the inside to make sure you have no signs of having this baby too early. Are you comfortable with that?"

"Oh, Ms. Kate, you do what you need to do."

Andrew's eyes follow my every movement, and I feel like he watches me to ensure I know what I'm doing. He is the teacher, and I am the student. I put on my gloves and begin my internal examination. I can feel Bupe's cervix, and it is hard and firm, exactly what I want to see at this point in the pregnancy.

"Everything looks great, Bupe. How are you feeling?" I pat her on her knee.

"Oh, I feel great. I'm taking the vitamins you gave me every day. I'm eating enough food, and I'm not lifting heavy things. I feel great. Different from last time."

Andrew stands up and smiles. "Bupe, I'm happy things are going well for you. I'd like to see you back at the village at the end of July, but sooner if anything changes. Do you understand?" Andrew looks at her sternly.

"Oh, Dr. Andrew. You know, I understand." Bupe smiles, and Andrew relaxes slightly. He puts his hand over hers.

"I worry about you is all, Bupe. I know you are doing everything you can to have a healthy pregnancy. You are a model patient." Bupe nods, and the sliver of light that shines in through the cracks of her hut shines against her glistening eyes.

Bupe looks over at me, and her grin turns mischievous. Bupe seems to know how to deflect attention from herself in a similar fashion to me. "Oh, Dr. Andrew, aren't you happy to have an assistant?"

"Of course, Bupe, very happy," Andrew responds, as he steals a glance in my direction.

Bupe continues, "And such a beautiful one. Don't you think Ms. Kate is beautiful?" My heart immediately flutters, and my face reddens, and I am thrilled there isn't much light in the hut.

Andrew glances down and clears his throat.

"I'm going to grab some bags of food I brought for you and the village. I'll be right back." Andrew leaves the hut hurriedly, and I am embarrassed on his behalf.

"Did you see that, Ms. Kate? I just got a Black man to blush."

Bupe rolls her head back and laughs loud enough to wake the wild animals surrounding the village. I know Andrew can hear her laugh from outside too. Bupe's joy is contagious, and as I look around her place, she has so little yet seems so content. I pull her into a hug, and we say goodbye for now.

Andrew and I are on the road again, with the windows wide open and the wind on our faces.

"I promise you. I did not put Bupe up to embarrassing you." I purse my lips and look over to Andrew.

His entire chest shakes as he laughs. "Bupe has really taken to you. She and Alvin were quite skeptical about seeking medical care, so she can embarrass me all she wants, as long as she's healthy and happy."

I laugh too. With my mouth wide open, I lean my head back and close my eyes and look up toward the sun.

"Why did you come back to Tanzania?" I ask. "I can imagine life is very different here than it was for you in England."

"It is a culture shock. I was always going to come back though. There is so much need here, and I want to invest in my people and country. My family invested in my education, and now I have to pay it back." Andrew turns to me, and lifts his sunglasses, and his dark almond eyes make it impossible to look away.

"Even though I've lived in England as long as I lived here, I never felt like I belonged. But now that I'm home, I don't quite fit in here either." Andrew slowly looks back at the road and lowers his sunglasses back over his eyes.

It would be strange not to belong anywhere. Many of his formative years were spent in England. I'm sure being away changed him, and now that he's back, I hadn't considered that he struggled to fit in here.

"How about you, Kate? Why did you become a midwife?"

I look forward to the windy road we travel on. We reach a fork in the road, and Andrew goes left.

"Honestly, it's all I ever remember wanting to do. When I was five, I had a baby sister who died during childbirth. It was a painful time for my family. As I got older, I became really interested in birth statistics, and how staggering they are, even in developed countries, and that interest turned into a public health interest. I think both my parents thought I'd lose interest, but I never did."

The words pour out of me, and I realize how little I've shared this story with anyone. Even in my master's program, when people asked me what motivated me to be a midwife, I never shared the story about my baby sister who died, and the trauma it left my parents with. Yet it feels entirely natural to be sharing this with Andrew.

He looks at me thoughtfully and pats my hand. "I'm so sorry to hear about your family's loss. I can only imagine how awful that would have been. So how, Kate, did you end up in Tanzania?" Andrew holds my gaze for what feels like an eternity as I ponder how to answer his question. My skin grows clammy and find it hard to breathe suddenly. A huge part of me wants to tell Andrew everything, but one thing at a time, and I've shared enough for one day.

"That's a long story," I say.

He looks at me as we pull into the inn. He stops the jeep in a parking spot directly in front of the building. He turns his entire body toward me and glides his sunglasses off his eyes and onto his head.

"Does the long story have anything to do with the messages you keep getting that make your eyes look sad?"

I look down at my hands, which press into my thighs on my lap. My heart quickens, and I wonder how Andrew sees me so clearly, after knowing me for such a short amount of time.

"Something like that."

CHAPTER 6

If we stand tall, it is because we stand on the shoulders of many ancestors.

—African Proverb

We walk inside the inn, and there are people drinking in a small bar inside the reception area. There are several high-top tables, and the room smells like sandalwood. Dark wood trims the ceiling and floor, and the floor has long black-and-white tiles arranged in a chevron pattern, which covers the entire surface. Andrew goes to the front desk, and after a short conversation, he comes back with two keys.

"We're both up on the second floor. I'll take you to your room." I follow Andrew to a back staircase, and he turns to me. "Are you hungry? The food at the bar is quite good. Would you like to grab a bite to eat?"

"I am hungry, but do you think I have time to shower first?"

"I would like a shower also. Why don't you come to my room when you are done getting ready, and we can head downstairs together?"

I smile and put the key in the keyhole and open the door, as Andrew turns and opens the door directly next to mine. My eyes scan the room, and I'm immediately brought back to my dormitory at university because this room is about the same size. The bed looks slightly wider than a single but not as full as a double. There is a tiny bathroom with a toilet, sink, and a shower. If Andrew's room is like mine, there is no way he'll fit in the shower.

My muscles ache after spending the day visiting women in the countryside. After seeing Bupe, we delivered two babies and visited a woman who wasn't ready to deliver yet. The dirt has found its way to my pores, and when I take my clothes off, it flies out and lands on the floor and lingers in the air, causing me to cough.

It is still warm outside and not much cooler inside. I pull on a skirt and shirt and quickly brush my hair and do a side braid. I glance at myself in the mirror and put on some makeup to finish my look. I walk out of the door and jump when my hotel door slams behind me, echoing through the empty hallway of the hotel.

Andrew opens his door before I have a chance to knock.

"Sorry if I took too long, I tried to get ready fast," I say. Andrew takes me in, and even though I'm only standing in the doorway, I can smell that his room has taken on the fresh linen and vanilla aroma that is Andrew.

"No need to apologize. I was just finishing getting ready myself."

Andrew turns his back to me and grabs something off the table in his room, and I allow my eyes to scan his body. Andrew dresses very well. He is in dark-gray shorts, a fitted black T-shirt, where once again, I have full visibility to his muscular arms. My eyes travel farther down to his backside, where his shirt meets his shorts, and his shorts frame his body perfectly. My stomach turns with nervous energy, and I quickly divert my eyes to the wall.

"I hope your shower wasn't as cold as mine," Andrew says, and I force myself to look at him once again.

I chuckle. "Unfortunately, it was, which helped me to get ready faster." We both laugh, and I feel his hand on the small of my back as he leads me to the small restaurant and bar in the lobby of the inn.

"Are you a beer drinker, Kate?"

I take a seat at a high-top table for two. "I am sometimes."

A waiter approaches our table, dressed casually in a white T-shirt and black pants.

"We would like two Serengetis, please, George."

"Of course, Dr. Andrew," the waiter responds. Andrew pats him on the shoulder as he walks away with our drink order.

"I hope you don't mind me ordering for you. If you don't like the beer, do not feel obligated to drink it. It is my favorite Tanzanian beer, and you're not experiencing the country if you don't try it." I straighten up as Andrew looks at me and then starts studying the menu.

The waiter comes back quickly with two large cans. I take a sip of the beer, and it's strong and full of flavor and very different tasting from beers I've had back home. The beer causes warmth that spreads across my stomach and then up to my chest and face, and I close my eyes for a moment, savoring the taste.

"What do you think of Serengeti?"

"I like it." I take another sip and look at Andrew above my can.

"Just be careful. There is more alcohol in that beer than you are probably used to," he says with a laugh. He then holds his can up and says, "Cheers to a successful day and successful deliveries."

I smile. "I will drink to that."

My beer goes down fast. We order bread and dip it in baba gha-noush, and I'm sure it's the best I've ever had. When Andrew orders another beer, I do the same. I feel light and carefree. Andrew's eyes are bright, with an expression I haven't seen before. Usually, when I'm with Andrew, it's in a clinical setting, and his eyes are intense and thoughtful, but now they shine. I could get lost looking into the depth of brown his eyes convey. I look around the quaint restaurant as tourists make their way through the doors. I can no longer hear Andrew very well as the volume increases tremendously.

"Is this a regular location for tourists?" I lean over and almost shout at Andrew.

"One of the most popular reasons to come to Tanzania is for a safari, and this is one of the stopping points before they head to their final destination. The Ruaha National Park is west of us a bit, and this is the largest town and last stop before arriving there. This inn gets a lot of business because of it."

I stare at the group who comes in, laughing and working their way to the bar. The language they speak is familiar, but I'm not sure what nationality they are.

"They are French. Let me know if you want me to translate." Andrew leans back in his chair after reading my mind.

"Wait, do you speak French?"

"It's my second language." Andrew's eyes cut to mine as he looks up from his food, and I'm sure my heart stops for a moment.

"Wait," I continue probing, "isn't English your second language?"

Andrew brushes his hand over his short hair. "I studied French before English."

Andrew quickly diverts the attention off the fact that I'm now aware of three languages he speaks fluently.

"It would be a shame for you to have come all this way and not to go on safari. I happen to know the doctor in charge of the hospital, and you are free to take time off for a holiday any time you want."

I smile up at Andrew, and his shoulders shake from his laugh, and every one of his unnaturally white teeth is visible. The background music turns up a few decibels, and I smile as the people standing around the bar and tables start swaying their bodies to the music. I watch as a man takes a woman's hand and leads her to the tiled dance floor. Every high-pitched step sounds like a purposefully placed beat in the song. More couples follow. There are laughs above the music, and the group of tourists takes over the entire lobby.

"Do you like this music, Kate?"

"I do! It's so different from anything I've heard before. It almost makes me want to dance!" I yell across the table so Andrew can hear me.

Andrew stands up and moves his chair next to me instead of across from me. "You should go and dance, Kate. I will not stop you."

I playfully push him in my arm and, for the first time, feel the hard definition of muscles underneath his shirt. I feel my cheeks heat and quickly drop my hand.

"I'm the worst dancer. I'm more of an observer than an active participant in life."

Andrew's expression changes slightly. "Everyone should star in their own life, Kate."

I look down and smooth out my skirt. His words seep into my head, and I try to shake them off.

"I've been told I'm a decent dancer, Kate. I'm happy to show you some moves."

"I haven't drunk enough to dance, but some other time perhaps." Andrew pats my hand as he looks toward the dance floor.

"Do you want to retire? I know it's been a long day," Andrew says.

I stiffen at the realization that I don't want to retire. I want to continue spending time with Andrew, even if that means we're watching other people dance.

"I'm not ready for bed yet. I may get another drink. Please don't feel like you have to stay. I understand if you are tired."

Andrew blinks away his expression.

"Then let's walk up to the bar and have another drink." Andrew puts his hand on my lower back once again and leads me to the bar. My body tingles as I feel his fingers spread on the outside of my shirt.

I turn to glance at Andrew as he pulls his phone out of his pocket and looks at it. "I have to take this call, Kate. Will you be fine?"

I nod at Andrew as he holds his phone in front of him. "Of course, can I order you a Serengeti?"

"That would be great." He smiles. "Thank you."

The crowd on the dance floor parts as Andrew wades through it. He is taller and more of a presence than everyone he passes. He walks out into the darkness and paces back and forth on the concrete in front of the large window of the inn. I pay for our drinks and lean back against the bar and watch everyone dance.

"Hello, miss."

I turn toward the voice next to me.

A man stands in front of me, with an accent as thick as the blond hair on his head. "Is it just you and your bodyguard here tonight?" I glance again at Andrew through the window and then look at the man speaking to me and chuckle.

"My bodyguard?"

"That African man you are with." He flicks his finger casually in Andrew's direction.

I laugh a little too loudly. "That's not my bodyguard. He's a colleague of mine."

The man slowly inches his way closer to me. "Oh, I see. I'm Paul."

"Nice to meet you, Paul. I'm Kate."

"You must be American, Kate?" Paul leans in closer, and I can feel the warmth of his arm on mine. I instinctively take a slight step back as I smell his whiskey-scented breath.

"What tipped you off?" I ask with a half-smile, as I take a large drink of my beer, avoiding looking at him.

"You have a very distinguishable accent."

"You as well. You must be French?"

"I am, yes."

My body tenses as Paul, the Frenchman, now reaches his hand behind me and rests it on the bar, extending it across my back. I'm boxed in, and I try to find the best escape route.

"Do you dance, Kate?"

"Very poorly, I'm afraid."

I stare at the door of the inn as Andrew walks in. I hold his gaze as he looks at me and then Paul. He quickens his pace through the lobby, and in a matter of a moment, he is right next to me.

I look up at him and point. "Andrew, this is Paul. He's visiting from France."

"Nice to meet you, Paul. I'm Dr. Andrew." Andrew extends his hand to Paul, and Paul hesitates before reaching his hand out to shake Andrew's. I notice the way Andrew emphasized the word *doctor* in his introduction, which is unlike him.

"You too," Paul says, as he looks around, uneasily. "It was nice to meet you, Kate, but I have to get back to my friends." Paul grabs his drink and walks toward people at the other end of the bar.

The crowd from behind me forces me closer to Andrew, and I brush up against him and look up to meet his eyes. I take a deep breath, and the smell of Andrew fills me. The fabric of his shirt brushes up against my cheek as I get pushed into him, and I feel so much safer in his presence than I did in Paul's.

Andrew bends over in my direction, and as I look up at him, I am only a few inches away from his intense brown eyes. He puts his mouth toward my ear, and my body fills with goose bumps as I feel his warm breath on me.

"Paul seemed a lot less interested in you once I joined the conversation."

I put my hand on the bar to steady myself, and Andrew steps closer to me. He pulls up a stool from underneath the bar, and when he sits, our height difference is a lot less noticeable. I feel the warmth of his body through his shirt, as the electricity works its way through me.

"He thought you were my bodyguard." I playfully roll my eyes.

"Of course, he did." The sarcasm oozes off Andrew's tongue.

"What do you mean by that?" I ask as I lean against the bar, facing Andrew.

"I'm Black, and you are White," Andrew mutters. "There is no other reason for us to be socializing with each other unless I was your employee, right?"

I instinctively pull gently at the back of Andrew's neck to force him toward me so we can hear each other better. His neck is warm, and I like the touch of his skin, but his eyes go dark, and I quickly remove my hand.

"No! That can't be the reason. Many people of different races spend time together. It's common in this day and age."

Andrew continues to lean into me, and his breath warms my face. "Do you have a lot of Black friends back home, Kate?"

My mouth shoots open, and defensiveness spreads across my body. "Where I live and the school I went to, there aren't a lot of Black people."

Andrew sits tall and throws me a sideways grin, and I feel disappointed—like, I've lost an important argument. I don't know if it's the beer or the adrenaline I feel or merely the need to be understood, but I put my hand on his arm, and Andrew looks down at me. I lose the courage to say what I want.

"It's getting late, Andrew," I concede. "I'm going to turn in."

"Sounds good. I'll walk you upstairs."

We walk in silence for a moment. My mind spins, and my heart races, and I fear I'm not giving Andrew a positive impression. I also don't like that I feel the need to have to explain myself to him, and I'm not sure how the conversation turned to race between us in the first place.

I flounder under the uncomfortable silence. "Andrew, I do know Black people. Maria lived with my family for a year, and there were some Black students at my school, just not very many."

"Kate, you don't owe me an explanation." My eyes meet Andrew's, and he looks sincere.

I sigh. "I feel like I'm saying all the wrong things right now."

Even though we have the space to spread out in front of our hotel room doors, magnetism keeps our bodies so close together we nearly touch. I glance at his fists, which are in tight balls, and his eyes don't leave mine.

Andrew's chest slowly rises and falls. "I want you to understand that the French man thinking I am your bodyguard is not because I'm tall or muscular or because he thinks you need a bodyguard to travel with you. He said that because I am a Black man." Andrew closes his eyes tightly and then looks at me. "He purposely approached you when I walked away, and if he thought I was your employee, he would have had no trouble approaching you while I was there. He was putting me in my place, letting me know that he's better than me. He wanted to humiliate me in front of you."

My shoulders slump down at the gravity of what Andrew is saying. I place my fingers to my lips, disappointed that I didn't see it for myself.

"I'm sorry I didn't recognize it. You're right," I say through my fingers.

"You don't need to apologize," Andrew says. "If you want to learn more about the experience of being a Black man, I'm happy to share my personal experiences. All you have to do is ask."

Andrew gently lifts my chin until our eyes meet. His hand is soft and warm against mine, and in this moment, I feel the energy shift between us.

"I still face racism, even here. It is not entirely common to see a Black man with a White woman, and even though we are colleagues, we will be judged and receive questions. My presence around you will not be well received. You need to prepare yourself for that."

"Oh," I say in almost a whisper.

I move my fingers from my lips and place my hand gently on my knotted stomach. I take a deep and deliberate breath at the gravity of this conversation and suddenly feel on the verge of tears.

"And you may not be racist, Kate, but people among you most likely are. You may not have noticed how those travelers were looking at me, but they did not like seeing me with you."

I exhale the breath I've been holding. Andrew places a hand on each of my shoulders and squeezes softly.

"Kate"—Andrew looks at me seriously—"it's been a long day. I think we both need to sleep." Andrew leans down, and his soft lips brush against my cheek, and we look at each other one more time before I go into my room and close the door behind me.

The next morning, the sun peeks through my closed curtains as my eyes slowly open and my arm stretches across the bed. For a moment, I don't know where I am, but then my head starts hurting, and last night comes vividly into my mind. I lie in bed, replaying our conversation, and I sigh. My phone beeps, and I look down to see a picture of Peter, and I realize I haven't thought about him for hours. I look at my phone and have one text message from him.

PETER

I love you, Kate. Can we talk? I have so much I want to say.

My head pounds even more, and I know this isn't going to go away.

ME

I walked in on you kissing Jane, and by the look of things, it was going to escalate further. Three months before we were supposed to get married.

I hit send, but have so much more to say.

ME

And instead of working things out immediately, you told me that you are confused over your feelings and that you have feelings for Jane.

Send. My body burns up, and instead of feeling sad, I feel angry.

ME

Your words verbatim, Peter, were 'maybe we should call off the wedding, at least for now, until we can figure things out.' I thought us talking was working it out. I still wanted to marry you, and you pulled the plug. I'm so mad at you!

I see the three dots and nearly throw my phone across the room as I await what he'll text me next.

PETER

I'm sorry, Katherine. I know I don't deserve a second chance, but I'd like one.

I turn my phone off, and hot tears fill my eyes. Peter is the only one who calls me Katherine, and as soon as I read it, I can't catch my breath. I place my phone on the table beside the bed. I walk into the bathroom and nearly gasp as I look in the mirror. Yesterday's makeup is still smudged on my face. I clean myself up, and then lie back down in bed for a moment. My phone is warm as I pick it up and contemplate turning it back on. I power it on and wait a moment for it to light up.

ME

Peter, if you love me, give me space. I have a lot to sort out. Let me use this distance to determine what I want.

I hit send and get ready to face the car ride home with Andrew.

CHAPTER 7

Unless you call out, who will open the door?

—Ethiopian Proverb

I sigh as I turn the corner on the second floor and see the waiting room, with not one chair empty.

"Hi there, Editha. It looks like the waiting room is full today. Who has been here the longest?"

Editha leans in on me. "That child right there." Editha points to a girl sitting in the waiting room, looking down at her lap, and from the looks of her, she is barely a teenager.

I walk up to her, and she is wearing a traditional Muslim dress and headscarf. "Hi, I'm Kate. Can you understand me?" She nods her head.

I smile at her. "Please follow me into an exam room."

I guide her into the room and point to the table where she takes a seat. I take a long look at the girl, and I can't help but wonder how old she is. She looks like a child. She is dressed plainly, in an all-black long dress and a black headscarf. The exam room we occupy fills with the odor of spices that cling to her clothing. Not only does she look young, but she's tiny. My five-foot, eight-inch frame dwarfs her.

"Let's first have a seat and talk. What is your name?"

"I'm Fatima," she says as she looks down, her hands spread flat against her legs, pressing into them. I can sense that Fatima is nervous, and she barely looks up at me the entire time we speak.

"It's very nice to meet you. Like I said, my name is Kate. What brings you here today?"

"I have a baby, and I want to make sure the baby and I are healthy."

I turn my head slightly and soften my voice. "How do you know you have a baby, Fatima?"

"I haven't bled for a while."

"I see." I smile again, trying to put her at ease. "How old are you?"

Fatima's hands tense as she digs her fingernails into her legs. "I don't know."

"Do you have a guess?"

"Thirteen. Maybe fourteen."

"Are you married?"

She continues to stare into her lap. "No."

"That's okay. You don't need to be scared of me. I'm going to take care of you."

She nods her head but avoids looking up at me. Her long dress is loose and flowing, and if she hadn't told me she was pregnant, I never would have guessed.

"Do you know how pregnant you are, Fatima?"

"It's been a while since bleeding."

"And you have had sexual intercourse?"

Her shoulders hunch further down, and her head slowly affirms my question.

"I'm happy you came in today. I will take great care of you. I will need to examine you by going inside. I'll be very gentle, and you tell me if I'm hurting you. I'm going to leave the room for one minute, and you can pull up your dress, but you'll need to remove your underwear. Here is a blanket to cover yourself up."

I step out of the room to give Fatima some privacy. Thirteen or fourteen? My heart breaks at her age. When I was that age, I still had no cares in the world. I hadn't even experienced my first kiss yet. My biggest concern was which parent was going to drive my friends and me to the mall or the movies. I knock on the door before entering, and Fatima is on the table, ready for her examination. Her face slowly turns toward me as I enter the room, and she tucks a black hair that has fallen out of her headscarf back in and then stares at the ceiling.

"I'm going to have you lie back, and you can put your feet here. The exam won't hurt at all, but I need to see how far you are in your pregnancy and make sure everything is okay."

Before I do my internal examination, I do an external exam. There appears to be trauma to Fatima's genitals. I take notice of bruising and discoloration on the outside of her vagina and inner legs. The bruising looks purple next to her dark-brown skin, and as I gently brush my hand against one of the bruises, Fatima's body stiffens.

"Is everything okay?" Fatima asks nervously.

"I'm checking everything to make sure."

I start my internal examination and see her cervix is still high. I press on her belly as I'm doing this, and I can feel the life inside of her. She is far enough along that I can do the rest of the examination externally. I feel her belly and take measurements, and she is almost twenty-six weeks pregnant, which is shocking because she is still barely showing. I take out my stethoscope and take note of a healthy heartbeat. This is usually the point in the exam where I break into a smile and say a silent prayer at the sound of life inside of someone. But Fatima is too young. She's a child herself.

"Fatima, where are your parents?"

"I live with my baba and two younger sisters. My mama died many years ago."

I remove my gloves and wash up and let Fatima know she can sit again.

"Everything looks good with your baby, but I would like to bring in Dr. Andrew as well. Are you fine with that?"

Once again, Fatima looks down but nods her head. I leave the room and rush to find Andrew.

"Editha, where is Andrew?"

"I believe he went to get a drink in the break room."

I walk down the hall and take a right into the breakroom, and sure enough, Andrew is pouring himself a cup of coffee. He glances up at me as I enter the room.

"Andrew, I'm hoping you will come to see one of my patients. She isn't sure exactly how old she is, but I'm guessing she is only thirteen. She lives with her father and two younger sisters. She's already around twenty-six weeks pregnant. Her age concerns me, but what concerns me more is that during my external exam, she has visible trauma to both her genitals and legs. I think she's being abused."

Andrew looks down at me and nods, and his eyes look heavy. "Show me to the room."

I guide Andrew to the exam room, where Fatima is still sitting on the bed, looking down at her hands. Andrew walks up to her and places a hand on her knee, and she jumps. Fatima slowly looks up at Andrew, and I wonder if patients are intimidated by him because of his size and because he's a male. Andrew hunches down and then pulls up a stool to make himself appear smaller, but his presence is commanding next to Fatima's small frame, and I hope he's able to put her at ease.

"I'm sorry to have startled you, Fatima. I am Dr. Andrew, and I work with Ms. Malone, and she told me some about you. How are you feeling today?"

"I feel fine."

"Is it okay if I examine you?"

Fatima slowly nods her consent. I watch Dr. Andrew do the same exam I just did. He stays calm as he prods around her bruising. Andrew finishes his examination and tells Fatima to sit up.

He gently places his hand on her chin, forcing her to look at him. Andrew lowers his voice, almost into a whisper. "Fatima, do you know who the father is?"

She nods and looks at me and then Andrew. I never thought to ask her that question.

"It would be helpful if you could tell Ms. Malone and me so we can help you."

Fatima forces her head down, out of the grip of Andrew's hand.

"My baba," she speaks into her lap.

Andrew repeats her words. "Your father is the one who put this baby in you?"

Fatima nods.

"Is he hurting you?"

"He makes me do it. I don't want to—"

Andrew rolls his stool closer to Fatima's face. He begins speaking in Swahili, and I am officially out of the conversation. I barely can make out any of the words spoken, so I lean against the far wall and make myself small. I observe Andrew, and a small part of me regrets letting Andrew see my patient. I'm no longer needed here. After a few minutes of discussion, Andrew stands up and pats her on her shoulder, and we escort her out.

The rest of the afternoon is full of patients, but I can't concentrate on anything but Fatima. I am sad and disturbed, and I want to protect her. She is just a child. And she's carrying her father's child? I feel the vomit threatening to appear beneath the surface. At the end of the day, I knock on Andrew's office door to see if he is still there. His eyes slowly look up at me.

"Can we talk?" His deep-brown eyes penetrate mine as he puts the paperwork to the side, and he folds his hands across his light wood desk.

"Sure. Sit down." Andrew's eyes follow me as I sit in the chair across from his desk. I inhale sharply to slow down my breaths and then exhale slowly.

"What did you say to Fatima, and why did you start speaking in Swahili? It cut me out of the conversation." The words pour out of me quickly.

Andrew looks down at his desk and then his eyes pop up to mine. "That was not my intention, Kate. Swahili is her native tongue, and I knew she would be able to have a fuller conversation with me if she had all the words she needed."

I soften slightly at his explanation. Fatima barely speaks English, and I should have realized that before getting defensive. "What are you going to do?"

"All I can do is provide a safe place here for her to receive prenatal care and have a safe delivery. That's what is in my power to do."

I wrinkle my forehead. "She's a child, Andrew. How is she supposed to raise a child?"

"I guarantee you she is already raising her siblings. She'll know how." Andrew breaks my gaze and starts organizing the papers on his desk.

"This isn't right. There has to be more that can be done," I say, as I stand up and start pacing in his office.

"What do you want me to do? Please tell me. How can I help Fatima?" Andrew speaks with more urgency, and his voice grows a little louder. I stare at him, and he stares back, neither one of us backing down. I'm sad and angry at this, at what I've seen today, at what this child must be going through.

"Her dad is abusing her. In addition to rape, did you see her bruises?" My voice sounds shrill.

Andrew flinches at the word *rape*, and he closes his eyes for a moment before opening them again. "We aren't in America. There are no resources for this type of thing. Children getting pregnant is common, and it's also common that it's rape by a family member. This does not make it okay. It is *not* okay."

Andrew paces back and forth in his office. "I can't march to her father's hut and beat him because he will take that out on her, and then she will no longer come to our clinic to receive care." Andrew stands behind his desk and pounds his fists, creating a low vibration in the room. "I can't find a sanctuary for Fatima because then her younger siblings would be at greater risk. There aren't social services that I can call, as that does not exist here." Andrew leans on his desk and stares at me. "You seem to have all the experience coming from America, Kate. So if you have ideas, I'm all ears."

Both my hands involuntarily find their way to my mouth, and I look at Andrew with surprise. His words cut through me, as he practically yells.

"So this is how life is here? And what?" I cross my arms dramatically, in a standoff with Andrew. "Are we supposed to accept that?"

Andrew walks from behind his desk toward me, and I hold my breath. "Again, Kate, I'm very willing to listen to any ideas you have on how to improve the life of pregnant women in Tanzania."

Heat envelopes my face and descends to my chest. I abruptly turn and leave the room. If I stay another moment, Andrew would see me either yell or cry, maybe both. My questioning Fatima's circumstances turns into Andrew and I in a screaming match. I can't catch my breath as I leave the hospital, and my blood continues to boil. I take a slight detour to Maria and Noor's bungalow instead of mine. I stayed at the hospital later than I was expecting, and I'm hoping Maria is home already. I want to unload on her and the day I had. I haven't even had a chance to debrief with Maria since my trip to the country with Andrew, and we're in need for a catch-up.

Maria answers quickly as I knock on the door. "Kate, come in. You just missed Noor. He ran out to Centro Market to pick up food."

I give Maria a quick hug and then pace in her kitchen. Before I have a chance to say anything, Maria pulls a bottle of wine from the fridge and grabs two glasses. She hands me the glass, and I take a long sip and enjoy the sweetness on my lips. I put the glass down gently, and Maria fills it up again. I finally take a seat at the table.

"Tough day, Kate?"

My loud sigh fills the room, and I look at Maria, who waits patiently for me to speak. "A tough few days actually. Maria, we're friends, right?"

Maria's laugh reverberates the space. "We're more than friends. We're family."

I nod. "It's never bothered you that I'm White, has it? I guess what I mean is, race has nothing to do with our relationship, right?"

"You're going to have to be more specific," Maria says with a confused expression.

A deep breath escapes, and I explain to Maria my conversation with Andrew when we traveled to the countryside. I also tell her about today's interaction and how we seem to be rubbing each other the wrong way ever since our conversation on race.

"Kate"—Maria places her hand over mine—"did you know that Andrew didn't feel comfortable traveling to the countryside with you alone? He asked me to attend also, but I couldn't on such short notice. There is a long and complex history of race in this world, and one of those issues is the weaponization of White women, and how all a White woman needs to do is scream foul about an interaction with a Black man, and every single person will believe the White woman."

My gasp is audible, and I cover my face with my hands. "Maria, I've never felt unsafe here or with Andrew. I would never do that."

"I know that. But I'm trying to help you see why he reacted the way he did regarding the man from France. Andrew is a very smart person. Ask him questions. I'm happy to talk about my experiences as well."

"Race has never been an issue for me," I blurt out.

Maria stares at me with pursed lips. "Race has never been an issue for you because you're White. Race follows me wherever I go. If you want to hear about how bad things were for me at times in Minneapolis, I have a long list of stories I can share."

"Maria"—I reach my hand out to take hers—"I do want to hear your stories." I continue, "But why are Andrew and I at odds so much? Today he practically yelled at me because I questioned him about a patient."

"Andrew is passionate about the work being done here. If I had to guess, it keeps him up at night that he can't do more. Be patient with him. You two are still getting to know each other."

I'm once again reminded of how much I have to learn in life. Maria and I have a long conversation until Noor returns home, and I excuse myself for the evening. I have a lot to process, and the general sense that I haven't educated myself enough on many issues, which I should have before diving into being a midwife in Tanzania.

I walk out in the evening air, and the wind is warm and dances around my face, making me feel less alone. I walk the few feet to my bungalow, and I see a couple of books in front of my door with a note.

Kate, please don't feel like you have to read these books, but I thought this may be a good starting point. Keep them as long as you would like.

—Andrew

The first book is a book called *Swahili: A Complete Course for Beginners*. The next book is called *Women and Pregnancy Health in Tanzania: Navigating the Class System*. I turn the book around, and the author is Andwele Mulungu. I stare at the name for another moment and open up the front sleeve of the book, and sure enough, the author is Dr. Andrew.

I grab the books and slam the door behind me. These books are another reminder that I'm not good enough.

CHAPTER 8

Travel teaches us how to see.

—African Proverb

I can't force myself out of bed. I pull my comforter up to my chin, and I can see the sun slowly rise through my window, and the chilly morning breeze cools my room. The sun inches further into the sky until it disappears from my view altogether. All that is left is the light it provides, reflecting off my white walls and calling me out of bed. Bupe continues to miss her appointments, and Andrew is asking me to accompany him to the countryside to see after her and one other woman who is close to delivering.

I want to say no, but Andrew corners me after I finished an exam at the hospital, and I try to decline and make up an excuse. Instead, I freeze and feel like I am having an out-of-body experience as I heard my voice say, "Sure."

I've been in a funk for a few days, so maybe the change of scenery will be good. Life can feel small in the village. I roll over and lie on my back and shut my eyes for another moment. I hear the birds chirp from my window, and for a moment, it feels like I'm back home. My phone buzzes from somewhere, and I start looking around to see where I could have put it. It lies on a pile of clothes in my room that I still haven't put away since arriving here.

PETER

I want you to know I'm going to fight for you.

I consider an appropriate response, but this is all I've hoped he would say the entire time.

Me

Okay.

At exactly seven, I hear the sound of jeep tires pulling up in front of my bungalow. Not only is Andrew much smarter than me, so he's proven, he's also annoyingly punctual. "Good morning, Kate. You look very rested."

When Andrew smiles, I relax a bit and can't help but smile back. It is unseasonably warm for this time of year I'm told, and the sun kisses my skin and warms my soul.

"Good morning, you look very rested too," I reply.

With a thud, Andrew throws my overnight bag in the back of his jeep and then hands me a coffee. I smile and hold it close to me, thankful for this cup of goodness in the morning. I steal a sideways glance at Andrew, and his orange T-shirt is a beautiful contrast next to his skin. I put my head back and shut my eyes and turn my face up toward the sun. Sometimes when I close my eyes, I like to imagine I'm somewhere else, but today, I want to stay presently in this jeep with Andrew.

The road twists and turns as we leave the village until it opens up to flat land and nothingness. Dust flies up from the gravel road, and the sun beats down on me through the open roof.

Andrew turns to me. "I haven't mentioned this to you, but I'm pleased that my good friend Ahmed will meet us at the inn this evening. He and I went to medical school together and discovered we were both from Dar. He is traveling through town and will spend time with us."

"That's great." My voice is weak after not talking for a while. "When is the last time you saw Ahmed?"

"He still resides mostly in London, so I haven't seen him since moving back to Tanzania. I'm looking forward to it."

"What is he doing in these parts?" I look out at the barren land.

Andrew's mouth turns up in a smile. "Ahmed is a bit eccentric, and he took a sabbatical back in London to be the head physician at Ruaha National Park. I believe he'll do it for three months only and then head back."

I can't imagine living in so many different locations and taking jobs everywhere in the world. The concept intrigues me. "I will not be offended in any way if you want to go and have a guy's night with your friend. I will gladly retire early and let you two catch up."

"You are, of course, free to do what you choose, but know that Ahmed looks forward to meeting you."

I point to myself exaggeratingly. "Me?"

Andrew laughs. "Don't sound so surprised."

Yet I am surprised. Andrew and I have a tense relationship, at best, so it's hard to imagine him speaking about me to anyone, especially in a positive manner. I consider telling Andrew that I've started practicing my Swahili and have been vigorously reading his book, but the moment doesn't feel right. The flat land quickly turns into rolling hills, and the terrain becomes familiar to me.

"We are here, Kate." I immediately see Alvin, and his eyes get big as he recognizes Andrew and me.

"Hello, Dr. Andrew." Alvin wipes his hands on his pants as he walks over to us. "I am surprised but happy to see you."

"It is good to see you," Andrew responds. "You and Bupe didn't come to the village for your appointment, and I have other business that brings me this way, so I thought we would come to visit you and do an exam on Bupe."

"Oh, she would like that very much." Alvin nods to us to follow him into their hut. He turns back to acknowledge me.

"Hello, Ms. Kate. Bupe will be very happy to see you."

"Hi, Alvin. Yes, I will be happy too." I look around at the huts, all the same in size and shape, as goats walk through the dirt paths between them.

I stoop down through the low doorway, while Andrew stays outside and chats with Alvin. Bupe's back is turned to me as she stirs something on the stove. The strong smell of spices wafts in the air.

"Hello, Bupe, may I come in?"

"Ms. Kate!" Bupe screams as she throws her hands up in the air and drops her spoon.

I laugh as she wobbles over and embraces me.

"I am surprised to see you, Kate. Is Dr. Andrew here too?"

"He is outside talking to Alvin. We were concerned about you because you missed your appointment, and we wanted to make sure you were feeling well."

"You didn't have to come all this way. I think Dr. Andrew is just finding excuses to get you alone." Bupe gently slaps a hand on her expanding belly as she laughs.

I playfully grab her shoulder. "Trust me, we are here for you and you alone." I laugh as I think of how tense things have been with Andrew. "Is it okay if we examine you today?"

"I would like that very much." Bupe sits down on her bed and starts disrobing and preparing for the examination. When she is ready, I step outside to bring Andrew in. Alvin stays outside as he prefers.

"How have you been feeling, Bupe?"

"I feel good. It is hard for me to move around as I'm so big." Bupe puffs her cheeks out and holds her arms out to show me how big. I take measurements and listen to the heartbeat as Bupe talks. Bupe has grown a lot, as she's measuring almost thirty-six weeks.

"Bupe, why did you miss your last appointment?" Andrew scolds her playfully as he puts his hand on his hips.

"Oh, I didn't want to, but Alvin's cousin used our truck, and he said he would return it in one day, but he was gone eight days."

"I understand, but don't let anyone else borrow your truck as I want you in the village soon. The baby could come at any time. Can you do that?"

"Yes, yes, Dr. Andrew. You don't have to worry. We will be there."

"Dr. Andrew," Bupe says after the examination, "did you drive Kate all this way just to examine me for a few minutes?" Bupe laughs as she looks at Andrew and then me.

"I, uh, Bupe, I have another patient closer to town that I'll also be checking in on, and then we'll stay at the inn this evening where a friend is in town from London."

"All this sun isn't good for Kate and her skin. If you are going to bring her on these long adventures, you must protect her." Bupe points in my direction with both of her hands, trying to show Andrew my pinkish skin.

Andrew looks at me and squints his eyes as he focuses on my skin. "You are right, Bupe. I'll make sure Kate doesn't burn while she's with me."

"Thank you, Dr. Andrew. Also, I don't want you to make a fuss because of me." Andrew squeezes Bupe's hand before leaving.

"Bupe," I whisper, "you are terrible."

She laughs hysterically.

"I like to see Dr. Andrew squirm." Bupe laughs and then looks at me seriously. "Your skin is quite pink, Ms. Kate."

I press my finger into my forearm, and the pink on my arm becomes white and then slowly disappears, and the pink spreads again. I am burned.

Bupe pulls me into a hug, and I feel her warm breath on my neck as she speaks. "Kate, are you sure everything looks fine with the baby?"

I pull away gently so I can look into her eyes. They are perfect circles, and the black of her irises are such a contrast against the white.

"Bupe, I'm sure. The baby's heartbeat is strong, as is yours. You look great, and you measure where you should. I would like to take more blood work when you get to the village just to make sure." I squeeze her hand and give her a reassuring smile. Bupe takes my hand and brings it to her face. She is soft and warm, and her skin is a beautiful mocha that glistens with the light coming through the window.

"Thank you, Ms. Kate. Alvin and I want this baby badly. Alvin is especially happy, and I am scared."

I pull Bupe into an embrace again and hold her for a moment. I can feel her baby kicking against my stomach, and I smile, feeling this life inside of her. "I will make sure everything is fine, Bupe."

Her glistening eyes look into mine. We say our goodbyes to Bupe and Alvin. But before Andrew pulls away, he reaches in his backseat and grabs a blanket.

He holds it out to me. "Bupe's right. Your legs and shoulders look burned. You should put this blanket around yourself."

I grab the wooly blanket, and my hand grazes Andrew's before I quickly pull away and become a deeper shade of red. "I promise you that my skin is fine, Andrew. And, it's hot. I don't want to cover up in a blanket."

"Kate"—Andrew leans in closer to me—"Bupe will skin me alive if I let you burn on my watch. Now take the blanket." He wraps it around my shoulders and pulls it around me.

"Fine, I give up."

Andrew looks at me and pauses before he clears his throat and moves over to his side of the jeep. Andrew and I are back on the road and headed to the inn for the night. The energy feels different from before, and we both steal glances at each other. I try to unwrap the blanket, and he reaches across my body and pulls it back on me.

When Andrew speaks next, I hear a subtle quiver in his voice. It wouldn't be noticeable to everyone, but I'm used to hearing the confident doctor when he speaks. He looks at me and says, "How old are you, Kate?"

"I'm twenty-four."

"Oh."

"Oh?" I laugh. "Is that what you expected?"

Andrew's body appears to relax. "I wasn't sure how old you were. At times, you appear confident and mature, but at other times, you seem naive and inexperienced."

My face burns with surprise, and I'm sure my heart stops beating for a moment, before it palpitates roughly against my chest bone, reminding me that I'm alive. I try to hide any reaction to Andrew's backhanded compliment, yet I'm starting to get a distinct impression that he's not my biggest fan.

"I'm sorry that I come off as naive and inexperienced." I'm defensive, and I break my cover.

Andrew's eyes cut to me. "I only meant that you have so much skill. I see confidence in you at times, but at other times, you seem so unsure of yourself."

I don't respond. His words injure my ego, but it's not the first time I've heard them either. My parents have told me many times, whether it related to my schoolwork, my relationships, or becoming a midwife, that I need confidence. I heard it from my nursing professors constantly. One even told me that if I can't at least fake confidence, my patients wouldn't have confidence in me. Looking back at these memories doesn't make Andrew's words sting less.

"I didn't mean to offend you," Andrew speaks slowly. "I think it's brave that you came all of the way here. You must have been planning it for a long time."

I laugh a little too loudly, and Andrew looks startled when he looks at me. "I don't mean to laugh. It's just that it ended up being a last-minute decision."

Andrew flattens his lips as he looks at me. "Is this part of the long story that's related to your text messages?"

I stare over at Andrew as he slows down the jeep. "I guess."

The jeep stops, and I haven't realized how long we'd been driving. We're now in front of the inn.

"We are here."

"Already?"

Andrew looks at me and chuckles. "Yes, already. Ahmed texted, and he'll meet us in the lobby in one hour. I'm hoping you'll join us."

"I'm going to rest in my room, and I'll come down if I get the energy." I avoid looking at Andrew as I get out of the jeep and grab my bag. He tries to help me carry it, but I pull it out of his hand.

"Okay."

CHAPTER 9

If everyone is going to dance, who, then, would watch?

—Cameroonian Proverb

I spend a few minutes decompressing in my room, thinking about how much Andrew gets under my skin. Honestly, I'm not sure why. He's my boss. He's going to have feedback, and it's no different from the feedback I've heard before. I've never cared so much that a boss is impressed with me, but I see Andrew watch my every move, and I want him to think I'm good at this. His opinion, for whatever reason, weighs heavily on me.

The evening is hot, and the air sputters through the air-conditioning vent slowly, barely cooling the room. I put some makeup on, but it sweats off my face almost instantly. I've gotten used to my skin always coated in glistening sweat while here. I'm bronzed from the Tanzanian sun, so there is little need for blush. My pink skin from earlier has already turned brown. I put on mascara and subtle eye shadow. I decide to wear a stretchy black dress and pair it with a gold belt that Maria told me I must bring on this trip. I look in the mirror and hope tonight helps me unwind, as I have knots in my stomach and feel uneasy. Sometimes I feel so alone. I shake my head, trying to remove the thought, and focus on finishing getting ready. It's nearly been an hour, and although Andrew isn't expecting me, I'm hoping he'll be happy that I decided to join him and his friend.

A few people sit at tables, and I don't immediately see Andrew. I sit down at an empty table near the window and glance around and finally see Andrew at the door speaking to a nice-looking man, who must be Ahmed. Ahmed is a few inches shorter than Andrew and wears his hair in twists. He is dressed nicely in jeans and a polo shirt, and I can tell from where I sit how happy they are to see each other.

I stand up from the table to walk over to them. Andrew's smile lights up when he sees me. If I didn't know better, I would think we were actually friends. He puts his hand on the small of my back. "Kate, I would like you to meet my good friend Ahmed. Ahmed, this is Kate."

Ahmed leans in and kisses both of my cheeks and takes my hands. "It is very nice to meet you, Kate. Andrew has told me so much about you."

"It's nice to meet you as well."

"Kate, I'm happy you decided to join us," Andrew says. I look at him for a moment, and his eyes shine, and he does look like he's glad I'm here.

The three of us enjoy a nice dinner, and I enjoy sitting back and watching the two of them catch up. They speak mostly English but keep resorting back to Swahili, and then they look at me apologetically. I don't mind. My Swahili book has been good for me, and I can pick up a few words here and there, but not enough to follow along completely. After dinner, we walk back to the inn, where the safari travelers have now arrived, and there appear to be about twenty tourists.

Andrew looks back at Ahmed and me and says, "I'll go to the bar and grab drinks for us." Ahmed and I walk over and stand at a high-top table.

"It's great to meet you, Kate, finally. Andrew has told me a lot about you." Ahmed leans in closer. "And I, for one, am happy he moved back to Tanzania and left Jasmine behind."

"Who's Jasmine?" My curiosity piques as I anxiously await Ahmed's response.

"The woman he was engaged to." Andrew arrives with three Serengetis and two shots. I wish I would have had more alone time with Ahmed to find out more.

A fast song comes on, and Ahmed claps his hands together and reaches for Andrew's hand and mine and pulls us to the dance floor. I don't have the chance to pull back. I laugh as I watch how excitedly Ahmed moves his body to the music. I do my best to move to the beat and blush as I watch Andrew dance. Ahmed takes the hands of a woman who seems to love the attention, and now I'm dancing only with Andrew. He takes my hand and leads me through the dance. My heart feels like it may explode out of my body, and my hand tingles where it touches his. This feels different from how negative I was feeling about him a few short hours ago. My heart flutters at his beauty and how my body reacts to touching his, ever so slightly. Andrew puts his other hand on my waist and pulls me in closer, and I feel like I'm going to faint from the excitement, as the space between us lessens. Our hips nearly touch as we move to the music. Andrew, so tall as I look up at him, spins me, and I'm no longer as close to him, and the song ends. Andrew's lips brush up against my cheek, and I flush, his hands still on my hips. Andrew becomes aware of his hands at the same time I do and abruptly removes them and puts more distance between us.

"I don't think you've given yourself a fair dance assessment, Kate. You are a fine dancer," Andrew leans in to say into my ear.

"That's one of the nicest things you've said to me." I laugh, but my mind thinks about all the critiques he has given me. "You keep dancing. I'm going to sit down for a moment."

Andrew smiles and goes back on the dance floor to join Ahmed. They are both in high demand with the European tourists, who all take turns being spun by them. The women especially fawn over Andrew. He moves so smoothly, and his clothes cling to every inch of his body perfectly. My mouth starts to water; only I don't think it's from watching Andrew dance.

Everything begins to look a little blurry. I put my elbows on the table and then rest my head in my hands. I close my eyes to stop the spinning. My face is hot and nearly scorches my hands. The music is loud, and rhythm beats against my two heartbeats—one in my chest and one in my stomach. I'm clammy and cold yet hot, and I can't open my eyes because the movement of people will put me over the edge, I fear.

A hand spreads across my lower back. "Kate, are you okay?" It's Andrew's voice ringing in my ears.

"I think I'm going to be sick," I moan into my hands.

"Let's get you to your room." I feel a hand hitch itself around my waist and pull me up. I open my eyes and see Andrew on one side and Ahmed on the other. I walk up the stairs, completely leaning on Andrew, almost unable to hold up my weight. My legs are jelly.

"Where is your room key, Kate?" I pull it out of my wallet and hand it to Andrew.

"Andrew, I'm going to be sick." This time it's said with more urgency.

The door to my hotel room opens, and I push Andrew and Ahmed out of the way and run into the bathroom and slam the door behind me. The vomit projectiles out of me and in and around the toilet. Every muscle in my stomach tightens as all its content flies out of me with startling force. I hear myself moan, and with my foot, I kick the bathroom door further closed. Just when I think nothing else can possibly come out, I start vomiting all over again.

The cold bathroom tiles sting my hot skin as I lie in a fetal position, holding my stomach between episodes. The tiles are a putrid yellow, the color of the contents that flew out of my stomach. I feel empty, but my stomach keeps constricting and cramping. I may never leave this bathroom again. I'll just lie on the floor and wait until someone finds my body. I lie back on the tile. My entire body shivers, and my teeth clatter together, and I stare at the flickering light above the sink. The whole room is silent except for my teeth violently clamoring against one another.

"Kate, can I come in?" Andrew's voice rings from the other side of the door, but I don't have the strength to respond. The door opens and I'm forced to sit up so it can open fully.

"You don't look so good." Andrew helps me to my feet. "Let me get you into the bed." I feel myself being lifted by Andrew, and I feel the stiff mattress beneath me.

"I'm so cold."

Andrew takes my shoes off. "You threw up on your dress." The back of his hand feels my forehead, and his hand feels like it's going to leave burn marks on me.

I need to take my dress off, but my arms feel like dumbbells, and I can't lift them. I think I hear Andrew rummaging through my bag. "You need to get out of that dress."

I slowly sway my head. I can barely move. I hear a heavy sigh from Andrew, and then he shimmies my dress over my head, and I feel soft cotton. Then he covers up my skin.

"Kate, you're burning up." There is shuffling and, perhaps, a faucet running, and then a cold towel on my forehead.

"Ahmed ran to see if there is a pharmacy open, and he also grabbed my medical bag. I think you have food poisoning."

I moan, and it's the only sound I can manage. Andrew finds a bag and hands it to me, and even more comes out of me. I hear the door open, but I don't open my eyes. Words are exchanged, and then the door closes again.

"Kate, Ahmed got medicine. I'm going to place this on your tongue."

I shake my head no, and he opens my mouth anyway. Andrew places a small pill there as his finger briefly touches my tongue, and then I feel Andrew manipulate a thermometer under my tongue. I doze in and out of sleep. I don't think I've thrown up in a while. I keep feeling Andrew's hand on my forehead, and then I fall back asleep. The cramps in my stomach are what I imagine childbirth will feel like. I open my eyes to slits. The room is pitch-black, and my teeth clatter, and I'm sure I'm going to freeze to death. I see a shadow in the corner of the room, and my eyes make out that it's Andrew on a chair.

"Andrew," I whisper painfully.

His body jolts up until he's kneeling next to me.

"I'm freezing. I'm so cold I think I'm going to die." The words come out slow, in waves, and at this moment, I don't feel like I'm exaggerating.

The bed dips, and Andrew hops in and gets under the covers. He pulls me into him and tightly wraps his arms around me and rubs my back. "Your fever is over 105. That's why you're so cold. I'm trying to get you warmer, but you need to keep that cold washcloth on your forehead."

I have forgotten how warm human bodies are but am reminded as I nuzzle my back into Andrew. He is the temperature I should strive for. I turn toward him, and his cotton shirt is soft and feels so good against my cheek that I want to wrap myself in it. He smells like soap and vanilla, and for whatever reason, the scent is intoxicating and also calming. His hand moves up to my head, and he rubs my hair.

My jaw relaxes as I start to warm slightly, and my teeth no longer clamor. "I'm sorry if I smell like puke."

Andrew's chest shakes as he laughs. "I assure you. You don't smell like puke." He moves his hand for a moment and feels my forehead. "Are you starting to warm up?"

"A little. Don't leave me. I'm still too cold to sleep."

I pull him in closer in case he tries to leave. His warmth is the only thing making me feel like I have a chance to survive the night. Andrew's chest goes up and then back down, over and over again. The sound of his heart against my ear is soothing and helps slow my speeding heart down.

"Tell me about where you're from, Kate." My body relaxes a little, and I further melt into Andrew's.

"I'm from Minneapolis. It's in the northcentral part of the country."

"Tell me about Minneapolis."

"It can be cold, but it can be hot too. It's a nice city. There are fun things to do. There are sport's teams and theaters and art." My words are sporadically spoken through the clamoring of teeth.

"Are you looking forward to going home?"

I continue to speak into Andrew's shirt without looking up at him. "I'm mostly excited. I didn't want to come here."

Andrew pulls me away from his body slightly and then pulls me back in. "Really? How come?"

"My dad made me. He thought I needed a distraction." My entire body shakes as I shiver. "Clearly, my dad thinks big."

I further melt into Andrew's hard chest. "What did you need a distraction from?"

"Life."

"What happened, Kate?" Andrew's words come out slowly. I feel his hand check my forehead again before he wraps it around my arm.

"I don't want to talk about it."

Andrew's chest stops moving rhythmically, but then he lets out a long and deliberate breath. My entire body feels warmer, and I don't want him to loosen his grip on me. His body is warm, and it's hard, and I can feel where his muscles come together like a jigsaw puzzle. I feel this strange safeness around him.

"Why are you so hard on me?"

"Because I believe in you," Andrew answers, and I realize I asked the question out loud and not just in my head.

"I've been meaning to tell you something," I say. *Because it's dark and I can't see Andrew's face, speaking truths to him seems easy.*

Andrew runs his long fingers through my hair, and his chest stops expanding against me as he waits.

"I've been reading the books you left for me," I confess. "And I was wrong to press you on Fatima, and I do want to learn about your experience with being Black." The words come out sleepily.

Andrew guides my head further into his chest and holds it there. I fall asleep to the smell of vanilla that instantly reminds me of baking cookies with my grandma when I was young. My last memory before dozing off is Andrew's soft and full lips, brushing against my forehead.

My stomach feels like I spent the night doing sit-ups. It's tight and in knots, and it also feels hollow. I can feel the sun on my face before I open my eyes. I open one eye first, and then the other, and Andrew sits in the chair, staring at me. When he sees my eyes open, he walks over to me and puts his hand on my forehead, but I already know what he's confirming; my fever has broken.

"How are you feeling, Kate?" Andrew sits on the edge of the bed and looks at me with concern.

I groan, remembering last night. I close my eyes as I remember Andrew changing me out of my dress. "I feel like someone beat me up."

Andrew smiles down at me. "You still look a bit green."

He hands me a bottle of water and helps me sit up. "I'm not sure if you'll be able to keep this down, but we need to make sure you don't get dehydrated." The room temperature water touches my lips, and I sip it slowly. We hear a light knock, and Andrew goes to the door.

"Hi, Kate. You almost look human again." Ahmed walks over to me and squeezes my hand.

"I almost feel human. Luckily, I had two doctors looking over me."

"I don't know how helpful I was. You had a pretty nasty case of food poisoning," Andrew says as he forces more water into me.

I look over at Ahmed and then at Andrew. "If it was food poisoning, why aren't you both sick?"

Andrew sits at the edge of the bed once again. "Because neither of us had the chicken dish." I think back to what we all ate. We all had bread, but then they both had a vegetable dish, and I was craving chicken. Now it all makes sense.

Ahmed places his hand on my cheek. "I'm sorry to leave you during a time of need, but I need to get on the road."

I give him my best smile. "I'm sure I made a great impression on you."

"You truly did, Kate." Ahmed kisses my forehead, and Andrew walks him out. I hear quiet voices by the door as they say their goodbyes.

I stand up, and the blood immediately rushes to my head. I stand a moment before taking a step, and I feel like a baby giraffe learning how to walk again. I go into the bathroom and look in the mirror, and my face is a pale shade of green. I brush my teeth and gag at the taste of the toothpaste. I rub my stomach, and it feels hard and lumpy. I will never eat chicken again.

Andrew walks back into the room. "I ran out and got you a ginger ale. I thought it might help your stomach."

I look at him curiously as he holds on to a garment bag. "I had your dress sent out to be washed last night. I hope you don't mind."

My face gets hot, and I imagine it looking redder than green at this moment. "I tried to get you to change, Kate, but you were unable." Andrew looks down. "I'm sorry."

I don't care how many naked women Andrew's seen in his line of work. The thought of Andrew seeing me in nothing more than a bra and panties makes me nearly die of embarrassment. When our eyes meet, I know he's thinking about the same thing I am.

Andrew pats me on my knee, and the bed dips down as he stands up. He turns to me as he reaches the door. "Keep drinking the ginger ale, Kate."

I lie back on the bed, knowing my ego may never recover.

CHAPTER 10

A good conversation is better than a good bed.

—Ethiopian Proverb

The sun penetrates my skin as I walk to the hospital with Maria. The sun is warm. There is a light breeze that doesn't allow me to get too hot, and the sky is the most beautiful color blue. I wish I could sit in my backyard with Maria all day, but instead, we'll both need to spend it at the hospital.

"Okay, Kate. So you're telling me you had a high fever, so Andrew got into bed with you and held you?"

I moan. "The entire night was a blur, but yes, I couldn't get warm because of the fever."

Maria squints her eyes, untrustingly looking at me. "I'm so sorry you were that sick. Thank goodness Andrew was there."

I close my eyes and look back up toward the sun. "Yeah, but now I'm scared to have to see him again."

"Don't be. Andrew is a consummate professional, and you needed help. He doesn't even see you as a woman."

Maria's words sting for some reason. My head still feels foggy, and I'm not sure how I feel or why I hope Andrew sees me as a woman. All I know is that I haven't been able to get Andrew out of my head since that night. To say I'm confused would be an understatement. Lately, I've been entertaining reaching out to Peter and having a much-needed conversation about what happened and our past and how he plans to fight for me. But there is this other part of me that can't deny the attraction I have to Andrew.

I shudder as the cold hits my shoulders as Maria and I get inside the hospital, and I know there is no point in thinking about Andrew in that manner. Andrew is my boss at work, and I'm his subordinate, and thinking of him in any way other than that would be counterproductive.

"I'll see you later, Maria," I say, as I wave while she steps inside her office, and I walk to the waiting room.

The waiting room is full, and Editha motions to me. "Kate, a woman is waiting in room 4 and room 7, and Andrew is with a patient in room 1. Take your pick, but room 4 seems more urgent."

I quickly change into my scrubs and tie my hair back into a top bun. Nyla has recently taken a leave from the hospital to visit family in Dar, and it's been hard to keep up. She's the only other staff at the hospital with experience delivering babies, so for now, it's only Andrew and me. There are days where hardly any women show up at the hospital, but other days are like today, where there is no way we can get to all the patients. It hasn't happened since I've arrived here, but Maria has told me stories of women giving birth on their own in hospitals because the doctors are busy with other patients.

I knock once on the door, then enter exam room 4. A woman sits on the bed and grimaces as I walk in. "*Jambo!*" I say enthusiastically, as I try out my Swahili.

The woman glances at me as she holds her belly. She is a tiny thing, and her belly protrudes straight out from her small frame. Her hair is uncovered, and her braids reach the middle of her back. She's already removed her skirt, and a blanket covers her legs.

"I'm Kate," I say as I grab my stethoscope. "It looks like you're about to have a baby."

The woman grimaces as she once again grips her belly. "My name is Adla. The baby is coming."

I instruct Adla to lie back, and I do an examination. The baby is already low, and I can see the top of the head starting to crown. Thick black hair is visible, and it shouldn't be long before the baby is born.

"Adla, is this your first child?"

She nods her head vigorously as she screams out in pain. I instruct her to push every time the pain comes, and Adla bears down.

The head descends slightly with every push and then goes back farther into the birthing canal. This hospital does its best, but I feel lost without the technology to monitor the baby's heartbeat during birth, as well as monitor the mother. Even in the States, not all moms request this technology, but I'm finding most do. So much of what Maria does is apply for grants and funding so this hospital can be better equipped, but there is so much further to go.

I wet a cloth and place it on Adla's forehead. She feels warm to me, and I'm nervous she has a fever. "Adla, you're doing great. For your next contraction, I want you to push with everything you have."

Adla screams out as she bears down. I attempt to maneuver the head out and can see the forehead, the eyes, the nose, and finally, the lips appear as well. With her next push, the shoulder seems lodged and refuses to pass through the birthing canal. Adla pushes again, and her scream pierces through the room.

"Adla, you're doing great. I can see your baby's head. You are so close."

I push on Adla's belly, just above her pelvic bone, hoping this will help free the shoulder. I do it once more with the next contraction, and I feel like the shoulder is starting to loosen, and I can see more of it. The exam room door swings open, and Andrew rushes toward us. He kneels next to me and then exits the room and yells something to Editha in Swahili.

Everything happens in slow motion, as I watch Andrew come back into the room, this time, with medicine, and he gives her a quick shot. He pulls a cart over to us, and I watch with wide eyes as he grabs a scalpel. Andrew cuts in a down and outward angle, and Adla's opening increases, and with one push, I catch the baby and quickly clean out his mouth, and the large baby boy cries out.

I place the baby on Adla's chest. "Congrats," I say through gritted teeth, "you have a healthy baby boy."

I stand back and watch as Adla holds her baby and cries. Andrew's eyes cut to mine, and I see his mouth go to say something, but I turn away from him before he has the chance and walk out of the exam room. Andrew can handle stitching Adla up and finishing up with her. I wash up and see the patient in exam room 7.

The anger boils in my chest as I continue to see patients. I was fooling myself when I thought that when Andrew and I got back to the village, that somehow things would be different. I thought perhaps he would stop undermining me at every turn. But the first time I saw him since returning, he pushed me out of the way and finished up with my delivery.

My cold shower is doing little to help with my anger. Logically, I know I have no reason to be upset, but I can't seem to stop fuming. I was doing everything I was taught in school. I gently applied pressure to Adla's pelvic bone to release pressure and help the shoulder pass. Everything was going fine until Andrew barged through the door.

*****

There's a loud knock at the door, and my eyes dart to it. I quickly pull on a pair of leggings and a shirt and towel dry my hair as I walk to the door. I swing my door open, and Andrew stands before me, and he wipes at a drip of water that starts running down his face from his hairline. He looks freshly showered himself, and when a breeze comes up behind him, the aroma of vanilla nearly intoxicates me.

"I am hoping we can talk, Kate."

I swing the door further open and turn my back and walk into the kitchen. I hear his footsteps follow closely behind. I pour myself a glass of wine and hold it up to Andrew, but he shakes his head.

"I want to discuss Adla with you," Andrew says. "I tried to give you space, but she'd been birthing too long. I could hear her from the other end of the hallway."

The anger starts in my stomach and works its way through my chest and out my mouth. "You undermined me."

Andrew puts his hand on his stomach as he winces. "I was nervous about shoulder dystocia. I've delivered babies who have died from that."

I sit down in a chair but stand up quickly. "I've also delivered babies with shoulder dystocia who were fine. I also work with medical professionals who consider episiotomies the same as genital muti-

lation." I furrow my brow. "Did you know that after having an episiotomy, women can have issues with intercourse for eighteen months
after the delivery?"

Andrew walks closer to me until we're almost touching. I strain
my neck to look up at him. "I do know that. I also know that Adla
had a fever. I could tell the minute I touched her skin. I also knew
that labor wasn't progressing."

"I was considering doing an episiotomy, but I hadn't exhausted
all the options yet. You intervened too soon."

Andrew puts his hand on the table and flicks his eyes to mine.
"I don't think you intervened soon enough, Kate. Adla and her baby
were starting to feel distressed."

"I know this is your hospital, and I know you are the doctor,
and I'm nothing more than a nurse and a midwife, but you undermined me today." The tears feel dangerously close to the surface as
the words pour out of me.

"Undermining you was never my intention. I made a quick
decision on what I thought was best for Adla and her baby."

My voice shakes. "You want me to have confidence, but you
second-guess me at every turn."

I look up at Andrew, and his almond eyes penetrate mine. For a
moment, I forget that I'm talking to my superior and not the Andrew
who laid in bed with me when I had food poisoning and definitely
not the Andrew who kissed my forehead as I fell asleep.

"My number 1 priority is the safety and well-being of my
patients. I did what I thought was best."

I turn my back to him and lean against my counter. I take a
slow drink of my wine and then turn to him again. "What bothers
me most is that you don't trust me." I turn around, as Andrew slowly
walks toward me, and I dig my palms into the counter and lean back.

"Kate, the problem is…is that you don't trust yourself. You have
no confidence in your abilities." He takes another step toward me.
"You paused today. I saw you. I stood outside the room and listened.
I didn't want to intervene, but I could feel your nervous energy from
the hallway."

My mouth opens, but no words come out. "Kate, you're young and inexperienced. I don't know if you've lost your confidence or you never had it but start believing in yourself."

"You have it all wrong, Andrew. I believe in myself plenty," I practically whisper.

"I don't see it that way," he retorts.

"You don't even know me."

"Kate," he says, pained. Andrew puts both arms on the counter I'm leaning on, boxing me in.

I hold my breath as I feel his warm breath on my face. His eyes look darker than usual, and his full lips are slightly open. My mind quickly remembers my first date with Peter as a sixteen-year-old. I haven't had a first kiss with anyone since then, but I'll never forget how dark Peter's eyes got, and I may be wrong, but I feel like I see the same look in Andrew's.

Andrew leans in, inch by inch, until our lips are a hairbreadth apart. I place my hand on Andrew's chest and spread my fingers. He's so hard underneath my hand, and his heart beats fast. Even with my fingers fully spread, they don't come near to covering his chest entirely.

"Andrew," I say as I exhale.

He blinks quickly and stands up straight and puts space between us. My eyes fixate on his lips, where he quickly pulls them into his mouth. Andrew turns away from me and walks to the door. He pauses with his hand on the doorknob and doesn't look at me when he speaks.

"You are great at what you do. I never want to contribute to you not believing in yourself."

"Thanks," I say to Andrew's back.

Andrew walks out of my bungalow, and I shut the door behind him. I lean against the closed door and attempt to regulate my breathing. I'm not always the most perceptive person, but there is no denying that something odd transpired between Andrew and me. We were mere inches from kissing.

I lie in bed and pull the covers up to my chin and watch the sun disappear slowly behind the fence in the backyard. I can already tell that sleep won't come easily tonight. I can't shut my mind off as I think about Peter and the chance of reconciliation and about Andrew and what just took place.

CHAPTER 11

The child who is not embraced by the village will burn it down to feel its warmth.

—African Proverb

Morning coffee with Maria at my bungalow has become my favorite daily routine. For so many evenings, I join Maria and Noor at their place for dinner, but mornings have been solely for us. The coffee here is dark and strong, and a cup keeps me sustained at the hospital all day.

I take a long sip and let the liquid warm my throat. "How are your wedding plans coming, Maria?"

Maria leans back in her chair and closes her eyes as she looks up and greets the sun with a smile.

"Everything is coming together great. It's hard to believe it's only a month away. My parents and some family back in Dar will arrive a week prior, and Andrew said wedding guests could stay at the empty hospital bungalows, which works out great."

We both slowly stand up, as it's time to get to the hospital and start our work for the day, and I take Maria's cup from her and place it in the sink with mine.

When the hospital was built over a year ago, ten accompanying bungalows in all shapes and sizes were built along the western parameter. Andrew's vision was that the bungalows would house people like myself who came from far away to work at the hospital. Most remain empty, as many of the hospital staff already live in the village.

Maria loops her arm in mine. "Speaking of the wedding, Kate, have you talked to your parents?"

We walk slowly up the stairs, in no hurry to start the day. "We've been playing phone tag. Have you talked to them?"

"Not on the phone, but I received an email from your mom yesterday. They will for sure be here for the wedding, and it sounds like they may extend their stay and travel around Tanzania."

I look down at my phone, and I don't have any missed calls or texts, but I need to get ahold of my parents. I know they are planning to come to the wedding, but I don't know how long they plan on staying. My parents consider Maria as their daughter; I know they will not miss her wedding. Yet the thought of my parents here and my two separate worlds colliding cause my throat to tighten.

"I'll see you after work, Maria." We wave and go our separate ways when we reach the second floor.

The waiting room isn't too full yet, but my eyes immediately cut to the young girl sitting with her hands folded in her lap, and I know instantly that it's Fatima. Her shoulders hunch over, and she avoids eye contact with everyone. It's as if the weight of the world sits atop her small frame.

"Hi, Fatima, how are you?"

"I am fine, Ms. Kate."

"If you're ready, I can bring you back." She reaches her hand out for mine, and I help her stand up.

I observe Fatima as I lead her into an exam room. She once again wears a dress that flows over her body and hides her shape, and I still can't see a pregnant belly through it. I'm learning, this village is small, and people talk, and if someone discovers that Fatima is pregnant, it will bring great shame to her and her family. I'm relieved to see her. The short time I have with her when she decides to show up, I know she's safe, if only for a moment.

"How are you feeling today, Fatima?"

"I feel good. I am feeling the baby a lot right now."

I place my arm gently on Fatima's and warmly squeeze it. I do my exam, and Fatima is right where she should be. My guess is she'll deliver sometime in late September, and I hope that I'll still be in Tanzania when it happens. Fatima's beautiful dark skin stretches where her stomach protrudes out and is no more than the size of a melon. The baby's heartbeat is high up in her belly, which means the baby is currently in a breech position. Although not uncommon at this point in a pregnancy, I still note it in her chart. I feel a gust from the door opening before I hear footsteps.

"Hello, Fatima, how are you feeling today?" Andrew walks directly over to where she sits and places both hands on her shoulders.

"I feel fine," Fatima says as she looks down at her hands.

Andrew's eyes cut to mine. "How did Fatima's exam go today?"

"Everything looks great with the baby, and Fatima says she's feeling healthy."

Andrew pulls up a chair and sits next to Fatima at the end of the exam table. "Fatima, you have a little over eight weeks until delivery. No decisions need to be made today, but the next time you come for an exam, we need to start discussing what the plan is for the baby. At your first appointment, you mentioned your father not wanting you to parent. However, it will take time for me to make arrangements if that is still the case."

Andrew speaks slowly as he explains everything to Fatima. She looks down and picks at her fingernails, never looking up to meet our eyes. Andrew sits patiently and turns his head, waiting for Fatima to respond.

"Is this something you can spend time thinking about?" Andrew asks her.

"Yes"—Fatima looks up at Andrew for the first time in minutes—"may I go now?"

"Of course"—Andrew stands up and pats Fatima on the knee—"Ms. Kate can finish up with you."

Fatima gets dressed, and I walk her out of the room, and she promises that she'll be back in a month.

The rest of the day flies by. I'm always surprised at how quickly time goes in this field. Even when there aren't many patients to see, there are still charts to review. The waiting room sits empty, and when I glance at the clock, it's already six in the evening. I put on my street clothes, ready to head out for the day. I hear footsteps come up behind me as I walk out of the hospital. I turn to look, and Andrew is a few steps behind me, also changed into his street clothes. He catches up to me and matches my pace.

"Do you have any plans for the evening, Kate?" I look toward my bungalow but keep walking.

"I don't have plans but was planning to walk to Centro Market to pick up food."

"I have the same plans. Is it fine if I walk with you?"

A few excuses run through my mind rapidly—like, we almost kissed, and now things feel awkward for me. Or you continue not to have confidence in me, which isn't helping my confidence in myself. But it isn't easy for me to tell people how I feel, so instead of saying any of those things, I let out an audible sigh.

"Of course."

Centro Market is the main market in the village, and it sits in the middle of town. Nothing in this village isn't walkable. It reminds me of a small Minnesotan town where the entire place is only ten blocks, and the action is compacted in the center of town. I look up at Andrew, who stares straight out. We walk in silence for a few moments, and when I stare straight ahead, I feel him turn and look at me.

I finally break the silence. "What are Fatima's options with the baby?"

We reach Centro Market, and it's busy. It looks like a farmer's market, with many tents and stands selling everything from meat to fruit and vegetables to junk food from around the world. Behind Centro Market, the street is lined with restaurants and shops, and few bars and music blasts from one of those bars.

"Fatima can place the child for adoption, parent the child, or find someone in the village like a friend or family member to parent the child."

I stop at a fruit station and examine the melons and oranges. Andrew knocks on the melon, and when he catches me observing, he shows me how to do the same to test for ripeness.

"What does adoption look like here?"

The man behind the counter watches us and then whispers to the man standing next to him, as he continues to stare at Andrew and me examining the fruit.

"Most of the orphanages in Tanzania reside in Dar es Salaam. I have a contact in Izazi who works directly with a couple of orphanages in Dar, and if this is what Fatima chooses, her baby would be transported to Izazi, and they would handle it from there."

I pay for a melon and some oranges, and we walk to the next vendor who is selling rice, which I also need. "What do you think she should do?"

"Honestly, Kate, I don't know what she can do besides adoption. Her family would be shunned if she came home with a baby at her age."

I scoop up the rice I want, and Andrew scoops up his own rice, and we pay and keep walking. Women stop and stare and then put their hands up to their mouths to cover up as they speak to one another quietly while glaring at us. We pass an older couple, and I don't think I imagine it when the woman glares at me and then says something to the man next to her. Whatever she says, she doesn't whisper, but she speaks too quickly for me to understand the Swahili.

I furrow my brow and say to Andrew in a whisper, "I feel like I'm being talked about."

Andrew lets out a heavy sigh. "You are." He clears his throat. "Or I should say, we are."

I'm uncomfortable with how many people stare at us. "Why?"

Andrew stops walking when we reach a wine tent, and he rummages through different varieties of red wine. "She called me dishonorable for being with you when there are many eligible women in the village to choose from."

My mouth hangs open. "And what is being said about me?"

"Kate," Andrew looks at me sympathetically.

"Please," I retort, "I want to know."

Andrew puts bottles of wine in the bag he brought. "The woman said that you should return home and find a husband there."

I look around in shock as people continue to watch us indiscreetly. I've been to Centro Market several times since I arrived in

Tanzania, mostly with Maria. I've also been here alone. Perhaps I am not as astute, but I don't recall anyone giving me long and disapproving looks like they are today. I look down at my outfit, and it's modest. My shirt is short-sleeved, but it flows, and my cotton skirt hits me mid-knee. Andrew and I pay for our wine, and his fingers spread on my lower back. He ushers me to the edge of the market and toward our bungalows. Andrew removes his hand as we exit Centro Market, where everything feels safe again.

"You should have told her I'm not in the village looking for a husband," I say, with a look of disgust that someone would think that of me.

A look of disappointment covers Andrew's face as I continue, "And you could have told them that we're not together in that sense."

"I find it best not to engage with people who express such archaic points of view," Andrew retorts. "Plus, it's not personal. They didn't like seeing us together, and neither one of us owes anyone an explanation."

We pass Andrew's bungalow, which is only a few down from mine, but he continues to walk with me until we reach my door.

"Call me naive, but was today's whispering because I'm White?" I think back to a few days ago when Andrew himself told me I could come off as naive.

"Yes, Kate. In the bigger cities in Tanzania, it would be a nonissue. Still, you have to understand this village is in the middle of nowhere, and for the most part, people aren't educated, nor have they experienced a lot of diversity."

"So do they disapprove of me or you?"

Andrew laughs and readjusts the bag in his hand. "Both. Kate, you seem to have a propensity for wanting people to like you."

Andrew isn't wrong, although I don't tell him that. I've always preferred to stay neutral in situations, knowing that not everyone will become a best friend but preferring the ease of not having anyone dislike me. Being like this has prevented me from having many close relationships, but it's also saved me the heartache of being the center of someone else's negativity.

"A piece of advice, Kate," Andrew says.

We stand in front of my door, and Andrew stands in the shade, and we both can quit squinting as we look at each other.

"Do what makes you happy and what you think is right, and don't let the opinion of others, especially strangers, help guide your decisions."

I chuckle as I picture me as Aristotle to Andrew's Plato, once again teaching me the ways of life. Andrew gives me lessons in the clinic and in life. I know he's older than me, and if I had to guess, he's in his early thirties, but sometimes I imagine how stupid and immature he must think I am. I have no world experience, and more than one time since being in Tanzania, it's shown.

My bags start to feel like weights in my hand, and my arms begin to ache. "Well, thanks for accompanying me to Centro Market. I'm going to get these bags inside."

Andrew leans across my body and opens my door for me. His arm grazes mine, causing my entire body to pebble with goose bumps. Without thinking, I lean into him slightly and inhale sharply and breathe in his scent. My eyes cut to his, and I know he's caught me.

"I'll see you tomorrow, Kate."

I turn to shut my door, and Andrew stands until the door is closed, and then I hear his footsteps outside as he walks toward his bungalow. I put my bags down on my counter and glance down at my phone and have several text messages.

Mom

> I'll try to call tomorrow, but in the meantime, I wanted to let you know, your dad and I have both been granted three full weeks off from work, so we're going to spend it in Tanzania. I also want you to know that the Jacobsons will be joining us. Let's chat more tomorrow.

My eyes nearly pop out of my head as I read and reread my mom's text message. Not only will she and my dad be in Tanzania for much longer than I expected, but the Jacobsons will be joining them? My mom has been best friends with Peter's mom, Barb, since before I was born, and Peter's dad went to medical school with my dad and Maria's dad, but the news still shocks me.

PETER

You may have already heard the news. My parents and I are both going to be joining your parents in Tanzania. This is me fighting for you, for us.

My phone hits the counter with a loud clunk. Time is no longer on my side to figure out what I want to do with my future with Peter. My worlds are about to collide in the biggest way possible.

CHAPTER 12

If you're a good person, even after death, your grave is loved.

—African Proverb

The next morning as I sit outside before work, I'm startled by the ringing of my phone. I see *Mom's cell* flash on my screen, and a picture of her at our lake house pops up on my screen.

"Hi, Mom."

"Kate, did you get my text from yesterday?"

"Yeah, it was too late to call, so I was hoping we'd connect today."

"I wanted to talk to you about our trip to Tanzania for the wedding."

"Okay." I stretch my legs out and hike my shorts up so the sun can reach as much skin as possible.

"I wanted to make sure you saw my text about the Jacobsons joining us."

I feel light-headed, and I'm happy I'm sitting down. When we first called off the engagement, I knew it was going to be awkward with our parents being friends, but I'd put that out of my mind for a while.

"Peter will come with his parents."

"Mom, won't this be a bit uncomfortable for all involved considering Peter and I aren't together anymore?"

"Barb told me that Peter is trying to get you back. Why didn't you tell me that, Kate?"

I take a deep breath and wish I wasn't having this conversation with my mom. "Because I'm processing everything still. Until I figure out some stuff, it's not worth a conversation."

"Kate, I can tell you firsthand how sorry he is. He came and spoke to your father and me."

"Mom, I don't want to discuss this, not now." I attempt to steady my voice but feel annoyed by my mom's meddling.

I hear a massive sigh into the phone. "Okay, but we leave in a few days, and Maria's parents will make sure we all get to the village. We'll stay for a little over a week, and we leave the day after the wedding for safari for a few days and then will end our trip back in the village."

"I'll think about it, but I really need to go." I end the call before I hear my mom say goodbye. I rub my temples, and then head to the hospital. The first people I see in the waiting room are Bupe and Alvin. I run over to her, not realizing how excited I am to see her.

"Bupe, you are here! I am happy to see you!" I give her a big hug, and we kiss each other on the cheeks.

"Alvin, it is great to see you also." I smile in his direction, not wanting him to feel left out. "Let's get you examined, Bupe. Alvin, you wait here, and I'll come and get you afterward."

I bring Bupe into the exam room and notice how much she has grown since the last time I saw her in the village. She wobbles when she walks and looks like she could have this baby any day now.

"How are you feeling?"

"I feel great. The baby is moving a lot. Alvin was starting to get nervous, so we decided to make the journey here to be safe."

"I'm happy you did. We can put you and Alvin in a nice room here, and then we'll all be ready the minute you go into labor."

I grab Bupe's hand as I guide her to the exam table. We look into each other's eyes, and Bupe gently squeezes my hand in gratitude. I start my measurements, and when I hear her baby's perfect heartbeat, I smile and start to relax. I bring Alvin in and show them to a room where they will both stay until the baby is born. I feel better they are both here, and I'm happy I will be able to check in on them daily.

"The staff here will take great care of both of you. Dr. Andrew and I will be here every day to check on you both." As if perfectly on cue, Andrew knocks and walks through the door.

Andrew smiles at me and then looks at Bupe and Alvin and smiles and greets them. "I heard you were both here."

"We are happy to be here," Bupe says as she smiles at Andrew and then looks at me and smiles. "Ms. Kate is going to get me settled into a room, and Alvin will park the truck."

Andrew looks at me again. "That sounds like a great plan. I'll check in on you later." Andrew squeezes Bupe's shoulder and then turns around to leave the room.

Bupe smiles at me. "Oh, Ms. Kate. Now you've made Andrew go and fall in love with you."

I put my hand over my mouth to stifle my laugh. "Bupe, what are you talking about?"

"He loves you, Ms. Kate. I know about these matters." Bupe takes my hand in hers and laughs.

Love. My only experience with it is how gradually it happens. I imagine a seed, and every day, it must be watered and tended to before it turns into a beautiful flower. I've only felt love once, and it was a slow process of getting to know each other.

"Do you love him too? You are harder for me to read." Bupe looks at me with sincerity.

I give Bupe my best side smile and turn my head slightly as I look at her. "I quit allowing myself to feel things like love a long time ago."

"Oh, Kate." Bupe crumples her face in pain. "I see what's going on. You've been hurt. I should have seen it sooner."

Tears threaten to fall, but instead, I laugh. "Bupe, I'm fine. I promise."

"Ms. Kate, I don't know if you know this, but I can read people. My mother could read people, and my grandma. It runs in our family."

I walk over and stand in front of Bupe, and she takes both my hands. "And what do you see when you read me?" I ask jokingly.

Bupe looks at me seriously, and I can tell this is not a joke for her.

"I can see that you're in charge of your destiny, but it will only work out the way you want it to if you stop listening to others and start putting yourself first."

I raise my eyebrows and help Bupe off the table and settle her and Alvin into their room. I play her words on repeat and wonder if there is truth to them. I can't get Bupe's round eyes out of my mind and the way they penetrated my own. It looks like she is seeing me. I mean, actually seeing me.

*****

Early the next morning, a loud knock echoes throughout my bungalow, and I sit up quickly in my bed and rub my eyes and see Maria standing at the doorway to my room. "Andrew told me to come and get you. It looks like Bupe is in labor."

I nod and throw on my shoes and run into the hospital with Maria. I quickly wash up and go into the delivery room where they are. The very first patient I met in Tanzania is about to have a baby. Bupe's eyes dart to me when I walk in the room. There is a nervous energy in the air—the kind of energy that only exists when life is about to change drastically. The life that Bupe and Alvin woke up to this morning will never exist again.

"Oh, Kate, this is quite the intense pain," Bupe says as she stretches her hand out to mine.

"I'm here, Bupe. You're going to be okay. Besides the pain, how are you feeling?"

"Dr. Andrew hasn't left my side. I feel good."

I glance in Andrew's direction as our eyes meet. I raise my eyebrows in my nonverbal attempt to ask him if he slept at the hospital last night. He shrugs his shoulder and gives a side smile in my direction.

I walk over to where Andrew is. "Have you checked her recently?"

"I checked her about thirty minutes ago, and she was dilated to five. That is when I had Maria go and get you. Let's recheck her in a few minutes."

I place a cold washcloth on Bupe's head. She moans as the cold and damp cloth touches her forehead. Her face scrunches as she breathes through a contraction. Somewhere in the process of caring for her, she's become my friend. Medicine has been entirely different in Tanzania compared to back home. I spend so much time getting to know the person. The relationships were always the reason I went into midwifery, but I'd forgotten that for so long. Bupe's contractions are happening every two and a half minutes, and she is steadily progressing.

"Bupe, I would like to check to see how close you are." She groans as she nods her approval. I put on my gloves, and she's nearly ready to push, and there is just a little lip remaining.

"Save your energy because you are very close to needing to push."

She grimaces through a contraction. Andrew moves to one side and Alvin to the other, and I grab the bassinet and warming blankets. Out of the corner of my eye, I see a technician, Adimu, walk in the room, ready to assist. Bupe's moans are steady and guttural. I stroke Bupe's face, and she hums a tune lowly. She lowly puts words to the song, and the Swahili drips off her tongue.

Andrew and I lock eyes for a moment. "She's singing 'Baba Yetu,'" he says in almost a whisper. ("The Lord's Prayer.")

Bupe smiles through her next contraction. "Remember what I told you about pushing, Bupe? Once it's time, I want you to do this slow and steady. I'm not going to leave your side."

I check her one more time, and she is fully dilated and fully effaced, and it is officially time to push. Alvin bends down and kisses Bupe's forehead and backs up into the corner of the room. Andrew and I take turns holding her hand while the other one prepares for the baby. Adimu stands to the side.

"You are doing great, Bupe," Andrew says. "You're having a contraction, so really push through it."

Bupe groans as she raises her knees higher and holds her breath through the push.

"Bupe"—I stroke her face with the palm of my hand—"I am proud of you. I just looked, and I can see the hair, so the baby's head is very close. You are doing amazing. You can do this." She turns her head into my hand, never opening her eyes.

I join Andrew between Bupe's legs and pull up a stool. I tell her when to push, but she's also figuring it out on her own based on when the pain comes. Andrew looks at me, and we speak without any words.

"Bupe," Andrew says, "one more push, and your baby should be out."

She screams out at the climax of her contraction, and I glance at Alvin briefly, who brings both his hands to his ears to shield them. Bupe pushes with all she has left, and I see Andrew hold the head and dislodge the baby's shoulder. Once the shoulder clears, the baby slides smoothly out, and I catch the slippery infant. I turn the baby around and practically scream.

"Congratulations, Bupe and Alvin! You have a beautiful baby boy." I quickly suction him out and place him on Bupe's chest.

I cover my face with both hands and tap on the bridge of my nose as I feel tears rush to my eyes. Bupe looks at her newborn and then presses her hands together and looks upward.

"*Asante, Baba. Asante, Baba,*" she says it over and over again, getting quieter each time until her voice is nothing more than a whisper.

Tears fall out of her eyes, rhythmically, one by one. A tear also escapes my eye, and I look over at Andrew, who looks on like a proud father. I walk over to him, and he looks down at me and takes my hand in his and squeezes it gently and then pats it with his other hand. His hand radiates warmth and electricity throughout my entire body, and it doesn't feel odd that we are holding hands. Andrew removes his hand from mine and places it around my shoulder as we watch Bupe and Alvin look at their healthy baby boy.

"Dr. Andrew, Ms. Kate." Bupe says as Andrew removes his hand from my shoulder. "Alvin and I would like you to meet our son, Andwele."

I raise my eyebrows and look at Andrew. He places his hand over his chest and purses his lips and nods at Bupe and then Alvin.

He walks over to her and kisses both her cheeks. "Thank you for this incredible honor."

Bupe reaches a hand up and squeezes Andrew's hand. After several minutes of fawning over baby Andwele and passing him around to the four of us, Bupe waves me over to her side.

"I need to use the bathroom, is that okay?"

"Let me help you get up. You might feel a bit faint, so I don't want you to walk unassisted," I reply.

I wrap baby Andwele up in a blanket after cleaning him off and hand him to Alvin. He's never been one to show emotion in my presence, but his smile stretches from ear to ear.

I walk over to Bupe and carefully sit her up. "How do you feel?" I place one hand on her arm and the other around her back.

Bupe grimaces but then smiles up at me. "I feel fine, but a little fuzzy in my head."

"I want to make sure we go slow. Let's sit here for a moment before getting up."

She grabs my hand and pushes herself into an upright position. I stay next to her, helping her support her weight.

"Ms. Kate, I don't feel so good." Bupe looks at me apologetically.

"It's okay, Bupe. Let's sit back down and let your blood flow get back to normal."

I gently sit Bupe back on the bed. I hold her one hand while stroking the cotton gown on her back with my other. Bupe's weight presses against me as she falls back in the bed, and her eyes roll back into her head. Bupe goes limp, and Andrew rushes to her side and does a pulse check.

"Kate, you need to go grab the cart!" Andrew yells at me.

I feel like I'm outside of my body, watching everything unfold but not really being there. I run out into the hallway and grab one of the crash carts we keep at the hospital. I run back into the room, and my eyes dart to Andrew giving Bupe CPR. I know CPR and practiced it extensively during my schooling. I've seen videos of it being performed as well but have never witnessed it live. As I watch Andrew, I realize how violent it is, and as the room spins around me, the only thing I can hear is him pounding on her chest. It all feels traumatic and desperate, and time stands still around us as Andrew continues with his compressions.

I turn the automated external defibrillator on and wait for the prompt. I quickly place the paddles in the appropriate location, and when I get the prompt, I shock her. Her body convulses upward, but her heart doesn't start. I do it again and again. Andrew continues with manual CPR, and blood trickles from Bupe's mouth. I'm light-headed, and I feel like I'm going to pass out. I see Alvin out of the corner of my eye, holding Andwele and looking on with sheer panic. I gently slap my face, forcing myself to stay upright.

"Breathe, Bupe, breathe. You have to breathe!" I yell at her.

Andrew pumps her chest as hard as he can, and I don't remember anyone else entering the room, yet it's full of staff assisting.

"Come on, Bupe, don't do this! Don't leave, you can't do this!" I barely recognize my own voice. Andrew continues pumping her chest, trying to find some semblance of a pulse.

I cry. "Bupe, breathe, just breathe!"

Andrew stops CPR, and the room is silent.

"Andrew, don't stop. Keep going!" I scream at him through my tears.

I run to Bupe and shock her another time. Andrew pulls my arms away, and I resist him and try to continue. Andrew wraps both arms around my shoulders and restrains me as I try with all my strength to reach her.

"It's been twenty-five minutes, Kate," Andrew says solemnly, as he tries to hold me. "We need to call this. Time of death, 1300 hours."

The entire room spins. I look at Andrew in disbelief. I look at Alvin, who is in shock, holding a perfectly healthy newborn baby. Finally, I look at Bupe's lifeless body. She was full of life just minutes ago. She delivered a healthy baby, and I don't understand this.

Andrew has lost all color in his face, and someone needs to comfort Alvin, who just lost his entire world. I look down, and my scrubs are full of blood. I walk over to Bupe's lifeless body, and I cover her up to her chin, and I want nothing more than to believe that she's fallen asleep.

I look back to Alvin, who is frozen. I take Andwele out of his hands. I bring the baby over to Bupe and stand next to her. Someone comes over to assist, and Andrew takes Alvin's hand and leads him out of the room. A nurse walks in, and I hand Andwele to her. And then I walk out. I don't remember who or what I pass. I don't remember seeing anyone. I walk down a flight of stairs and find myself back in my bungalow where the afternoon sun shines through the windows. The sun casts shadows in my tiny kitchen, and it feels like a betrayal that the sun dares to continue shining.

I sit at the table and put my head between my hands and cry. I cry harder than I've allowed myself in a very long time. I cry for Alvin, who will have to find a way to raise this child on his own. I cry for Andwele, who will grow up without a mom. I mostly cry for Bupe, who entrusted this hospital and me with her life. Bupe became my friend and loved me and made me smile and laugh. I cry for all she will miss. She wanted to be a mom more than anything. Life isn't fair. She only got to hold her precious son for a moment. I don't know how long I've been sitting at my table, but the sun has now set as I continue to sit in a completely dark room.

Chapter 13

He who has the choice has the pain.

—African Proverb

There is a low knock at my door, and it swings open. I look up and see Andrew, and he doesn't look much better than me, except it appears like he changed and showered. He turns on the light as he enters. I slowly lift my gaze until it meets his.

"Kate—"

I stand up and stay behind a chair that separates me from Andrew. I bite my lip as I hold my breath. Andrew looks as broken as I feel. We stare at each other for what feels like a long time. He doesn't move from his position near the door, and I make no effort to close the space between us.

Irrational anger bubbles up through my body. "Andrew, why did you stop? Why didn't you let me continue?"

Andrew walks over to me and moves the chair between us. I ball my hands into fists and push them into his chest. He doesn't move. My fists pound at his firm chest, and he doesn't wince or change expression. I don't want to hurt Andrew, but it feels good to hit something, and he lets me. Andrew grabs me by the wrists and holds my hands away from him. I cry, and his strength overtakes me as he pulls me into his chest. He releases my hands, and they hang at my side, unable to hold him back.

"Kate," Andrew quietly speaks into my hair, "there was nothing else to try. It had been too long."

I know he's right. I nod into his tear-soaked shirt.

Andrew grabs me by my shoulders and pulls me away from his body. "I'm going to make you tea. I think it would feel good for you to take a shower and clean off."

I look down at my scrubs, and the dry blood is a reminder. I still feel like I'm outside of my own body, and I see myself walk into the bathroom and take a cold shower. I don't even feel self-conscious as I walk out of the bathroom in nothing but a towel covering me. Andrew glances in my direction and quickly glances down. I go into my bedroom area and put on a pair of pajama shorts and a tank top. I sit on my bed and stare straight ahead at the darkness that watches me through the window.

"Can I come in, Kate?"

"Yes," I answer quietly.

Andrew walks in and sits next to me on the bed and takes my hand and holds it. We both look straight ahead as our legs brush up against each other. Andrew turns toward me.

"There is nothing we could have done, Kate. All signs point to a pulmonary embolism, and there was no way we could have predicted this. Her blood work was perfect. Every appointment, every ultrasound, every heartbeat. It was textbook."

I look up at Andrew and take a deep breath. The pain and tightness I feel in my chest is a reminder that I'm alive. The tea kettle whistles on the cooktop, and my hand feels lonely as Andrew drops it and rushes to the kitchen. I follow him, where I find him pouring my tea. My room feels too lonely without him. I walk up behind him, just as he's about to turn around. My eyes feel puffy and almost swollen shut with wretchedness. Andrew looks down at me, and his strong arms wrap around me. He feels like refuge and comfort at this moment.

"Her delivery was textbook. She barely lost any blood. There were no signs, Kate."

I take my hand and wipe at my tears, unable to say anything.

"What did I do wrong?" I ask.

I look up at him, and he places his hands on my shoulders. "Kate, this is not your fault."

A single tear runs down my cheek, and Andrew wipes it away with his finger. "Why Bupe?"

"Why anyone, Kate?" With my tea in hand, I walk back toward my bedroom and sit back on my bed.

"Do you want me to get Maria?" Andrew's voice is low.

I wipe my eyes with the back of my hands. "No."

I grab Andrew's hand and pull him down on my bed. He takes my cup and places it on my nightstand and pulls the comforter over my body and tucks in my cold feet. I look up at him, and his pain feels as palpable as mine. I'd love a hug from Maria right now, but only Andrew knows how this feels, and there is comfort in that. We now have this excruciatingly traumatic life experience that connects us, and no one else will do but Andrew.

Andrew brushes my wet hair back. "Do you want me to leave?"

"No."

I move over toward the wall to make room. Andrew hesitates, and his chest slowly rises and falls. I prop myself up on my elbow and turn to the side, and Andrew slides into the bed next to me.

"I've never felt further from home than I do right now," I confess.

"You have me, Kate. I'm here for you." He props himself up on his elbow as well.

Andrew gently places his hand behind my head and pulls me into his body. I have flashbacks to the night at the inn when he held me. The circumstances are entirely different, but the comfort of Andrew feels the same. I wrap my arm around him and explore the intricacy of every muscle in his upper back. When we lie down like this, the height difference is less noticeable, and I'm able to nest myself in Andrew's neck. We're so close; my lips press into his skin as I breathe. Andrew's heartbeat is fast as it pulsates against my own.

"She was my friend, Andrew. I feel like this is my fault." I speak into his neck.

Andrew stiffens his body and then lets out a deep exhale. "I know she was. Kate, look at me." Andrew takes my chin in his hand and gently raises my head to look at him. "There is nothing you could have done. Nothing. We can't blame ourselves."

"I feel so…" I shudder against him. Traumatized, shocked, in utter disbelief. When I close my eyes, all I see is Bupe's lifeless body convulsing off the bed with each shock, and Andrew desperately pounding on her chest. I see Alvin's face with a look I'll never be able to get out of my head.

"I know," Andrew responds quietly. And he does know. I know every time he closes his eyes; this is all he'll see too.

I squeeze Andrew harder. I feel him hold his breath for a moment before silently exhaling. I try not to think about the fact that I'm lying in bed with my boss. Andrew's eyes flick to my lips, and my eyes do the same to his. I allow myself to stare longer than I've ever allowed myself to. His lips are so full and form a perfect heart shape at the top where both sides meet. I slowly inch my face closer to Andrew. He doesn't back up, but his eyes go up in surprise.

"Kate"—I feel his warm breath on my face—"are you sure?"

The question catches me off guard. He doesn't want to kiss me. No one pauses and asks that question if they want it to happen. I pull back, surprised.

Andrew runs his hand through my hair. "Kate?"

"I'm sorry. You don't want to kiss me." I lower my eyes in shame.

"I want to kiss you," Andrew says. "I wanted to make sure you consented first."

I look down, as I've lost my nerve, but Andrew pulls my face back up to look at him.

Andrew wets his lips. "I always want to kiss you, Kate."

I part my lips and slowly nod my head. If it's my consent Andrew is after, he has it.

Andrew's strong hand pulls the back of my neck forward, and I lean in and firmly press my lips to his. Andrew's lips are as soft as they look, and I push further into him and feel like I'm pressing into a soft pillow. Neither Andrew nor I shut our eyes as we hold our lips together and help breathe air for the other person. I move my hand to his face and feel the definition of his cheekbones that I could get lost in for hours. But it's his eyes that tell such a compelling story. We pull away from our chaste kiss, but neither of us looks away.

His hand moves beneath my chin, forcing me to look at him. He puts his hand behind my back and pulls me closer. He lays me on my back and hovers over me, and I move my hand to his arm and stroke the muscle right above his elbow. I've spent hours looking at this beautiful man, admiring him from near and far, and it feels glorious to have permission to touch him.

Andrew pulls my head up, and our lips crash into each other. At first, it's soft. He takes my bottom lip in his mouth, and my lips involuntarily part. When he pulls away from me gently, I wrap my arm around the back of his head and pull him toward me. Andrew breathes into our kiss as he lightly bites my lip, and I feel his tongue dance with mine.

He spreads my legs with his knee as he balances on his elbow. I can feel his response to our kiss as he presses against me. All of Andrew's breath is released into me, and he's breathed me back to life. My teeth gently scrape against his bottom lip, and Andrew's weight becomes heavier on me as he groans into my mouth. He takes my hair in his fist and lifts me further into him. My knees are shaky, and my heart is near exploding. I open my eyes, and Andrew's deep-brown eyes stare back at me. He slows down the kiss, and I stare into his almond eyes. I've never kissed like this, and no one has ever made me feel this desired before.

Andrew slows down the kiss further as I feel his hand loosen on my head until he removes it completely, and my head is back on the pillow. He moves his hand to my cheek and gently rubs it, and then he gives me one final kiss on my forehead before he lies down on his back beside me. We both lie on our backs with only our arms touching. We breathe heavily. Andrew finally props himself up on his elbow, and I do the same, so I'm once again facing him.

"You really know how to kiss, Kate." Andrew deeply exhales, and he seems at a loss of words.

"So do you."

I'll never forget that kiss for the rest of my life. Andrew knows what he's doing. I blush when I imagine all the other things he's good at too. I look at Andrew's lips again, and I think I will never be able to get enough of them.

Andrew smiles as he catches me, staring at his lips. "That's enough for one night."

"Are you sure?" I say through a heavy sigh.

Andrew laughs. "I need to leave you wanting more."

I lie back down on my pillow but still face Andrew. He lowers himself and pulls me in, so my face is once again buried into his shirt. Andrew rubs my back with one of his hands. My mind goes to Bupe, but then it goes to my kiss with Andrew. I can feel sleep coming, and I want nothing more than to have a temporary escape from this reality and pain.

Andrew's heart has slowed down, and with each rise in his chest, I imagine the ocean waves, methodically rising and falling. Andrew rhythmically caresses my hair. With each stroke, my breaths become longer. My heart feels broken, and as I lie on Andrew's chest, I imagine us stitching each other's brokenness until it's no longer felt. My mouth rests against his cotton T-shirt, and I breathe him in deeply.

"Try to sleep, Kate."

I close my eyes and finally doze off into the night.

*****

I wake up with my face still tucked into Andrew's shirt. I breathe in quietly because I'm not ready for him to know I'm awake and face him.

"Kate, are you awake?"

I jolt up more dramatically than I intend, avoiding looking at Andrew. "I'm going to make coffee." Andrew grabs my hand as I attempt to get off the bed.

"Lie with me a little longer."

I relax into his arms again, thankful that he has a way of us waking up together feel as normal as possible. I let Andrew hold me for a few more minutes, and then I get up to make us coffee. I lean both elbows on the cold and sterile metal of the counters and put my head in my hands and stare out my window at the hospital. Bupe is still there, but she isn't. The grief crashes into me and pierces my stomach and makes my throat feel like it's closing. My feet feel connected to the floor. The weight of it all is such a heavy thing to carry.

I know what it's like to lose someone I love, but not a spouse. Then again, grief is grief, not meant to be compared and contrasted. I remember when my baby sister died, but I was only five. I was sad about it, as much as someone that age can be. But I was mostly sad because her room would have to be taken down, and because for months, my parents prepared me for a relationship that was never to be.

Seeing my parents' grief will stick with me for the rest of my life. I had a front-row seat to it all, and it changed us as a family. My mom's grief was the most outward. It was the thick kind of grief, that casts a wide net, and anyone in its path will feel it too. Our entire house felt like an albatross around our necks. Late at night, when my mom thought everyone was sleeping, she'd tiptoe into my baby sister's bedroom, separated from mine by only a bathroom. I'd hear the rocking chair rock back and forth and the sobs that escaped from her through the melody she hummed. Most nights, the rhythmic sound of the rocking chair would put me to sleep, but on other nights, I would contemplate whether I should go into the room and be with her. I would lie awake for hours and listen to her rock.

Many of the days and months after her death were spent at my parents' best friends, the Jacobsons. Mrs. Jacobson was kind to me, and Peter and I would play for hours. One day, my dad picked me up from their house and brought me home, and my baby sister's room was painted gray, and there were no longer signs that this was ever going to be a baby's room. We never discussed our grief or the daughter or sister that never made it home from the hospital. We all bottled it up and dealt with it on our own.

Andrew's hands squeeze my shoulders from behind as I'm lost in thought, staring out at the hospital. I turn around and hand him a cup of coffee.

"Thanks, Kate."

We stare at each other, but I don't say the words on my mind. Instead, I study his face, and I may be wrong, but I think he regrets our kiss.

"I have to get to the hospital. When you have a chance, stop by. I want you to review Bupe's chart," Andrew says.

As quickly as Andrew fell into my bed, we are back to being teacher and student, and the reality of Bupe's death can no longer be ignored.

CHAPTER 14

Your previous lie damages your present truth.

—Somali Proverb

The door to my bungalow swings open, and Maria runs to me and nearly knocks me over as I stand at the counter. I bury my head in her braids, and she wraps her delicate hands around my waist.

Maria looks at me. "Kate, I just saw Andrew and came over as quickly as I heard."

I didn't realize I had any tears left in me, but they start to fall again, and Maria wipes them away with the back of her hands.

"Why didn't you come and get me last night? I'm so sorry you were alone."

I gently pull back from Maria and pour us both a cup of coffee. I hand Maria her cup and then blow on mine.

"I wasn't alone."

Maria takes my face in her hand. "Kate?"

I look down at my coffee cup and then cut my eyes to Maria's from above my cup.

"Andrew stayed."

"Oh." Maria puts her hand on her hip. She walks to the table and then turns to me again. "Are you going to make me beg you for information?"

Maria follows me as I walk around to get ready for the day. First, I walk to the bedroom and then the bathroom, with Maria on my heels the entire time. I share so much of my life with Maria, yet I hesitate to say anything to her. I don't want her looking at us differently, especially as I'm figuring out what last night meant.

"It's nothing, Maria. I don't think either of us wanted to be alone."

"Are you sure that's all it was to Andrew?" Maria asks me thoughtfully. "I mean, you two have spent the night together twice."

I grab Maria's hand, and we walk out the door. "When you put it that way, it sounds like more than it is."

Maria stops walking and looks at me. "Okay, Kate. It's just"—Maria pauses and furrows her brow—"I know you have a lot to figure out in your life, and well, Andrew has been hurt, and I know he's cautious in his life."

"Maria," I cut her off, "you don't need to worry."

We continue to walk to the hospital. My words are cavalier, yet in my head, I am worried. My feelings have been coming slowly, but they've been growing for a while. The waiting room sits empty, and I can hear a pin drop on the second floor of the hospital. Editha glances up from her magazine and acknowledges me but then quickly looks back down. Andrew's office door swings open, and our eyes meet, and he waves me over.

"Kate, I need to go meet with Alvin about bringing Bupe back to their village. It's slow right now, and I'd like you to go through Bupe's entire medical chart and highlight and take note of anything significant. Okay?"

Andrew glances at a stack of papers on his desk. "Sit at my desk, and I'll be back in a few hours."

Before I have a chance to say anything, Andrew walks out, and the slamming of the door echoes in the empty corridor. The difference between the Andrew I woke up with and the one asking me to review medical records is vast.

Bupe's medical records are thick. I open Andrew's top drawer and pull out a pen and a highlighter, and I start at the beginning. Bupe first visited Andrew and the hospital in late December. The record indicates that a woman in her village told her she should come here because the hospital could help her have a healthy delivery. Bupe hadn't thought twice about her mom dying during childbirth, but then when she delivered a stillborn, she started worrying that something runs in her family.

I study the many exams Andrew gave Bupe, and nothing jumps out as abnormal. She had two ultrasounds during her pregnancy, and all the measurements were perfect. I study the many blood tests Bupe was administered, and those appear normal too. One of her blood tests indicated a small amount of protein in her urine. Still, her blood pressure tests were normal, and it looks like Andrew prescribed an antibiotic for a possible urinary tract infection.

The last blood test Bupe had was a month ago, and those results, too, looked good. I read Andrew's notes, and they were from my exam, where it shows everything was on track, and both mother and baby appeared healthy. Bupe dying makes no clinical sense.

I read Andrew's final note in the chart from last night. After Bupe died, I retreated to my bungalow fairly quickly, and I realize that Andrew hung around here to handle everything. His note indicates that although Bupe felt dizzy after childbirth, no other signs presented themselves. The postmortem exam, although not an autopsy, shows that Bupe barely lost blood during the birth and that everything occurred normally during delivery. Her heart stopped suddenly, with no other signs.

Andrew finishes the chart with the following note:

> The village hospital does not have the appropriate medical professionals to conduct an autopsy. My postmortem exam, absent of any obvious trauma during childbirth and based on how quickly the patient expired, it would appear that she expired due to a pulmonary embolism.

I close Bupe's chart and stare at Andrew's computer in front of me. I learned about pulmonary embolisms during my studies and also learned how rare they are. One of the case studies I did in my master's program was around a mother who died during childbirth from a pulmonary embolism, but it was nothing more than a case study and not something so close to home.

I move the mouse to bring Andrew's computer to life to learn more about this condition. A picture on his home screen stares back at me. It is Andrew, with his arm around a very attractive female, her holding her finger up and displaying a diamond ring. I move my face closer to the photo. The woman looks like she could be on the cover of a magazine, and Andrew stands behind her, with his arms wrapped around her and a smile on his face. Her hair is straight and hangs down well below her shoulders. Her brown eyes are magnified, and her lips are red and full.

The door swings open, and I push my chair back suddenly, like I was doing something wrong and got caught.

"Hey, Andrew, I finished studying the chart and was going to do an internet search on a few things."

He glances at the computer and then back at me, his face expressionless.

"Kate," Andrew says, rather shyly, "would you like to join me for dinner tonight?"

Andrew stuffs his hands into the pockets of his khaki pants and takes a step toward his desk. I stand up quickly and speak before I have a chance to overthink what dinner means.

"Umm, thanks. That would be great."

Andrew smiles warmly. "Great. Come over in about an hour."

"I'll bring the wine," I say.

We both stand, staring at each other, and I realize I'm in his office, standing behind his desk. I quickly walk around the corner and step by Andrew and give him an awkward wave.

"I'll see you soon," I say as I hurry out of his office without looking back.

I quickly change my clothes and decide on a flowy blue summer dress. I take a quick peek in the mirror and apply a little blush and lip gloss. I smack my lips together, grab a cold bottle of wine, and walk to Andrew's bungalow, which is only a few away from mine. I try so hard not to overthink going to Andrew's. I spend too much time thinking, and I want to try to be somewhat spontaneous.

I stop in front of his door and put my hand up to knock and then pull it back to my side. I have an excessive amount of nervous energy. The door swings open, and I nearly fall inside. "Kate, I thought I heard you approach. Sorry if I didn't hear you knock."

"Ah, it's fine." I glance around his bungalow, and it's much bigger than mine, which makes sense because he lives here permanently. His bedroom seems to have an actual door, and there is a whole other room in his that mine doesn't have.

Andrew laughs, and I can see every one of his teeth. "Here, let me take the wine and pour us a glass. Feel free to take a tour."

"Yeah?" I shrug my shoulders.

Andrew laughs at me and nods his head. I start in the extra room his bungalow has that mine doesn't. It has a couch and two chairs, with a large window that looks into his backyard. The room has a warm ambiance, and I would spend all my time there. Andrew's kitchen looks similar to mine, but his table is much larger. I quickly glance into his bathroom, which is slightly larger than mine and is a lot cleaner than I keep mine too. I open the door to the backyard, and he has four lounging chairs around a firepit. I can almost taste the smell of bonfire on a crisp winter evening here.

I step inside, and Andrew's back is turned to me. He changed into a pair of jeans that hug his thighs. His black T-shirt is snug on his muscular arms, and I can see his muscles flex from here as he cuts something on his counter. I lean back against the door, enjoying looking at him without being noticed.

Andrew looks at me over his shoulder and smiles. "You can come closer to me, Kate. I won't bite."

I look down and smile and walk toward Andrew. "Is there something I can help you with?"

Andrew hands me a glass of wine and then holds up a piece of mango. "Try this. It's the mango I got at Centro Market with you, and I don't think I've had better."

I put my hand up to take it and realize he plans to put it in my mouth. I open my mouth as he gently drops it, and his finger grazes my lips. The mango is soft and sweet. I wash it down with a sip of my wine, and the flavors complement each other perfectly.

I moan from the satisfaction. "That is good."

"Here, have more."

Andrew points to a bowl where he has cut some up. I grab another mango and let it slowly dissolve in my mouth, enjoying every moment of it. I sip my wine and feel helpless as Andrew cuts up food and turns down the burner so the rice can simmer.

Andrew bends over and grabs a zucchini from the refrigerator and holds it out for me. "Will you cut this?"

I take the zucchini from his hand and nearly melt into his touch as our hands make contact. I haven't acted like a schoolgirl in, well, forever, so why am I being one now? I wash it and stand next to Andrew, cutting it. It feels like we do this every night—stand next to each other, our arms touching, making dinner together.

"Here you go." I step back from the counter, and Andrew takes the zucchini and puts it in a pan and adds spices.

"I purposely avoided meat as I don't want you to get some sort of food poisoning again."

I cover my face with my hand and shake my head as I smile. I have avoided meat ever since that miserable night. "I appreciate the thoughtfulness."

Andrew hurriedly sets the table and places a bottle of wine down. He then puts our food in bowls, and we sit down.

"Thanks for inviting me to dinner, Andrew."

"Honestly, Kate. I'm not sure why we didn't do this sooner. It's much easier to cook for two than one anyway."

I have been in the village for over two months, and I'm very aware that this is the first time I've been in Andrew's bungalow and dined with him alone. I realize that I'm halfway through my time in Tanzania, yet it's gone so fast.

"If the food is good, I may come back."

"Oh, yeah?" Andrew laughs, and I'm convinced he should always laugh and smile. It's impossible not to feel better with his smile that makes his eyes shine, especially when I feel like this particular smile is meant only for me. I take a bite of food, and I am not surprised to find out that Andrew is an exceptional cook. It's flavored to perfection, and the spices on the zucchini bring out wonderful flavors.

"Well?"

I look over at Andrew's searching eyes, wanting to hear what I think of his food. "Hmm, it is so good. I'll definitely come back."

Andrew laughs. "Good, that's what I was hoping for. I'm happy it's up to your standards."

"Definitely up to my standards." I smile as I take another bite and look over at Andrew, who looks pleased with himself.

I help Andrew clear the dishes, and we stand at the sink while he washes, and I dry. My stomach is full, and being with him feels like the most natural thing in the world. I try to stay in the moment because I know in a couple of days, the entire energy of the village will feel different with my parents and the Jacobsons' presence.

"One of the first times I met you, Kate, we did dishes together."

I look up at Andrew and laugh. "You're right. That seems like forever ago."

"It does, but I knew the first time I met you that we'd be friends."

"Yeah?" I ask.

Andrew nods thoughtfully before looking down at me. "Of course, do you want to sit by the fire and eat mango?"

I look at my watch, and it's not too late, but I'm very aware that I keep walking further into this. "Sure."

Andrew grabs the bowl of mangos and leads me outside. He starts the fire in mere moments, and he sits in the chair next to mine.

"I like your backyard." I look around the space. It's the same size as mine but much more put together.

"I put in the firepit. There is something about sitting by a fire that clears my mind. I make all my big life decisions around the fire."

I nod because I can relate to exactly what he's saying. "I know what you mean. We have a firepit in our backyard in Minneapolis. It's one of my favorite things."

I pop a mango into my mouth and close my eyes and take in the taste. Eating mango reminds me of a summer day, sitting on a beach and looking out over blue water and the sun on my face.

I turn to face Andrew. "So what big decision have you made while sitting by this fire?"

"Well"—he turns to me also—"asking you to dinner. I was afraid you'd say no."

I cover my face with my hands. "Andrew, of course, I wouldn't say no to dinner with you."

Andrew smiles, and I stare ahead at the fire. I'm so relaxed I close my eyes and enjoy the warmth all around me.

"What are you thinking right now?" Andrew asks.

I turn to face him. "I'm sorry. I have a lot on my mind."

"Bupe?"

Hearing her name cuts at me sharply, and the pain and grief find its way to my stomach once again. She's all I think about, except moments I'm with Andrew; the grief doesn't feel as heavy.

"Yes, and my parents. They are arriving in a couple of days, with their best friends from back home and their son, Peter."

"That's a good thing, right?"

I pull my lips into my mouth and close my eyes once again. "I hope so. I've kept these two worlds fairly separate from each other, and I'm nervous to see how the two worlds get along."

"I can actually relate to that entirely," Andrew says, as he intertwines his fingers with mine and holds my hand.

My body tenses, both at how natural it feels, but also how I feel like I'm betraying Peter. Andrew feels me tense up, "We're just holding hands, Kate."

"I have a past," I say between breaths.

"I would hope so, Kate."

I lean back and look at Andrew. "An unresolved past."

Andrew releases my hand and looks toward the sky. "I see."

Without thinking, I grab Andrew's hand and thread my fingers through his. Andrew looks at me and smiles and squeezes my hand tightly in his. Logically, I know I don't owe Peter anything. I'm a single woman, yet I feel like I'm doing something wrong.

With a deep and heavy breath, I open up. "There is so much we don't know about each other. And well, you're my boss."

Andrew squeezes my hand tighter. "I don't see myself as your boss. I run the hospital, and you're nice enough to volunteer. And I hope you can learn from me as I'm older and have been in this field for much longer than you. I'm learning from you too."

I look ahead at the fire, and the reds and oranges are mesmerizing. There is a small blue center that looks like it's dancing against the black sky.

"You're learning from me?"

"Kate"—Andrew moves his body closer to me—"you teach me patience and kindness. All the women love you. And you're so much braver than you ever admit."

Andrew slowly looks at me, and my entire body catches fire. I know what my next move means, but there is something about him that's intoxicating, and I don't want to stay away. I have the rest of my life to be settled down, but right now, I want to be closer. I stand up and sit on the foot of his chair. He moves over and pats a space next to him like he was expecting me to cross over this entire time. I lie down on the chair, and his hand makes it hard to breathe as he strokes my cheek.

"I don't know what I'm doing." My eyes meet Andrew's, and it feels like the most honest words I've ever spoken.

"Sometimes, that's okay." Andrew wraps his arms around my waist and pulls me in further.

I stare into what are becoming my favorite eyes. My face is inches from Andrew's, and his eyes are almost as familiar to me as my own at this point. He pulls in his bottom lip and sucks on it. I stroke his face, which is soft with a little bit of stubble that I don't usually get to see. His eyes close for a moment, and I see his chest sharply inhale.

I spread my fingers and slowly move my hand to his chest. I can feel every muscle under his thin shirt. I slowly move my hand over his arm and feel every muscle and bulge. My hand massages his forearm and finally reaches his hand, and he quickly intertwines my fingers in his, and I raise both of our arms over our heads. Andrew lets me feel in control, even though it would take a small movement for him to gain dominance.

I lean into him and turn my head, and Andrew's lips slightly part as my lips brush up against his. He releases my hand above our heads and, with his fingertips, slowly strokes my arm until my entire body fills with bumps. I pull Andrew's face into mine with urgency, and our tongues immediately battle for dominance. My neck tingles as I feel Andrew's hand, pulling me into him. I wrap my leg around his body and instinctively roll my hips, and I feel his breathing change as he moans into my mouth. We fill each other's lungs with air, and then Andrew pulls away, testing me, with little bites.

The fire has gotten dimmer, but instead of the air getting cooler, all I feel is the heat off Andrew's body. Our lips fit each other's perfectly, and each kiss leaves me willing to lose myself and push out any rational thought. Andrew gives me a chaste kiss, with finality, and when I try to kiss him again, he holds me tightly in his arms. I feel his throbbing heart against my ear as we both struggle to catch our breath. We lay like this for several minutes until I feel his lips kiss my forehead—a soft kiss.

Andrew is a gentle giant, and he surprises me with his restraint and how tenderly he kisses me. "You always stop me," I say to Andrew, as I pry myself from his arms and sit up.

"Trust me when I say this. I'm doing it for you."

I close my eyes and look up toward the stars. "You know me, huh?"

"I know that I care too much about you to ever go beyond what I think you're ready for."

I chew on my lip, knowing he's right. "Walk me out?"

"I'm going to need a moment longer. I'll meet you inside." I look in his eyes and don't question him.

CHAPTER 15

We must go back and reclaim our past so we can move forward; so we understand why and how we came to be who we are today.

—Ghanaian Proverb

I'm up before the sun to tidy up my bungalow and myself. Showering this early has its benefits as the water is mostly warm at this hour. I close my eyes as the water runs over my body, touching every part of me. I had a restless night. I watched the moon through my window get lower in the sky. I counted the individual squares of the hardwood in my bedroom.

I constantly think of my kiss last night with Andrew. He lets me feel in control, and he doesn't take things too far. I know he reacts to us kissing the same way I do. I'm not always the most confident person, but I know the way we kiss is special and not just to me. I rub my hands over my stomach, which is tight and in knots.

I feel so unsettled right now. I'd feel this anyway with Peter coming to the village, but then add on top of it that my relationship with Andrew has taken on a new dynamic, and I feel like I'm living a double life. I take a deep breath and remind myself that Andrew hasn't shared much about his past, nor have I shared much about mine. I think of the beautiful woman on his computer. Mostly I feel unsettled because I'm going to have to make decisions. I feel comfortable holding Peter at bay until I figure out what I want moving forward. I don't want to be unfair to anyone, but I've never been so unsure about what I want from my life. Losing Peter, and subsequently regretting it, is my biggest fear right now. I'm also not willing to take him back until I feel like we've addressed the concerns I have in our relationship.

I make my bed because I know my mom will notice if I don't, and I quickly wash my dishes. The sun has now made an appearance, and I send a quick text to my parents.

ME

I'm hoping you're both sleeping in after the long journey. I need to be at the hospital this morning, but come by anytime. Love you!

*****

I get to the hospital and am happy to see Fatima in the waiting room. I've been worried about her, and I know there is little I can do to right all that is wrong in her life, but her face brings me joy today. I go over and greet her.

"Fatima, it is good to see you. How are you feeling?"

"I am good."

She looks down, and I place my hand over hers. I can see her belly has grown quite a bit since the last time I've seen her. I instruct her to get in a gown, and I start my examination. The baby's heartbeat sounds strong, and Fatima's heart also sounds good.

"I wasn't expecting to see you so soon."

Fatima nods. "I have been thinking a lot and want to talk to you."

"How are things at home?" She looks down at her hands again, like she always does when she's hoping to disappear and go unnoticed.

"Things are not good." She slumps further down.

"Does your father hurt you?"

Her head methodically moves up and down, and she inhales sharply. I feel simultaneous rage and compassion. If I were back home, I would call in child and protective services. As I think of this,

I realize that would also mean life in foster care for Fatima. I act like things are so ancient in Tanzania, but I don't know if her outcome would be much more positive back home. The one good thing about being back home is that a father who raped his child would spend a lifetime in jail.

"Does he still force himself on you, Fatima?" Our eyes meet, and her eyes fill with tears. She takes the backside of her hand to wipe a tear.

It looks like Fatima is going to say something. I wait for what feels like several minutes.

"He is mad at me for having his baby inside of me. He tells me to hide it and is scared people in the village will find out. He says it is my fault for having the baby inside me, but it isn't my fault."

"No, Fatima, it isn't your fault. You did nothing wrong. You didn't make your father force himself on you. That was his choice, and it is the wrong choice."

Fatima continues to wipe at her tears. "I worry my father will kill the baby if I bring it home."

I've tried to anticipate every scenario with Fatima, and her father harming the baby never entered into my mind.

"I will never love this baby. I can't. I know it's not the baby's fault for being here, but I won't love something that came this way. I love my siblings because they are part of my mom and have my mom's goodness. I will never love this baby." Fatima slumps further down and gazes at her hands folded in her lap.

I take Fatima's hand in mine. "It's okay to feel that way."

"Dr. Andrew said there are options. I want to discuss those options. I don't want this baby."

I breathe in slowly, knowing what she is saying and feeling the weight of it. I don't disagree with her choice. I only hope that this is her choice because she'll need to have peace with it to move forward with her life.

"Would you like to speak with Dr. Andrew about this?" Fatima looks up at me and nods. I instruct her to get dressed and tell her that I will find the doctor.

It's a slow day at the hospital. It's been a slow few days, so I'm not even sure if Andrew is here. I knock on his door, and he is there, sitting at his desk, and it's impossible to act naturally as if our relationship hasn't entered some slippery slope of unclear boundaries.

"Good morning, Andrew. Fatima is here."

"How'd you sleep, Kate?" My heart quickens as his eyes flash to mine. Andrew smiles at me, and he looks tired. Is he having a hard time sleeping too?

"Umm, Fatima would like to speak to you about her options."

Andrew stands up and turns his head slightly and walks toward me. I'm positive my legs are going to betray me and give out underneath me. "I couldn't get the kiss out of my head all night, Kate. I tried, but it's all I thought about."

I put my hand up to cover my hot face, but Andrew grabs it midair. "Don't hide your face, Kate. I want to see you."

Andrew holds my hand for a moment, but I gently pull away, squeezing his hand first. "I'm just trying to get through the day." He turns and smiles at me. "Let me show you to Fatima."

I bring Andrew into the examination room where I left Fatima, and she is now fully clothed and sitting in a chair instead of on the table.

"Hi, Fatima, it's good to see you."

"Dr. Andrew, I do not want this baby," Fatima blurts out as soon as the door is closed.

Dr. Andrew's face is full of compassion and concern. "You are sure, Fatima? Anytime you want to change your mind, you can. You have to be at peace with this decision."

I watch as Dr. Andrew makes himself smaller and looks at Fatima with pursed lips and kind eyes.

"Thank you. I will not change my mind. I want this baby to have a chance at another life, not this life."

Andrew looks up at me and holds my gaze for a moment. He then looks up at Fatima.

"I am going to start making arrangements and preparing for this. I want you to come back again in two weeks, and I'll have some plans in place by then."

Fatima confirms her understanding, and Andrew helps her out of the chair. "Fatima, let me walk you out." Andrew smiles at her and leads her out of the exam room.

I strip the sheets off the table and work on turning the room around when the door opens again. I look up, and the door shuts behind Andrew, and I see him turn the lock, and he slowly walks toward me.

My voice shakes slightly. "I have this under control."

Andrew continues to close the space between us. I stand up straight and look around, and there is no way to escape. I'm not even sure I want to. I lean against the wall, and Andrew's hand softly brushes across my face. I pin my hands behind my body and sharply inhale, unable to breathe.

"I wanted to check in, Kate." Andrew takes my face in his hand. "Are you ready for your visitors?"

My eyes glance at the door and then back at Andrew. "I mean, I guess I have no choice. Are you ready to meet my family?"

Andrew laughs. "Yes and no. I don't feel ready to share you."

Andrew puts his hand under my chin and pulls my face toward his, and his lips gently brush up against mine. The gesture feels intimate as if we do this every day. Like, it's the most normal thing in the world for Andrew to check in on me and greet me with a kiss. I continue stepping further into whatever this is, and it will no doubt complicate everything else going on in my life.

I place my hand on his chest as I move away. "I'm going to see if there are any more patients here." I pause at the door and slow my breathing down and then open it.

Editha sits at the desk and looks at me suspiciously, or perhaps I imagine it, and then she looks down the hallway. My parents are standing there, talking to Maria animatedly. It feels like time stands still when I see Peter. He stands between my mom and Maria and laughs at something Maria says.

His sandy blond hair is longer than it was the last time I'd seen him, and gel appears to hold it back and brushed to the side. He looks tan underneath his khaki shorts and T-shirt, with stark white tennis shoes. It's only been a little over two months since I've seen him, but I feel like I'm seeing him for the first time. He's bulked up, and from here, it looks like he has new muscles he didn't have before.

Peter's eyes jolt up, and he sees me watching from a distance. He smiles shyly and puts his hand up and waves, and then my parents both look in my direction. They walk hurriedly toward me with Peter a few steps behind them. Peter hangs back as I greet my parents.

"Kate, look at you. You look so grown up." My mom wraps me in her arms, nearly suffocating me.

I laugh. "Mom, you saw me two months ago." She pulls away and puts both of her hands on my face.

"I know, honey. It's just so wonderful to see you." My mom turns her head and looks at me deeper. "You've gotten so tan, Kate."

"Give her room, Paula. Let me hug my girl." My dad pulls me in, and the scent of his Old Spice aftershave makes me want to melt into him.

"Hi, Dad." I squeeze him a little harder before letting him go.

"We're happy to see you, kid." My skin warms as I sink into his kiss.

Peter steps forward and joins our circle. "Hi, Kate."

Peter leans in and gives me a quick hug and releases. He feels foreign to me, and it feels like ages since we've had physical contact. For nearly eight years, I've been hugged and kissed by Peter. I think I know him almost better than he knows himself. I feel like I'm meeting him for the first time.

"My parents are back in the bungalow, but they can't wait to see you," Peter continues.

I smile and am relieved our first encounter is over. My dad looks over my shoulder.

"Is that the head of the hospital, Kate?"

I glance over my shoulder, and Andrew is at the intake desk, having a conversation with Editha. I don't want to do this right now but have no way out of it and decide it's best to get this first meeting out of the way. I feel like a fraud, like I'm lying to everyone about who I am and what my intentions are.

Andrew keeps glancing over at us, and I know he expects an introduction.

"Yes, that is Dr. Andrew. The founder of this hospital. Come on, and I'll introduce you to him."

Andrew turns to us and watches as we walk toward him. My head feels fuzzy, and I was hoping I would be able to keep my visitors away from Andrew altogether. Crashing my worlds together means I'm going to have to make decisions about my future. Decisions I don't feel ready to make. We reach Andrew, and he stands tall.

"Mom, Dad, this is Dr. Andrew. Dr. Andrew, my parents."

Andrew smiles and extends his hand to my dad first and then my mom. "Dr. Malone and Dr. Malone, it's lovely to meet you both. And please call me Andrew." Andrew speaks with formality.

My dad vigorously shakes his hand. "It's great to meet you, Andrew. Please call me John, and this is my wife, Paula."

Andrew smiles and then looks at Peter and then me.

I sigh. "Andrew, this is my...this is Peter." I stumble over my words as Andrew extends his hand to Peter.

"It's nice to meet you, Peter." Andrew is all politeness and smiles, but not the open smile my parents received.

"Yes, you as well." The men both stand taller as they size each other up, and I want to escape and run far away from here. Peter is a handsome man. He's always been handsome—however, he's like a boy-child next to Andrew. Andrew is about six inches taller than Peter's six-foot-two frame.

My face flushes, and I'm confident that it's the color of a tomato. I look at my parents and Peter. "As great as it is to you see all, I have a bit more work to do, but I can stop by later."

Andrew immediately interjects. "Kate, it's not that busy here. Go. Be with your family." He nods toward the stairwell.

I turn and look at Andrew. "Are you sure?"

Andrew smiles at me, and for some reason, I feel as if my heart is breaking in two, piece by piece. Andrew doesn't know what Peter has meant to me. And Peter doesn't know what Andrew is beginning to mean to me.

"I'll see you tomorrow?" I anxiously wait for Andrew's response.

"Of course." Andrew looks at my parents and then at Peter. "Again, it was lovely meeting all of you, and I hope you find your visit here enjoyable."

My dad once again shakes Andrew's hand and then places his hand on my shoulder as the four of us walk out of the hospital. I glance over my shoulder, and Andrew continues to watch me as I walk away.

CHAPTER 16

A pearl is only a pearl once it's out of its shell.

—Nigerian Proverb

Maria gets back to work, and Peter and my mom walk a few steps ahead of my dad and me. My mom appears engrossed in a story Peter is telling her. My mom's hand goes up to her mouth and her other hand grabs onto Peter's shoulder as her shoulders shake from laughter. My mom has always loved Peter.

My dad leans his head in my direction. "I'm wondering if Andrew would mind sitting down with me while I'm here. I'd like to pick his brain about medical stuff."

I laugh because, of course, this is what's on my dad's mind. "I can make sure that happens. Andrew likes geeking out about medical stuff too."

"Great. We'll get along well."

"Would you all like to see my bungalow?" I gesture toward my parents and Peter.

My mom turns to look at me excitedly. "Of course!"

I open the door for my dad, mom, and Peter, and it feels odd again to have them see this part of my life. Tanzania has been my experience, just for me, and now they are in my space. My mom looks in my fridge and then glances in my bedroom, and I'm happy I made the bed. She inspects my bathroom and then opens the door and looks in the backyard.

"Well?" I ask, knowing every inch of my space is being judged.

"It's so tidy, Kate. It's not a large space, but it's nice." My mom's lips turn up in a smile, and she claps her hands together as she continues to look around.

I smile and am relieved I passed my mom's judgment, which isn't easy to do. "It's the perfect size for one person."

"Yes, I suppose. Well, we are going to go see Maria's parents shortly." My mom dramatically looks at her watch. "Peter, why don't you stay here? It would be boring to hang out with us grown-ups as we catch up on the past twenty years."

I look at my mom and roll my eyes. I see through this. My mom kisses my cheek and walks out the door. My dad turns to me and shrugs his shoulders and then turns to follow her.

I look at Peter and shake my head. "My mom's never been subtle."

Peter's shoulders shake as he chuckles. "That's for sure."

Peter steps toward me and wraps his arms around me and holds me. His touch feels familiar, and my face rests easily on his shoulders. I can smell his shampooed hair as I deeply inhale and can smell the Acqua di Gio cologne on his clothes and skin. It's the only scent Peter has worn in all the years I've known him. Peter takes deep breaths against me, and he looks at me and smiles as he lets go. He pulls me away and smiles at me, and I find it hard to smile back.

I grab a bottle of wine on the counter because being alone with Peter is going to require wine. I hold up the bottle for him, and he nods, so I pour us both a glass and motion for him to come to the backyard. I sit in a chair, and he sits next to me.

"So this is Tanzania." Peter looks around my backyard and then at me.

"Well, Tanzania is a large country, but this is my slice of it."

Peter nods, and I stretch my legs out in front of me. I stare ahead at the fence in front of me.

"Should we make small talk, or do we address the elephant in the room now?"

Peter audibly gasps and then sighs. His mouth turns up in a smile as he looks at me. "Let's address it."

The person Peter knows me as would never take charge like this. I take a long and slow drink of my wine.

"You first." I look at Peter.

Peter turns his chair to me and takes my hand in his. "I messed up. I want you to forgive me and give me another chance."

I close my eyes and can see Peter and Jane kissing. I remember exactly how I felt at that moment, and the nausea that has been at bay since arriving in Tanzania makes its way to my throat and threatens to come out. I can see the day like it was yesterday. It was a Wednesday, and I was supposed to be doing rounds at the hospital until late, but I got violently ill and couldn't stop throwing up in the bathroom, so my instructor sent me home.

As soon as I walked into the apartment I shared with Peter, I could sense something was off. The aura of the place felt different, and I walked around to follow my intuition. I ended up being brought to our master bedroom, where the door was closed. I opened it up, and Peter, with nothing more on than unbuttoned jeans, jumped off the bed. Jane and I locked eyes, and she tried to hide her bare chest, and I stood frozen. Jane had been my very best friend since being together in Mrs. Lawson's class in kindergarten. I couldn't form a word, let alone a thought, and they both followed me around the apartment, pleading with me. They were sorry. This had never happened before; this would never happen again.

"Why, Jane? What were you thinking?" My voice grows loud, and my heart beats faster.

I think back to high school when Peter and I first started dating. I hung out with a popular group of friends, but I wasn't necessarily popular. I was lanky and a book nerd. Jane was the ringleader. She developed before everyone else and always had a maturity about her. I was quiet and a follower. I liked hanging out with type-A personalities because it meant I could blend into the background. When Peter started showing interest in me, Jane was nearly as surprised as me. Guys like Peter didn't go after girls like me. They dated girls like Jane.

Peter puts his glass of wine down and puts his head in his hands for a moment. When he looks up at me, his hair is disheveled. "I started panicking as we got closer to the wedding. All we talked about was the wedding. We were spending more time separated as I finished up my second year of law school, and you were constantly doing rounds."

I rest my elbows on my knees, and my hands hold my face up.

Peter continues, "I started freaking out. I mean, legit freaking out, Kate. Here I was, a twenty-four-year-old, and was already in a relationship eight years old. I'd never experience a first kiss again, the excitement and anticipation. I felt stuck."

Talking about this, reliving what happened, brings the feelings so close to the surface it's like no time has passed at all. I exhale the breath I didn't realize I was holding.

He looks over at me. "I'm sorry if that's hard to hear, but it's the truth. Jane was coming around more, and because you were busy doing rounds, she and I would hang out. It was so stupid, Kate. I don't have feelings for her, I never have. But she was there, and I wanted to see what someone else felt like."

I shudder thinking back to seeing them kiss. I felt so betrayed and entirely naive. I should have seen it coming.

"I know you don't believe me, but I would not have slept with Jane had you not come home."

My lips barely move as my question comes out. "How was the kiss, Peter?"

"It was…different."

I laugh, but it sounds more like a snort. "Would you take me back if it was me who kissed someone else?"

Peter looks at me thoughtfully and then down at his hands. "I think so. I mean, I hope I would."

I think to last night, lying in Andrew's lawn chair, our bodies pressed up against one another. The warmth and hardness of his body as I explored it with my hands. I think of nothing else when I kiss Andrew, except that I want to find a way for it to last longer. Peter and I are broken up, but am I any different than him?

"What if I told you I'd kissed someone since we've broken up?"

Peter looks at me, startled, and his face turns red. I see his fists ball up as he tightens them. His chest rises and falls slowly. "I would have no right to be mad at you." Peter looks down and then back up at me. "Have you kissed someone?"

I sigh dramatically, not ready to tell Peter the truth, but not ready to lie either.

"My feelings are all over the place. I was devastated, Peter. Being apart has made me think about our relationship more. Kiss or no kiss, our relationship wasn't perfect."

"I know that, but we're perfect for each other." Peter puts his hand on my knee. It's something he's done a million times before, but now it feels too intimate.

I shudder once again. "I feel like this is all my heart can handle for a day." I stand up, and Peter reluctantly joins me. He chews at his bottom lip, which he has always done when he's nervous.

We walk inside and place our wine glasses on the counter. "I can walk you to your bungalow."

"No need. I can see it from here." Peter smiles.

I open the door for him, and he turns to me. "I'll see you tomorrow, right?"

I smile and put my hand on his shoulder. "You'll see me every day. It's a small village. It sounds like there is an event almost every night for Maria and Noor's wedding." Peter leans in and hugs me. He smells familiar. The laundry detergent he uses, his aftershave, it's all Peter.

I look up from our hug as Andrew walks out of the hospital. Maybe I imagine it, but it looks like Andrew picks up his pace as he walks in our direction. I try to hurry my goodbye to Peter, but it's no use, Andrew has reached us, and Peter's still here.

"Hi, Kate. Hi, Peter." Andrew looks at me and then Peter. "Peter, how are you finding the village?"

"I haven't seen much of it yet, but it's good." Peter puffs out his chest slightly, and his eyes widen as he checks Andrew out. With one hand, Peter runs his fingers through his sandy blond locks.

I attempt to insert myself. "Andrew, my dad is hoping he can have time with you. He wants to talk medical stuff, I guess."

Andrew's countenance softens slightly. "Yes, I would enjoy that."

"Peter, I'm right next to the bungalow you're sharing with your parents. Can I walk you?" Peter looks at me as if seeking my permission. I nod and shrug my shoulders.

"Sure, I was headed there now."

Before I have an opportunity to relax, Maria and Noor walk toward us from the hospital. Maria nearly skips toward us, excitement and joy plastered across her face.

"Good, you're all here." Maria smiles brightly at all of us. "The parents are getting together tonight, so Noor and I wanted to invite you all over to our place for drinks and appetizers."

Noor smiles at me and then to Peter and Andrew. "Yes, please come over. Let's say in one hour."

I jump in quickly. "I'm sure Peter is tired from his travels. Maybe another night."

Peter waves his hand in the air. "I'm not tired at all. I'd love that. And I'd love time to get to know your fiancé better." Peter smiles at Noor.

Maria claps her hands together. "Then it's settled. Come over in an hour. No need to bring anything."

Maria waves and grabs Noor's hand, and they walk into their bungalow. Andrew, Peter, and I stand there for a moment, with no one saying a thing. I finally turn my back and walk to my bungalow, and the two of them walk off together.

I know I am going to be forced to confront my past as well as figure out my future, but I didn't think it would happen on day 1. I'm not sure what Maria is up to, but I look forward to the words I'll say to her when I get her alone. It was awkward enough standing around with Andrew and Peter for the few minutes that we were all together. Now we're going to be having drinks and appetizers together. For someone who's only had one boyfriend ever, in her entire life, I've sure managed to create a mess. I wonder if anyone will notice if I don't show up.

I throw a dress on and trudge over to Maria and Noor's bungalow. The door is open, and I hear voices from her backyard. The evening is warm and perfect for sitting outside with friends.

Peter arrives next, shortly followed by Andrew. Noor puts his hand on my shoulder and says, "Kate, white or red wine?"

I look at the bottles on his counter. "I'll have red. Thanks, Noor."

Maria comes from her backyard, with music playing, and a smile painted on her face, which makes it impossible to be upset with her. "After you all get a drink, come to the back."

Tanzanian pop music plays from a speaker on the table, and we stand around and catch up. Peter comes and stands next to me, and his hair is still damp from the shower he must have just taken. He's a good-looking man. No one could deny him of that, and his skin has become so bronzed this summer. He now wears jeans with a T-shirt. Our eyes meet, as mine lingers on him for too long.

"You all don't need to stand," Maria says, as she takes a seat at her outdoor table. "Let's sit."

I walk over to the table, and Peter sits directly next to me, and Andrew sits across from me. I try to keep my eyes neutral and focus on Noor and Maria instead of looking back and forth between Andrew and Peter.

"Peter, what do you do back home?" Andrew asks.

Peter smiles, seemingly happy to answer. "I'm about to start my third and last year of law school. I also clerk for one of Minnesota's state judges." Peter then adds, "And one of the largest law firms in the city has promised me a position upon passing the bar exam."

Maria jumps up and runs around the table to hug Peter. "That's so great, Peter." They laugh as Maria smothers him.

Peter puts his hand on my knee, which is visible to everyone due to the low table. I tense up but don't move his hand. "Thanks, Maria. Yeah, I'm excited about it. It's hard to get into this firm as a new lawyer, so I'm excited about it."

Andrew's eyes burn holes in me from across the table. He looks at me and then down at Peter's hand on my knee and locks his eyes on mine. Andrew looks like he's close to jumping across the table and swatting Peter's hand away. Peter moves his hand and then looks at Andrew.

"What's your story, man? Kate's parents were telling us that you are the founder of this hospital." I cringe at how informally Peter addresses Andrew.

Andrew takes a drink of his wine and then slowly puts it down. "My story isn't entirely interesting. I studied to be a doctor in England, and after practicing there for a few years, I decided to open a hospital in my home country."

"Did you bring your family with you?" Peter asks him, and I tense up.

"My parents live in Dar es Salaam, as well as my three sisters."

Peter continues prying, "I meant a wife and kids. I mean, I'm assuming you are married."

My entire body tightens, and I'd do anything to be somewhere other than here. Andrew smiles slowly. "I'm unmarried, I'm afraid. I came to the village all by myself."

Peter nods his head and puts his hand up to his chin. "I must have heard wrong about you being married. Sorry about that."

Andrew waves him off, and I stand up and take my empty drink inside to pour myself another glass of wine. I take my time pouring, wondering if anyone would notice if I sneak through the front door and leave. I lean back against the counter and breathe in my glass of wine, before peeling myself away from the counter, and begrudgingly walking back outside. I regret not telling Maria about kissing Andrew. If she knew, she hopefully wouldn't have put me in this awkward position.

When I walk outside, Maria grabs Noor's hand as a song comes over the speakers, and the two of them laugh as they start dancing joyfully. I stay standing and smile as I watch them, and Peter stands up to join me. His arm brushes up against mine as he also watches them dance, but all I can see is Andrew watching me and every interaction.

Peter puts his arm around me, and my body once against stiffens. "Isn't it great that we get to see Maria get married? I mean, who would have thought when she came to live with your family so many years ago that we'd be in Tanzania together."

"Yeah," I say as I squirm out of his hold, "it's crazy how things work out sometimes."

"Sorry I keep touching you. I can't help myself. I've missed you."

I look up at him and his deep blue eyes. "I know but please don't."

Peter leans into me as I face him. "I don't think your doctor friend likes me." Peter and I both look at Andrew, who watches us and looks like he's about to be sick.

"Your questions were intrusive," I respond, unamused.

He leans in further to me. "There's something I don't like about him, but I can't place my finger on it."

I wonder if something he doesn't like about him is the same something that I don't like about Jane.

The sun keeps getting lower, which I'm going to use as my excuse for why I need to leave. The song ends, and I jump at the opportunity to announce before the next song starts.

"I'm tired, so I'm going to say good night to everyone."

Everyone looks at me, and Maria starts to protest. I dramatically yawn and quickly say my goodbyes and shut the door tightly to my bungalow. It's not my bravest move, but tonight, I'm avoiding everyone, for at least one more day.

CHAPTER 17

Only a fool tests the depth of a river with both feet.

—African Proverb

The door to exam room 6 swings open, as I hurriedly clean up the room and put fresh sheets on the bed. This is my practice after every patient. Sure, in most hospitals, there is a staff that cleans up after appointments and gets rooms ready for the next patient, but this isn't most hospitals. I enjoy the cleanup work, however. It's a moment where I can unwind for a moment before jumping in with a new patient.

"Kate, there are patients in rooms 1, 3, and 4. Are you almost done in here?"

I look up at Andrew, who has taken this tone with me since the moment I showed up at work today. Nothing I do is good enough and clearly not fast enough today.

"I needed to get the sheets on the bed. I'm ready now. Which patient should I take?"

Andrew looks annoyed at my question and walks out of the room, but not before yelling, "Take the patient in room 1."

I roll my eyes at Andrew's abrupt dismissal but hurry to room 1. A large woman sits on the exam table, and I smile as I walk over to her.

"*Jambo*, I'm Kate. How can I help you today?"

"I'm Zuwena. I'm from the village and newly pregnant and would like to be examined."

I smile and do my examination. The more people hear about the village hospital, the more patients that show up. But because very few pay anything for our services, Maria's fundraising efforts are even more important. The good thing is, the more people who are aware of our services, the better their outcomes will be. But the downside is, with Nyla still visiting family in another part of the country, Andrew and I are the only ones available for women's pregnancy health.

I learn that Zuwena is in her midthirties and already the mother of five children—all of whom she delivered in her home. The last two babies were large and challenging births, and she wants early intervention. Zuwena is fourteen weeks pregnant, and because her size worries me slightly, I order blood work for her and ask her to come back in a month.

As I clean up the room, the door swings open again. "Kate, what is taking you so long?" Andrew leans against the open door. "I need you in exam room 4."

I look up at Andrew. "I'm going as fast as I can. I can't help that it's busy, and we aren't going to have exam rooms to use if I don't clean up afterward."

Andrew grunts as he walks out of the room. "Exam room 4, Kate."

I decide not to say anything else. Something that I've learned from him specifically is to take our time with the patients. We should get to know them, their stories, their background, and that is exactly what I've been doing, and now Andrew doesn't think I'm fast enough.

When I get home at the end of the day, I'm exhausted. I realize I didn't pause to eat, and I've been on my feet all day, and they ache. I'm due at my parents' bungalow for dinner with them and the Jacobsons, but I can barely keep my eyes open. I decide to text my mom.

ME

I had an extremely long day at the hospital today. I can barely stay upright, let alone have a conversation, so I'm out for tonight. I'm not at the hospi-

*tal tomorrow, so let's plan to spend the entire day
together.*

The sun set hours ago, and I didn't lie to my mom. I am
exhausted, but I can't turn my mind off, and something has been
bothering me. I walk out my front door, and the hospital is lit up by a
few of the hospital rooms. Most of the bungalows are dark, including
my parents' and Peter's. I imagine they went to sleep hours ago, still
fighting jetlag. I put on my sandals and throw a sweater over my shirt
as the night has turned chilly.

I walk in the direction of my parents' bungalow, but as I look
over, I can see the kitchen light on in Andrew's. I smell the scent of a
bonfire, and I follow the smell until it leads me to where I knew I was
headed the moment I ventured outside. I pause in front of his door,
wondering what magnetic energy brought me here. I knock lightly,
and there is no answer. I tap a bit harder, and there is still no answer.

I've completely lost my mind because now I turn his door handle and push the door open. I stay halfway outside but put one foot
inside. I can see a glow shining through his back door. I close the
door behind me and walk through his kitchen, feeling like a colos-
sal intruder. I slowly open his back door and push it open. Andrew
reclines in front of the fire with a glass of wine and a book and flash-
light, and he must not hear me because he doesn't look up.

"Andrew," I say quietly, so I don't startle him. Andrew flinches
as he looks at me. He puts his hand over his heart, and I can tell he's
surprised.

"I'm sorry. I saw your light on, and then when you didn't answer
the door—I should leave."

"No, no, Kate. It's fine. I just wasn't expecting anyone."

Andrew stands up to greet me, but there is a lack of friendliness
from both of us.

"Why were you so rude to me today?" The words spill out of
me.

"Kate," Andrew says through a heavy sigh.

"You rode me all day," I say through gritted teeth. "Do you have
feedback you want to share with me? Am I not pulling my weight?"

Andrew sits back down in his chair and motions me to the chair next to him. "Are you with him, Kate?"

I sit and face Andrew. "Who?"

Andrew throws his arms up in the air. "You know who. Are you with Peter?"

I sigh, knowing that there is no more delaying this conversation. "No."

Andrew rests his elbows on his knees as he turns to face me in his chair. "But when you said you have a past, you meant him, didn't you?"

I close my eyes for a moment. "Yes."

"I wish you would have told me, Kate. I was ill-prepared to see you with him yesterday and the way he touched you. I wanted to—"

"We don't tell each other a lot of things," I interrupt, "like who's the woman on your screen saver with the huge diamond? We never talk about that either."

Andrew folds his hands. "I wasn't hiding her from you. That's Jasmine, and we were engaged, and we're not anymore. Her picture is only still there out of my laziness. I'll remove it."

I clench my jaw. "You don't have to remove her photo. I was only making a point."

Now it's Andrew who clenches his jaw. "I would have given you the courtesy of a heads-up if Jasmine were to visit the village. That's all I'm saying, Kate."

"You're right," I concede. "I handled things poorly."

"Kate, I like you." I lose my ability to breathe. "Yesterday made me feel weird. I didn't like seeing him touch you, and I could tell I was missing out on a lot of the backstory. I don't need the details, but I don't want to look like a fool either."

I take a deep breath and look into Andrew's eyes. "I was engaged to Peter. We were supposed to get married this summer but broke up a month before I came here."

My body shivers as Andrew puts his hands on my knees.

"And I didn't know he would be coming here until recently, but I'm not ready to talk about it, and I may never be."

Andrew's thumb circles the skin underneath my bent knees. "I respect you not wanting to talk about it, but can I ask you one thing?"

My body tenses, but I give Andrew permission to ask.

"Does he want to get back together?" Andrew stops massaging my skin and looks down. "And do you want to be with him still?"

As much as I don't want to discuss this with Andrew, I know his questions aren't unfair and that he deserves answers. "Yes, and I don't know."

I lie back in the chair and look at the stars because I couldn't continue looking at the broken look on Andrew's face after I responded. I shiver from the nighttime air, and Andrew hands me the softest blanket, and I rub it against my cheek before covering my legs. Andrew lies back too, and neither of us says a thing, and the air feels heavy between us.

"Andrew, I wasn't trying to hide anything from you. I'm simply trying to give myself space to figure things out."

"I understand."

Andrew and I turn toward each other, only inches apart, separated by our own chairs. Yet we feel millions of miles away at this moment. I look into his eyes and see so much vulnerability. Andrew seems so willing to put it all out there, and I realize it's me that is holding back. His chest rises as he inhales. He turns his head to the sky.

"Look"—Andrew points upward—"you can perfectly see Alpha Centauri. It's the closest star to us after the sun, only four light-years away."

Andrew and I simultaneously recline our chairs further down, so now we are both lying completely flat. I smile as I listen to Andrew, who seems to know something about everything. I'm thankful for the change in subject.

"What's that?" I point over to the east at what looks like a massive star in the distance.

"This is a rare sighting, Kate. That is Jupiter rising and can only be seen on the clearest of nights." Andrew looks at me as our eyes once again connect.

I stare at Jupiter and can't wrap my mind around how far away it is and how immense our universe is. The sky is complete darkness but littered with a million spots of light. It occurs to me that when I'm back in Minnesota, Andrew and I will still look at the same sky. Our universe is massive, yet we all look at the same sun, moon, and stars. It makes me feel so connected and like I'm part of something much bigger than myself. I turn to Andrew and lie on my side, so I'm facing him from my reclining lawn chair.

"It feels hypocritical to ask after my unwillingness to share, but why didn't things work out between you and Jasmine?"

Andrew smiles slightly and puckers his lips in thought. "I wanted to move here after my residency. I told her that when we met, and she always acted on board. But once it was time, she wouldn't come."

Andrew turns to his side now too, and we are both wrapped in our blankets.

"Where'd you meet her?"

"Medical school. She's a doctor too. She moved to London at the age of three from Ghana and apparently wanted to stay in London more than marry me."

"That must have been hard for you."

Andrew looks thoughtful and pulls his blanket up to his chin. "At first, yeah."

I watch as his eyes close in a long blink and then open and look at me. "If I thought she was my person, I would have stayed for her."

"Yeah?"

"Yeah."

I squint my eyes, thinking about what it feels like to love someone so much that you would sacrifice where you live for them. I pull the blanket up over my face and then slowly pull it down, where Andrew's expectant eyes continue to watch me. I know I just got done telling Andrew I didn't want to talk about, and I appreciate that he's putting no pressure on me, but I decide to open the subject of Peter back up.

"The day I got on the plane to come here, I was so mad and completely broken. The broken engagement was sudden, and I hated

Peter's guts. And now that he's here, I realize that for whatever reason, I've been softening toward him for a while. I don't feel angry anymore. But now I have to work through how I do feel."

Andrew purses his lips, and they turn up in a half-smile. But it's genuine and meant for me. "If you're still in love with him, if he's your person, do everything you can to end up with him."

I rest my head on my hand and don't blink as I look at Andrew. "You'd be okay with that?"

"No," Andrew says, "but how you feel is entirely up to you. I wouldn't sit around and watch though."

"What do you think I should do?"

"I'd quit asking other people to help you make this decision." Andrew puts a finger over his lips and then removes it. "If you dig deep, Kate, you already have your answer."

"I don't trust my gut anymore. I feel like I have a lot to lose if I get this wrong."

Andrew smiles at me, the smile where I know no one else has ever been lucky enough to see. This smile is only meant for me. The smile reaches his eyes, and his eyes soften, and it makes me want to jump out of my chair and squeeze him. Andrew sits up and puts both his hands on the arms of my chair and leans in until his soft lips touch mine. Our lips are the perfect fit. His full lips surround my smaller lips, and it feels like a force of magnets that keep us together. I want more of him, but I also want to be fair. I push back gently on his chest until we're separated.

"Andrew, I need to be fair to everyone involved. Until I make some life decisions, I think we should stay only friends."

Andrew looks at me knowingly and sits back down in his chair. "If being your friend means I'm in your life, then I'll be your friend."

Andrew takes my hand and squeezes it and doesn't let go. We both roll to our sides, with our fingers intertwined, and look at each other without saying a thing. I put up a boundary with Andrew, and now that he's respecting it, I want to lean across the imaginary line and have him hold me. I never thought it was possible to have feelings for two men at the same time, but I do. My heart feels like it's breaking, being this separated from Andrew. But I've sent this man enough mixed signals for a lifetime.

"I was a jerk to you today, I'm sorry," Andrew says sleepily.

"You're forgiven."

I pull up my blanket to my chin and pull my knees up. My eyes feel like weights, and I try to keep them open as long as possible so I can look at Andrew's almond eyes.

CHAPTER 18

One who causes others misfortune also teaches them wisdom.

—African Proverb

I can see the light through my eyelids, but I'm too comfortable to open them. The sun warms my face, and I feel a breeze on my skin and hair. I pull my blanket up to my chin and feel the soft, plush material stroke my face. I slowly open my eyes, and Andrew is inches from me, in his lawn chair, watching me sleep.

"You have freckles on the bridge of your face and cheeks," he says through a smile.

I shut my eyes and then open them again to make sure I'm not dreaming this. Andrew is still here, so this isn't a dream.

"I don't have them all the time. It's from the sun."

Andrew continues to watch me, and I jump slightly. "I slept here all night?"

"No, you went home, and then I carried you back here to sleep on my lawn chair." Andrew laughs at his joke, and I roll my eyes.

"Yes, Kate. All night. You fell asleep, nearly midsentence. I didn't want to wake you up."

"Did you sleep out here too?"

"I did, and it's one of the best night's sleep I've ever had. I should sleep out here more often."

I laugh but pull the covers over my head. "I think I slept well too." I sit up and stretch my hands high above my head and yawn. I look at my watch but realize I'm not wearing one. "What time is it?"

Andrew pulls out his phone. "It's nearly nine."

"Ugh, I have to get up."

I take my hair out of the hairband it was tied up in. I start running my fingers through my hair and attempt to smooth out the curls and tangles. Andrew watches me as I then take my hair and tie it to the top of my head. I look down at my clothes, and they look put together enough.

"Can I use your bathroom?"

Andrew nods. "Let me make you coffee before you leave."

I brush my teeth with my finger and look at myself in the mirror. Waking up in the sun made my freckles highly visible, and Andrew was right, they are sprinkled across my cheeks and nose, just like when I was a kid. I walk into the kitchen, and Andrew leans against the counter, with a coffee mug in hand, and he hands it to me. I take a drink, and the first touch to my tongue awakens my senses. I don't know how people can start their day without a cup of this magic.

"I'm going to attempt to walk out of here without being seen." I lean toward Andrew to peek out his window.

Andrew chuckles. "You're that nervous, huh?"

"Well, it won't look good."

Andrew shrugs his shoulders. I know he doesn't care whether I'm caught or not.

"Thanks for letting me crash your party of one last night."

Andrew reaches his arm out for me and pulls me into a hug, and my skin prickles as his soft lips kiss my forehead. There is such intimacy in this benign gesture.

"Crash my party anytime. I enjoyed the company."

I smile and take one more sip and put the cup down and then slowly open Andrew's front door. I look toward my parents' bungalow and then toward mine and don't see any movement. I look back at Andrew and then close his door. I walk toward my place, and the dust fills my sandals as I take slow and deliberate steps.

"Kate, what are you doing?"

I whip around to see my mom standing there. My stomach moves into my chest. "I needed to talk to Andrew about a patient."

"How long have you been there? I came by your place earlier, and you weren't there."

I go to lie, to dig myself further into this but decide against it. "What's up, Mom?"

"Your dad is in the shower. Why don't I walk you to your place?"

My mom falls into step with me, and I feel like a teenager who just got caught sneaking out of the house. My mom's face, everything about her, makes me tense up.

We arrive at my bungalow in a short minute. "Can I get you coffee?"

She nods and then puts her hands on her hip. "Did you spend the night with that doctor?"

"Andrew?" I know who she is referring to, but I don't like her cheapening him to *that doctor.*

"I came by your place at eight, and you weren't here. I assumed you were at the hospital, but then I saw you walk out of his bungalow an hour later."

"Mom, it's nothing. I went over there to sit by the fire, and I fell asleep in a lawn chair."

My mom takes a dramatic sip of her coffee and then sits at the table.

"That doesn't sound like nothing, Kate."

"Please. It's nothing." We have a stare-off, and I have a new-found confidence and refuse to look away.

My mom takes a moment before responding. She picks at her fingernails and then finally looks back up at me. "I don't like how he looks at you."

"Who?"

"Andrew. I don't like how Andrew looks at you."

My hand moves up to my cheek as I laugh. "And how does Andrew look at me?"

"Like you are meat, like you are something he can obtain or acquire. I'm telling you, no matter where you are, Andrew watches you."

I roll my eyes. "You've met him once. That doesn't sound like a fair assessment."

"What would Peter think of you spending the night with Andrew?"

The heat reaches every inch of my body. "Mom, quit saying I spent the night with him. That means sex. I promise you that there was no sex."

"Kate Malone!" my mom squeaks as she feigns shock at my use of the word *sex*. "Do you like him?" she asks me pointedly. Her lips are pursed, and I anticipate this conversation is going to go south, and quickly.

"Andrew is nice. In fact, he's quickly become a very good friend."

"This isn't fair to Peter."

The heat in my face may actually cause me to spontaneously combust. I feel a rage I haven't felt in ages.

"Peter cheated on me. Peter called off the wedding, not me." I try to get the words out but have to hold back not to yell.

"He's here to make things right, but you have to give him a chance."

I pace back and forth and take deep breaths, attempting to regulate my heartbeat. A flip switches in my head. My mom never seems to have my back. It's as if she doesn't care at all what's best for me. The anger bubbles up, and I've lost all ability to have a logical conversation.

"Maybe I will date Andrew." I cross my arms over my chest.

"Kate! What are you thinking? You'd date someone outside of your race?" My mom takes a step closer to me, and I can practically see every pore in her face.

"Mom," I say softly, her words piercing the armor of my heart as she says it, "this is about Andrew being Black?"

"I don't have a racist bone in my body, but I also don't want things for you that will add complications to your life, and being with a Black man would make things more complicated."

The tears well up in my eyes, and I tap the bridge of my nose because my mom doesn't deserve my emotions.

"Thank you, Mom."

"What are you thanking me for?" Her words are cold, and as much as I love her, I have a moment where I can't believe she's *my* mom.

I lose all attempts at holding in the emotion, and now I practically scream through the tears. "For not making me guess your thoughts. For coming right out and saying this is because Andrew is Black. You've saved me a lot of heartache figuring out your true thoughts. So thank you." My tears now flow down my cheeks, and I can't stop them.

"Don't you dare make me the bad person. I'm pointing out the truth." My mom puts her hand on my shoulder. "I have Black friends, Kate. But Black men can be—"

"Stop. Just stop." A sob escapes, and my entire body shakes. I can't let her finish the sentence. If my mom and I are going to have a relationship moving forward, I can't know what she was going to say. It may be a place she can't come back from.

"Kate, I didn't mean to upset you. I'm being pragmatic."

My mom sighs and tries to hold my gaze, but I can't look at her. I remember the first time Andrew and I traveled to the countryside when the French tourist asked me if Andrew was my bodyguard. Andrew tried to educate me on how the world is, and I remember brushing off his insinuation that I was witnessing racism. But here I am, sitting with my mom, and she is telling me that a relationship with a Black man would be too complicated.

Why didn't she lead with the fact that we live thousands of miles away? I would have agreed with that point. Andrew was right, and my mom just proved it to me. The disappointment makes me want to curl up in a ball and cry or maybe even scream. We never had a reason to converse about race before. I always thought racism was obvious and overt. This has nothing to do with Andrew being in Tanzania. Instead, this is all about Andrew being a Black man.

"Mom, we have the entire day to spend together as I don't work. Can we talk about anything else?" I recoil as her palm cups my cheek.

"I love you, Kate. This isn't about race. I just think you and Peter have a history I don't want you to give up on."

"So this conversation has nothing to do with Andrew being Black, do I understand this correctly?"

"Kate, I will never welcome difficult things in your life, and I'm not going to stand here and lie to you. You will have an uphill battle if you date outside of your race. That is the truth."

I close my eyes and take a deep breath. This is about race. "I'm going to take a quick shower, Mom, and then I'll head over to your bungalow."

I openly cry during my shower. The noise of the water drowns out the sound, but I cry to the heavens. I ball my fists and hit them against the stone wall and lay my head against it and weep. I don't cry because of the complicated future I could have with Andrew. In fact, no part of me thinks he and I have a future at all. I cry because of my mom's words. I know I have a lot to learn. I know I haven't handled race perfectly in my life, especially here in Tanzania, where I'm actually exposed to different races. But my mom didn't mince words, and I don't know if I'll ever look at her the same.

I throw on my sunglasses as I walk to my parent's bungalow, as my eyes are red and puffy, and I don't want to draw attention to myself. Mr. and Mrs. Jacobson stand in front of their bungalow, with Peter right next to them, and the six of us walk toward Centro Market, where I promised I'd show them all the market and then grab a coffee at one of the shops near there.

Peter and I walk a few steps behind the grown-ups, and he looks at me and smiles. "Is the weather always so perfect here?"

I laugh softly. "It drizzled one evening since I've been here, but yeah, it's been pretty perfect so far."

We reach Centro Market, and I start at the fruit vendor. The mangos remain my favorite fruit here, and it's so much more flavorful than all the mangos back home. I feel Peter's hand on my shoulder, as he leans in from behind me to sample the mangos that sit on a plate.

"Kate, you have to try this." Peter places a piece of mango in my open mouth.

The vendor behind the table smiles at us and says in Swahili, "*Wanandoa wazur.*" I know the words well, as I've said it to people in the hospital. It means "beautiful couple."

We walk through more of the market, and my mom and Mrs. Jacobson nearly buy all the wine at the wine vendor. All the villagers and the vendors smile at our group of six foreigners, and everyone admires Peter and I as we hang back and walk together. No one whispers under their breath or gives us disapproving looks. Everyone is the epitome of kindness and acceptance.

My mom comes over and wraps her arms around me. "Everyone is so friendly here, Kate. I can see why you like it here so much."

I force a pained smile and nod. "Yeah, everyone is great here, Mom."

Peter takes my hand in his, and I don't have the energy to pull away. Peter and I have held hands a million times. The mold of his hand is familiar, and I look down at our hands, his slightly tanner than mine, but we are mostly the same shade. I don't know why, but my mind goes toward our senior year of college, walking around the convention center.

We were there for a career fair in medicine. I already had been accepted into the university to study nursing, but I was still unsure what type of nursing I wanted to focus on. I stopped in front of a booth for Doctors Without Borders. I slowly looked through a brochure that talked about the program, and all the different countries I could live in and work. My grand idea was to spend our first year of marriage, while Peter was finishing up his third year of law school, living abroad and truly making an impact. The brochure said that experience in midwifery was especially desired.

I took the brochure and discussed it with Peter that same evening. I'll never forget how upset he was. He said it was a terrible idea to spend a year apart, especially right after getting married and then reminded me that once he makes partner at a law firm, I won't have to work at all. Instead, he said, I can stay home and raise our children.

I let out an audible sigh.

Peter squeezes my hand. "Is everything okay, Kate?"

I am so far down a rabbit hole I have forgotten where I am. "Yes, I'm fine."

After visiting almost every single vendor at Centro Market, we walk back toward the bungalows. My dad walks with Peter and me and puts his arm around me.

"Andrew stopped over at my bungalow this morning, Kate. He said he has a lot of free time today, so I think I'll take him out for a beer at one of those bars we just passed and talk medicine."

My body warms, and the thought of my dad and Andrew sharing a beer warms me in ways I can't explain. "I'll walk you to the hospital whenever you are ready, Dad."

He smiles and then catches up with my mom and the Jacobsons.

Peter leans closer to me and, in almost a whisper, says, "There is something about Andrew I don't like."

"You've already told me that."

"I know, but I can't stop thinking about it."

My body stiffens, and I put space between the two of us. "He's been great to me, so you'll have to find a way to get over it."

Peter visibly tenses up too. "I'm sorry I said anything."

I drop everyone off at their bungalows, and I walk my dad over to the hospital. I'm grateful for a moment alone with him, as I haven't had one since he arrived.

CHAPTER 19

No matter how many times you wash a goat, it will still smell like a goat.

—Ethiopian Proverb

My chips fall from the vending machine, and then Maria's follow right after mine.

"Kate, it was seriously the cutest thing I've seen. Noor and I were a few tables away, but your dad and Andrew were laughing so hard and seemed to have the best time together."

I laugh as Maria recounts seeing my dad with Andrew at the bar, talking about all things medical. I pop a chip in my mouth and chew it before opening my mouth to respond.

"I'm not surprised they'd get along so well. Now that I think of it, Andrew reminds me of my dad in some ways."

Maria rests her head on my shoulder as we walk toward her office. "I can see that actually. That's probably why I loved your dad the first time I ever met him."

The waiting room is once again full, so I pop the last chip in my mouth and hurry down the hallway. "Maria, I have to go see patients but let's chat later. There has to be something I can be doing to get everything ready for your big day."

Maria laughs and waves me off. "I'll let you know, but I'm telling you, everything is ready to go, including our outfits."

I go to the waiting room and grab a patient and bring her into the exam room. No babies are ready to come today, and I spend the entire morning examining women and having talks about pregnancy health. The patients are diverse in religion, age, and circumstances, but with each one, I learn something new. As I clean up the room from the last patient, Andrew walks through the door.

"Hey, Kate. I wanted to let you know Peter is in the waiting room, looking for you."

I look toward the door and then Andrew and then the clock. It is getting late, but I am not ready to leave for the day yet.

"Thanks, Andrew."

He opens the door for me, and I walk out, and he follows me. Next to Peter, only one other woman is waiting, and I smile when I see it's Fatima. She's a couple of chairs away from Peter, but I see her steal glances in his direction. Peter and I make eye contact, and I give him the one-moment look and walk over to Fatima.

"Hi, Fatima. I hope you haven't been waiting long. I can take you to an exam room now."

Fatima stands up and follows me, and Peter's eyes pierce into me as he watches my every move. Andrew follows us into the exam room as well.

Fatima sits down and looks at us. "I came back to discuss the plan."

Andrew looks at me and then Fatima. He pulls up a chair and sits next to the table.

"I have updates for you too, Fatima. You go first."

Fatima nods her head. "My father knows I have a baby in my belly, but I don't want him to know what happens with the baby. He says that adoption is not Allah's way and that there are family members who can care for the baby. I don't want that."

I inch closer, and Andrew wraps his hand around hers. "Why don't you want that, Fatima?"

"I don't want a daily reminder that I bore my father's child. All our family lives in the village. The child would live in the village too. And people will talk. But my dad will never accept adoption."

I take Fatima's other hand in mine. "What do you want to do, Fatima?"

"I want to deliver the baby here and then tell my dad that the baby died during birth."

Fatima looks down, as Andrew continues to hold one hand of Fatima's and I hold the other. Andrew looks at me.

"Fatima, we'll do our best with that plan." Andrew agrees. "But while you're here, may we make sure everything looks good and healthy?"

Fatima nods, and I back up as Andrew does his examination. Everything continues to look great with the baby, and she continues to measure on track. After the examination, I walk her to the door. I glance at the waiting room, and Peter no longer sits there. I watch Fatima walk down the hall, and I go back into the exam room where Andrew is stripping the bed of sheets.

"Andrew, please. We're not so desperate that the doctor has to turn over the rooms, are we?" I smile at him playfully.

He puts the dirty sheets in the hamper, and I pull out fresh linens to line the bed. Andrew grabs one end of the sheet, and I grab the other.

"What do you think of Fatima's wishes?" I ask Andrew.

"I'm not entirely surprised. Adoption is a point of confusion in Islam. Many Muslims say it is forbidden in Islamic law to adopt a child, but it's permissible to take care of another child. It's semantics, really."

Andrew walks over to where I lean against the exam bed. "Here's what concerns me, Kate. I know she has a while to go in her pregnancy, but the baby remains breech. There is no way Fatima can tell her father that she had the baby in the country somewhere and then come back with a cesarean scar. We'll need to ensure that the baby is born vaginally."

Andrew puts his hand next to where I lean, and I like the closeness. The muscle of his forearm is visible, and I catch myself staring. "Couldn't Fatima tell her father she delivered at the hospital, but the baby died?"

"No, if her father knows she is coming to the hospital for treatment, and that people here knows he impregnated his thirteen-year-old daughter, he'll kill her."

"I worry about how small she is," I say in response.

The door swings open, and Andrew and I both look toward the door. Heat envelopes my face as Peter stands in the doorway.

"Sorry to interrupt, but I saw that woman leave, so I was hoping we could talk, Kate."

If my face is as red as it feels, it's now the color of a tomato. "Peter, I was just finishing up discussing a patient. Can you wait a moment?"

Andrew quickly interjects, "It's fine, Kate. We can discuss more later."

"Are you sure?"

Andrew nods at me, reassuringly, and I walk out of the exam room. I quickly change out of my scrubs, and Peter and I walk out of the hospital. The anger is close to overwhelming me, but I don't want to say anything until we are privately back in my bungalow.

We walk through the door, and I can't wait another moment to speak. "Peter, what were you thinking?"

Peter looks taken aback, as he opens up my fridge and grabs himself a beer. "What do you mean?"

"I was discussing a patient with Andrew, who happens to be my boss. What were you thinking just barging in there?"

Peter opens his beer and takes a slow sip of it. "Kate, I'm sorry, but I have a bad feeling about the two of you. Why do you need to see a patient together? You're a midwife. You don't need his help. And why do you need to discuss the patient for so long after she leaves?"

I slam my hand down on the counter and look up at Peter. "You don't understand the nature of my work, and that's fine, Peter. But I've been working extremely hard trying to gain Andrew's respect for me as a healthcare provider. You barged in tonight, and it was embarrassing and made me look small."

"I don't like him, Kate."

"So you've said."

Peter paces in my kitchen and then stands in front of me. "Well, when you want to tell me what's going on here, I'm ready to listen. Because I know you better than anyone else knows you, and I can tell something isn't right." Peter downs his beer with another sip and slams the door as he leaves my bungalow.

I lean on the counter, trying to catch my breath, entirely embarrassed by the way he conducted himself, but also realizing I need to start being honest with everyone in my life. I almost told Peter about kissing Andrew, but I hesitated. I'm not a cheater. I kissed Andrew as a single person. And if I decide to reconcile with Peter, I'll be honest with him, but I'm still figuring things out. I lie in my bed, staring at the ceiling, and I know I'll never be able to sleep tonight. My heart has finally slowed to a normal pace, but I know I need to address what happened with Andrew. I throw on a pair of yoga pants and my favorite Minnesota sweatshirt and peek out my front door. Once again, the bungalows look dark. The moon is high in the sky and the only light I see. I glance in the direction of my parents and, once again, see a dim light on in Andrew's kitchen. I close my door quietly and tiptoe in the direction of his bungalow. I once again can smell the embers of the fire and the sweet wood burning in contrast to the cool breeze. I pause, knowing this is a bad idea, but feeling like the smell of fire is inviting me in. I don't even knock lightly. I turn the doorknob and walk in and immediately see the light from the backyard. I walk through Andrew's kitchen and open the back door. Andrew doesn't even glance in my direction, but in my lawn chair is a folded blanket and on the ground is a glass of water.

"Am I that predictable, Andrew?"

I walk up to the chair and look over to Andrew as I sit down. His lips go flat, and I'm not greeted with the smile I was hoping for. "Not predictable, Kate. I was just hoping."

"I wanted to apologize for Peter barging into the exam room. It was extremely unprofessional, and it won't happen again."

"Kate, you have nothing to apologize for."

I sit on the chair next to him and put my face in my hands. "I feel like I have something to apologize for. Everything feels so disjointed, but you are my boss, and today wasn't professional."

"Again, Kate. I'm not your boss. I'm a mentor, helping you improve your craft."

I nod at Andrew and try to smile. I bring my knees to my chest and wrap the blanket around me. Andrew reaches across the boundary I set and squeezes my hand before asking, "Light or heavy?"

I turn my head sideways. "What do you mean?"

Andrew drops my hand, as I can see him register that he's crossed a boundary.

"Do you want to talk about a light topic or a heavy topic?"

My head jerks in his direction. "We've had options this entire time?" I laugh as I think of all the deep discussions we've had. "Light, definitely light."

Andrew bites his lip and smirks as he looks at me. "Here's mine. I'm a tall man, Kate. I'm six foot, eight inches. When I moved to London for boarding school, everyone was excited about the African man who was extremely tall and loved basketball. I was even tall back then. The problem was, I was terrible. I wanted so badly to be good, but I was the worst player on the team. Everyone thought I was a sham."

I place my hand over my mouth, and the laugh escapes through my fingers. "I don't know if I'll ever look at you the same. So you were really bad?"

"Kate, it was embarrassing. Tanzanians like futbol, not basketball." Andrew smiles and looks relieved that he's shared his secret.

I shake my head and am thankful for the moon tonight so that I can see Andrew's face. I turn on my side so I can face him better.

"So I tell everyone that I could make a better impact as a midwife than a doctor, right? I think I told you that. But the truth is, me, the daughter of two doctors, failed the Medical College Admission Test. I mean, failed it big time. I am terrible at math, which by the way, isn't a good indication of who will be a good doctor, but I didn't have the heart to try again."

Andrew gasps but doesn't laugh at me. "You are a wonderful midwife. Forget the MCATs."

Andrew leans forward in his chair. "Okay, before wanting to become a medical doctor, I wanted to be a paleontologist."

"That's not so bad." I laugh hysterically as I picture a younger Andrew, obsessed with dinosaurs like so many young boys are.

"Now this is embarrassing, Andrew, so please don't judge me. When I found out Maria was going to live with my family, I told everyone she was visiting from the country of Africa." I put my face in my hands and shake my head.

"Kate, no, you didn't?" Andrew rolls his head back and laughs. I'm sure I've never seen anything as beautiful as a real smile from Andrew.

Andrew turns on his side, and we face each other, inches apart, separated by our own chairs. His eyes hold my gaze, and he folds his hands underneath his face. His face turns serious.

"I'm afraid I'm not doing enough in Tanzania. I'm not reaching enough people. I'm not making a difference."

"That wasn't light, Andrew."

"No." For a moment, he looks smaller than he is as he stares at me. The moon reflects off his almond eyes, and it looks like they are an entrance into everything Andrew holds inside of himself.

I breathe in sharply at his confession and stop myself from telling him he's doing more than anyone else.

"I'm worried that when I go home, the first-world problems I see won't be enough to keep me interested in this profession. I'm worried home will never feel like home again."

Andrew reaches his hand across the threshold and squeezes my hand, and I immediately feel safe and warm. "I stay up at night wondering if I missed something with Bupe. If I could have saved her."

I take a long blink as I hold my breath and then release slowly. "I stay up at night wondering if I killed Bupe."

A pained expression floods Andrew's face, and it looks like he is in physical pain.

"Kate, no. Never say that. Never think that." He reaches out for my hand again; this time, he doesn't let go.

Andrew massages the inside of my palm with his fingertip as he continues. "I worry that you always put people ahead of yourself, that your decisions are more based on not hurting people than doing what's best for you."

I feel a tightening in my stomach. "I worry about that too," I say in almost a whisper.

Andrew lifts his head off his chair and leans into me.

"I worry that you're going to make a decision you'll regret for the rest of your life."

I take my bottom lip in my mouth and put my hand on my chest as I quietly protest. "Andrew—"

"Kate, I'm sorry."

"No, no." I look down and then slowly raise my eyes to his. "I worry that I'm going to be sixty years old someday and think to myself, if only—"

Andrew leaps off his chair and lies with me in mine. His long, strong arms wrap around me and gently pushes my face closer to his chest.

"Kate, as long as you always put yourself first, you'll never need to entertain these fears you have."

I lift my face to look at Andrew and, for a moment, decide my boundaries are arbitrary and completely unnecessary. I lay a soft and chaste kiss to Andrew's lips and then bury myself again in his shirt.

CHAPTER 20

A happy man marries the girl he loves, but a happier man loves the girl he marries.

—African Proverb

My eyes dart open, and I sit up abruptly in my bed. It's Noor and Maria's wedding day! It's already been a long week with my family here, Peter, and the wedding festivities, and it all leads to today.

There is a pounding on my door and then footsteps. "Kate, it's my wedding day!"

I run out into the kitchen, and Maria has a silk bonnet on her head, and she's bouncing up and down. I throw my head back and laugh, and Maria grabs me and bounces while dancing. "What can I do for you?"

"Just have snacks and drinks ready for us ladies as we get ready. Everyone will be here in a couple of hours. I want champagne as we get ready. I need something to relax me."

"Done. I have completely stocked up. What else?"

"Honestly, nothing. Everything is ready. I'm going to look fabulous." Maria sways her hips and dances to the music only she can hear.

I laugh. "Tonight is going to be what dreams are made of."

"I need to get back to my place, but Noor asked Andrew to drop off some things, so he'll be here at some point this morning."

"Got it."

Maria gives me another hug and dances out of my bungalow while I laugh.

I bring a pair of shorts and a tank top into the bathroom and take a long, mostly warm shower. I would never have thought I'd be here for Maria's wedding, especially after how much I resisted coming here. Now I'm the maid of honor and can't wait to see a Tanzanian wedding and all the traditions. I turn off the shower and hear footsteps in my kitchen.

"Hello?" I call out through the closed bathroom door.

"Sorry if I startled you. I'm dropping stuff off per Noor's instructions." I would know Andrew's voice anywhere.

"Maria said you'd be stopping over. I'll be out in a minute." I throw on my pair of shorts and tank top and quickly brush through my wet hair.

The aroma of fresh flowers overpowers me as I walk out of the bathroom. I don't see Andrew. Perhaps he went to get another load. There are bouquets of lilies, all in vases, and my small bungalow has been transformed. I bend down to get closer to the flowers and inhale sharply and close my eyes, imagining I'm in a field full of them.

"They smell good, don't they?"

I turn around, as Andrew comes in, holding a few bottles of champagne. "Noor wasn't sure if you had champagne, and it was Maria's request."

"Thank you. The flowers smell amazing. I think I need flowers in my bungalow at all times." I smile as I take another long inhale.

Andrew puts several bottles in my fridge and turns to look at me. I observe the once-over he does of my body, and I watch him pause on my lips and then move his glance back up to my eyes. He leans back against the counter and continues to look at me. He isn't even attempting to be subtle.

"You're staring at me, Andrew."

Andrew chuckles and looks down and then back to me.

"I'm sorry." Andrew places his hand on his cheek. "I had all these great excuses, but you'd see right through them. I like looking at you, Kate."

I shake my head but smile. "Well, try being subtler next time. Is this everything?" I motion to the fridge and flowers.

"For now, until Noor or Maria gives me further instructions."

"I guess I'll see you at the back of the aisle."

"It's a date." Andrew walks toward the door and then turns to me. "I'll be the man in back who gets to walk the most beautiful woman down the aisle."

Andrew closes the space between us, and my insides are quickly a puddle. "You're walking Maria down the aisle?" I joke.

"I meant you, Kate." Andrew breathes into my ear, and I'm sure the only sound we can hear is my beating heart.

Andrew pulls me into him, and for a moment, my arms hang at my side. I slowly bring them up and wrap them around his waist. We stand in an embrace for a moment.

"Andrew?"

I feel his chest expand as he releases a breath. "I'll see you at the wedding."

*****

It's wedding time. Maria is a sight to behold in her beautiful lace wedding gown, and her braids are pulled up on top of her head, and she has a beautiful red lip. Maria's dress fits her petite figure perfectly. It hugs her in all the right places and then darts out slightly at the knee. She's the most gorgeous bride I've ever seen.

My dress is aqua blue, with thick straps and an organza overlay. I decided on flat shoes as I expect to be on my feet a lot today. I wear my hair down in big curls, and Maria's mom put a few flowers throughout my hair. We walk out of the bungalow, holding hands. We don't have far to go as the tent is set up just around the corner.

Maria hangs back slightly, so no one, especially Noor, will see her before she begins her walk down the aisle. Her parents hang back with Maria, and my mom walks me to the ceremony, where my dad is already seated and waiting for my mom to sit. The music is already playing, and Andrew stands at the back of the seated area, presumably waiting for me. I see him before he sees me, and he is a vision.

My heart feels like it's going to stop as Andrew's eyes slowly turn to me. I've never seen him in anything other than smart clothes, but today, he wears traditional Tanzanian attire. His shirt is a loose white blouse, with gold stitching around the neck, and it tucks into a wrapped skirt, almost to his ankles, that is the same color of my dress. The outfit is paired with casual sandals.

Andrew watches me approach, and he doesn't look away, as his eyes smile. He has a peculiar expression, and not for the first time, I wish I could read his mind, to know what he's thinking. I wish he would look away, as the gaze he gives me makes me self-conscious as I walk toward him. I finally reach him, and he puts his arm out for me, and I clasp my arm through his. Before we walk down the aisle, he leans over to me. My hand caresses the fabric of his skirt, and it's the same fabric as my dress.

"You look breathtaking, Kate."

"So do you," I say, and my reward is Andrew's smile.

Andrew puts his hand over his heart, and I smile up at him, and my skin fills with goose bumps. Andrew and I receive the cue to start walking down the aisle. There are flower petals that make up the aisle, laying over the dirt of the terrain we are on. I am to the right of Andrew, and my left arm is wrapped through his right arm. I smile at the guests, many I recognize from the village, and a few I don't recognize at all. I see my parents up toward the front, with Peter and his parents. We reach the front of the aisle, and Andrew guides me to a chair in the front near Maria's parents, and he sits down next to me.

"Tanzanian weddings are long, so the witnesses sit through the ceremony." Andrew leans over and whispers to me.

The song changes, and Maria enters the back of the aisle, her mom on one side of her and her dad on the other. I can tell from here that she is crying. I look over at Noor, who also has glistening eyes. I always love watching the groom at weddings to see their reaction to their bride walking toward them. Maria walks slowly down the aisle, and my heart nearly bursts with gratitude that I'm here.

The ceremony starts, and Noor speaks in Swahili. He points to people gathered, and when he points, to them, they stand up.

Andrew leans over too, and I can smell the mint of his breath and his lips nearly touch my ear as he whispers, "Noor is introducing everyone who has come to the wedding from his side."

Maria then speaks and must be introducing those here for her.

"Stand up, Kate, you are being introduced." I'm glad Andrew said something as I didn't recognize my name when spoken.

After everyone is introduced, Noor's parents walk up to the front and take Noor over to Maria's parents, and they have a conversation and exchange something.

Andrew leans over once again. "This is the ceremonial dowry ceremony. There isn't actually a dowry, but it's tradition." I nod as I lean toward Andrew to take in his every word.

The vows that Noor and Maria share are beautiful, at least, the ones I understand. The ceremony switches between English and Swahili. At one point, Noor and Maria are tied together and walk in a circle. Approximately two hours have passed. Noor and Maria kiss, marking the end of the ceremony.

"They are now married," Andrew says as he smiles at me and pats my hand.

The DJ who is off to the side starts playing loud music, and everyone stands up. Andrew grabs my hand and leads me into a circle. Everyone at the wedding now stands in one large circle and dances. Maria and Noor are in the middle dancing, smiling, and stealing kisses from each other. Everyone claps to the music, and the mood is celebratory. After the song ends, the circle disperses.

The music continues, and after I enjoy some fantastic food, I get up to get myself a drink at the bar. I talk to a few of the staff members from the hospital, and I take in the scenery. There is no first dance like I'm used to or a father-daughter dance; instead, anyone who feels like it makes their way to the dance floor. The rhythm of the music creates vibrations on the ground and on my feet, which are now bare so I can move around on the dance floor easier. I have grown to love the different music I hear in Tanzania, and I love how freely everyone dances here like they don't care what people think or who is watching.

Maria sees me working my way to her, and she grabs my hand and pulls me in. I wipe away the sweat that pools at my brow. It's a fast song, and I feel carefree as I move around and dance. Noor also dances with us, and then Editha comes and joins us. It's a song I've heard before, but I have no idea what the name of it is. When the song ends, I go to refill my wine. My dad joins me at the bar just as the song turns slow.

"Want to dance with your old man, Kate?"

I grab his hand and bring him to the dance floor. "I'd love to."

I place my hand on my dad's shoulder and hold his right hand, which he presses against his chest.

"Have I told you how beautiful you look today, Kate?" He winks at me.

"Thanks, Dad," I say as I look down.

I breathe in and smell the same comforting aftershave that my dad has worn since I was a young girl. We dance in silence, and then I break the silence with something I've wanted to tell my dad for a long time.

"Dad, I'm glad you made me come to Tanzania. It turns out, you were right once again."

My dad laughs and puts both his hands gently around my neck.

"I'm happy you are happy. That is all I ever want for you, Kate." I watch as my dad's smile turns into something else. "Can I ask you something?"

I look up at him and nod.

"I believe that you're happy, but it also seems like something is bothering you. Are you sure everything is okay?"

The wine tingles through my body and makes me feel light and honest, as if I have nothing to hide.

"What am I going to do about Peter?"

My dad nods, slowly and deliberately. "Follow your heart, Kate."

I purse my lips and stare into my dad's blue eyes. "And if it leads me away from Peter, you're fine with that?"

My dad breathes out quickly in a gasp.

"A parent is only as happy as their unhappiest child. I want you to be happy, and if that's with Peter, great. But if it's not with Peter, that is great too. You and your happiness, Kate, that's what I want most for you."

The song ends, and my dad squeezes my shoulders and kisses me on my cheek. I hold him for a moment. Whether he realizes it or not, he's permitted me to make my own choice, and that means everything to me.

The atmosphere is celebratory, and my moves are out and proud tonight. Peter comes and stands by me. "You look beautiful, Kate."

"Thanks, Peter," I say with a smile.

We stand next to each other, barely saying a word, instead, stealing glances at each other. The song once again turns slow, and the crowd parts as Andrew finds his way to me.

"Will you dance with me, Kate?"

"Umm"—I look over to an uncomfortable Peter, whose eyes meet mine at the same time—"sure."

I go to take Andrew's hand, and I feel Peter's hand around my elbow. I look back at him quickly.

"Kate, stay with me," Peter pleads with me.

I look to Andrew, who still holds my hand in his, and then back to Peter. "Peter, it's fine."

He slowly pries his hand off me, and I turn and walk with Andrew to the dance floor.

Andrew takes my hand in his, and instead of holding it, he guides it to his neck. I move my hands to his shoulders, as his neck is too high. Andrew puts his hands on my hips and pulls me into him.

He looks down at me. "Your dress matches your eyes." I'm happy he didn't mention the uncomfortable interaction we just had with Peter.

I look down at my dress. "I guess you're right."

"I've never seen anyone as beautiful," Andrew says into my ear.

My hands are tired being on his tall shoulders, so I remove them from his neck, and I put them around his waist. Andrew pulls me in closer to him, and my hand wanders up under his untucked shirt accidentally. When my hand meets the skin on his back, right above his pants line, I go to remove it quickly, but I immediately feel the warmth and electricity of his skin, and I find myself unable to lift my hand.

We are more in an embrace than dancing at this point. There is no space between us, and I rest my head on his chest while I hold his back under his shirt. Andrew rests his head on mine, and I feel like we are the only two people in existence. His heart beats steadily underneath his hard chest muscles. He smells heavenly, like clean linens and vanilla. We don't say a thing to each other, yet I know I'm not the only one who feels like no one else exists in this moment. We stop dancing and gaze at each other for a moment, as people and music moves around us.

"Andrew," I say, as he continues to hold me, but says nothing.

He looks down at me, and time stands still as we look into each other's eyes.

"Kate—"

I feel a hand on my shoulder and turn to see Peter. Andrew clears his throat, and when I turn back around to look at him, he's walking away.

"We haven't danced yet." Peter takes my hand as the song turns slow again.

"I know I already told you this, but you look beautiful tonight, Kate," Peter says to me.

I place my hand on Peter's shoulder. "Thanks."

"I mean it, Kate. You've always been breathtaking, but something about Tanzania has made you... I don't know, but I've never seen you look better."

I look down and then back up at Peter. "Are you having fun?"

"I am. I can't believe we leave tomorrow already. I'm looking forward to the safari though. I wish you were coming, but I'll be back in a few days."

My eyes somehow find Andrew. He's dancing with Maria, but he watches me. "I know. You'll have so much fun."

Peter pulls me into him. He looks handsome in his white dress shirt, and I'm close enough that I can see his faint freckles on his face. I've danced with Peter a million times before, and we move our hips and feet in rhythm. Peter and I hold each other's gaze. We barely need to speak. We know each other that well. I know every inch of his skin. I know every look that he gives. In many ways, I feel like an extension of him.

"I love you, Kate."

Peter looks at me as the music stops. His eyes plead with mine, and he waits for my response. He holds a finger up to my lips and then removes it and leans in and kisses me. His lips feel so familiar on mine, even though it's been so long since we've kissed. I don't pull away, and I keep my eyes open the whole time. After a moment, Peter pulls away and smiles. He walks away toward the bar, and I stand, surprised by the kiss. People dance around me, and I turn to see Andrew, watching me. By the look on his face, he saw the kiss. I hurry toward him, but I'm too late, and he's disappeared.

CHAPTER 21

He who loves the vase loves also what is inside.

—African Proverb

I go into my bungalow and shut the door and look down at my feet, and the dirt feels rough. I've been dancing barefoot all night, and I want to wash them off before going to bed. As I walk into the bathroom, I glance in the mirror, and my hair is still mostly intact, and the flowers are still in place. I turn the spigot of the shower on and lift my dress to my knees and start rinsing my feet. I see all the dirt leave my feet and toes and swirl down the drain. My feet start to look clean again. I think I hear a knock at the door over the sound of the shower.

I walk into the kitchen, leaving a wet trail behind me. I don't know what the emotion is when I see it's Peter, but it feels like a twitch of disappointment.

"Can I come in?" he asks.

I hold the door open for Peter as he enters. I shut the door behind him, and he stares down at my feet, and I laugh. "They were filthy, trust me."

Peter looks around my place and then back at me and smiles. "You've never been a dancer, but you were on the floor all night tonight."

"Yeah, I promised Maria I'd dance."

"You looked good out there. Carefree."

"Uh, do you want to go sit on the couch?" I motion to the room. "I'll meet you there. I need to get into something more comfortable."

I take my beautiful blue dress off and lay it across the bed. I feel magical in that dress, like I can do anything. I walk out of my bedroom, and Peter sits on the couch, with one of his legs crossed over the other. I sit next to him like I've done a million times before, with my legs crossed.

"I leave tomorrow, as you know," Peter looks at me intently.

"I know. But you'll be back in a few days before you drive to Dar and fly home."

Peter inches closer to me. "That's the plan."

"I'll be home in a little over a month." My body tenses as the words come out of my mouth. It doesn't seem like my time here is almost done, but it is. I don't know if I'll be ready to leave this village in a month, but I know I'm not ready now.

"I kept our place back home." Peter looks at me shyly and then looks down. "I don't want to presume anything, but if you're ready, you can move back in anytime."

I pucker my lips as I chew on the inside of my cheek. Reality smacks me in the face, I'm going to have to go home, and I'm going to have to figure things out. I can't leave Peter in limbo for much longer. This isn't fair to him. I put my hand on Peter's shoulder and turn my face to him. "I'm not purposely leaving you hanging, Peter. This isn't even about you kissing Jane anymore. But that happening has forced me to reevaluate things."

Peter looks down, and his face looks wounded. "I know. I just, I feel like I'm losing you. It's taken everything in me to come here and watch you live your life. I don't even recognize you anymore. Not in a bad way, you're just so different. It's like, you've moved on, and I'm not part of this new reality." Peter puts his hand on my knee. "It's taken everything in me not to punch that doctor in the face."

I shake my head slowly. "Please don't say that."

"I'm not stupid, Kate. I can tell there is something there, so quit lying to me."

I rest my head on my elbow and look into Peter's blue eyes. I can't begin to explain something to him that I don't understand myself. Peter pulls himself closer to me, and with his other hand, he strokes my face. I watch in slow motion as Peter turns his head slightly, and then gently, his lips touch mine. He removes his lips and then kisses me again. I part my lips, and Peter's tongue slowly and deliberately enter my mouth, and we stay this way for a while, in a sweet, affectionate kiss. My lips match his in size, and the kiss feels like licking an ice cream cone, slowly and evenly. It's the kind of kiss that can go on forever. It's a pleasant kiss, but it will never lead to anything.

His expression is difficult to read. He studies my face, and I give him my side smile and ask, "How did that feel to you, Peter?"

Peter chuckles and wrinkles his face. "What do you mean?"

"I mean when we just kissed. Did it feel, I don't know, passionate?"

Peter pats my knee and then keeps his hand there. He chuckles slightly. "Kate, you know I don't believe in stuff like that. It felt familiar, in a good way."

"You don't believe in stuff like what?" I want to rip Peter wide open and have a real conversation about how he feels.

"I believe in love, and perhaps eight years ago, when I first kissed you, it felt explosive. I don't remember. But now it feels comfortable and stable. We've spent eight years getting to know each other. That's worth more to me than any passion ever could. I don't think that stuff lasts." Peter rubs my arm with his fingers. "What lasts in a relationship is trust and friendship, and that's what I'm trying to get back with you."

I prod further. "It doesn't bother you that you'll never feel that again? It doesn't feel like settling to you?"

"Look, Kate," Peter continues to caress my arm. "I messed up big time. I was having all the thoughts that you are now having, so I tested it out. Kissing you was a hundred times better than kissing Jane. I made the biggest mistake of my life for chasing something that doesn't exist."

I place my hand on Peter's knee and turn my head. "You didn't think kissing Jane was... I don't know, remarkable?"

Peter picks at a lint on my shirt. "No, I thought of you the entire time."

Peter's words confirm what I've known. Peter and I aren't the same. When I kiss Andrew, Peter is the last thought in my mind. I see fireworks and feel things, deep inside, that I know I've never felt before. And I fear it's not because it's a kiss with a new person. I don't remember ever feeling that when Peter and I were first together.

"Don't you think you can have both, Peter? Passion and familiarity?"

Peter looks at me, surprised. "I've never heard you speak this way."

There are so many things that I've never spoken to Peter. He watches me as my mind goes in many different directions. I lean forward and put my hand behind his neck and pull him to me. Our lips meet, and I forcibly spread his, so I can feel more of him. Peter falls back, and I lay on him and run my hand through his hair. Peter pulls back and looks at me.

"What are you doing, Kate?" he asks breathily.

I try to hide my surprise at how little I felt when we kissed, by how off our chemistry feels. I prop myself back to a sitting position and put space between us.

"Don't you want this?" I gesture toward him.

He furrows his brow. "I've never seen you like this."

I stare at him blankly, unable to articulate all the thoughts that run through my mind. Peter gently lifts my head off the back of the couch and guides me to his lap.

"Here, lay your head down." I willingly lay my head in Peter's lap and tuck my knees into my chest. Peter strokes my hair, and my eyes get heavier until I quit fighting it and close them again.

As Peter strokes my hair, I think of what life will be like when I go back home. I'll move back into our place, and we'll quickly fall back into our old routines. We'll need to reevaluate if Jane is in our lives. Peter will finish his last year of law school. I'll apply for jobs at the local hospitals and will need to start at the bottom, working mostly nights and weekends. We'll get married, but to save humiliation after canceling our first wedding, we'll do a small desti-nation wedding, probably to Mexico. We'll wait a few years and then start trying to have children. We'll have two children, and life will get busy, so besides a trip to Mexico or the Caribbean, we won't see much of the world. So many people would dream of that life, why does it make me want to cry?

I wake to Peter shaking his leg. "Kate. Hey, Kate. I hate to wake you, but I need to get back and pack. We're taking off soon."

I rub my eyes, with my head still in Peter's lap. "What time is it?"

"It's eight."

I slowly get off Peter and feel like I've barely slept. "I'm so sorry. Did you sleep at all?"

"I got some sleep. I'm fine. I'll sleep on our drive today."

Peter's hair is tousled, and I'm sure he barely slept in the upright position he was in. I get up and turn on the coffee maker, as I rub the sore muscles in my neck. I hate to say it, but everything will be easier once I have space from Peter; I'll be able to think through things.

"Here, drink this." I hand a mug to Peter. "I'll walk you back. I need to say goodbye to my parents, anyway."

I feel like a vampire stepping out into the light for the first time, as my eyes adjust to the sun. I need to tell Peter that I have too much to work out in my head before I start examining a future with him, but it doesn't feel right to drop that on him right before he goes on a safari. We glance at each other, and Peter puts his arm around me and pulls me closer to him.

"I'm happy I'll get to see you in a few days," he says.

"Me too." I smile at Peter, and he squeezes my shoulder. As we walk by, Andrew walks out of his bungalow.

I try to divert my eyes away from Andrew, but I see him pause in his tracks. His gaze burns with anger, and he doesn't look away. Peter glances over at him and pulls me even closer to him. It all feels like a game, like I don't even matter. There are so many words not being spoken. I look away from Andrew but know he continues to watch our every move.

Peter takes both my hands in his, and I don't like the intent behind it. "Please, Kate, don't go there."

I turn my head to the side, as Peter looks beyond me, most likely looking at Andrew. "Peter, when you get back to the village, let's talk about everything."

Peter kisses me on the lips, and I don't pull away, but I don't kiss him back either. "Fine. But, Kate, please don't." He pulls me in for a hug before releasing me.

"Have fun on your safari. See you in a few days."

Peter smiles and pulls me into a long hug. I watch as he walks into his bungalow, and I go to say goodbye to my parents. I walk into their bungalow, and my mom is running around like a crazy lady, throwing things into bags.

She glances up at me. "Hi, Kate. Because we're coming back to the village, I'm going to leave a lot of my stuff here and only take the essentials. I don't know what to pack though." My mom looks around at her piles of clothes and puts both her hands on her face.

My dad walks up to me, a lot more calmly. "Did you have fun last night, Kate?"

I smile and lean into him as he kisses my cheek. "I did. I've never seen such a beautiful bride."

"Well," my mom interrupts, "you'll be next, Kate. I saw the way you and Peter looked at each other last night."

"That's enough, Paula," my dad quickly interjects.

My mom zips her overly stuffed bag and walks over to me and puts both hands on my cheeks. "Kate, your father and I will be back in a week. Please make good decisions." Her eyes plead with mine.

I glance over at my dad and shrug off her statement.

"Don't worry about me, Mom. I always make good decisions."

My dad grabs my mom's arm and picks up her bag.

"Paula, our ride will leave without us if we don't hurry up. We can trust Kate to do what's best for Kate."

I smile and kiss them both goodbye, knowing I'll see them in a few short days. I also know that once they come back, I'll only have about three weeks left in Tanzania, and I'll be home, shortly behind them.

My chest feels tight at the thought of leaving. Last night with Peter felt safe. We know each other. We love each other and always will. Yet my heart aches, and if I allow myself to think about it, I know why.

CHAPTER 22

You know who you love, but you can't know who loves you.

—Nigerian Proverb

Day quickly turns into night, and the shadows in my bungalow continue to move and shift until they no longer exist. The next time I open my eyes, there are no more shadows, only darkness. Even the moon shines dully tonight. Maria and Noor took off for an adventure in the country. My parents have left; Peter and his parents have left as well. I'm all alone. Again.

It's been an exhausting week—a collision of two distinct and separate worlds—and not surprisingly, the worlds didn't go together well. The juggling makes my eyes even heavier, yet I find myself slipping on my sandals and pulling on a sweater. I want to take a glance outside, see if everything is in order, and perhaps see if I can smell a fire from a few bungalows over.

The outdoors is nearly as dark as my bungalow, with only faint lights coming from the hospital. I look up at the moon, and a perfectly oval cloud hangs on top of it, refusing to allow it to light my path. I glance at Andrew's bungalow, and it is dark, and no fire lights the sky or awakens my senses. It's the day after the wedding, and it is dark everywhere. I feel this renewed sense of energy and purpose, but the village sleeps. I walk back inside my bungalow, defeated by the darkness.

Although the days have no meaning here, the universe knows it's Monday morning, and the hospital waiting room reflects it. There is hardly an empty chair, as women sit and watch me with expectant eyes, hoping I bring them to an exam room next.

I look around, and there is no sign of Andrew, so he must not be here yet, or he's already with another patient. I approach the most pregnant-looking woman and bring her to an exam room.

"Hi, I'm Kate. How can I help you today?"

"My name is Zaina. I think this baby is coming." Zaina grabs her stomach and moans. I bring her into an exam room, and after a quick check, I confirm that Zaina is going to have this baby. She's another woman at the hospital, all alone. I've learned that most of these women have husbands, but it's not entirely common for men to attend the births of their children.

I quickly but calmly swing the door open, and luckily, Editha is walking by. "Editha, I have a child ready to be born. Where is everyone?"

Editha glances down one end of the hallway and then the other. "Dr. Andrew is delivering another baby a couple of doors down." I look at her wide-eyed, and she shrugs her shoulders. I go back into the room where Zaina lies on the table, crying out in pain.

"Zaina, it's just you and me today." She turns her head sharply to me, and her eyes look as panicked as I feel. I hope everything is textbook as I don't welcome difficult today.

I quickly prepare everything, so I'm ready when the baby comes. "Zaina, your body is ready. When the pain comes, that is your body's signal to push."

Zaina's eyes are shut, but she affirms that she understands. With each push, a wave of baby's hair extends through the canal, only to be sucked up again.

"Zaina, I know you're tired, but this time, I want you to hold your push for a count of ten. We need you to progress more than this."

Zaina screams out, and when her contraction comes, she bears down and pushes. I can now see the forehead, and I gently rotate the baby. "One more push, and your baby will be here."

With one large grunt, a baby boy fully emerges and, with a little pat on the back, immediately screams out. Zaina cries out in relief, and I wipe down the baby.

"Zaina, you have a baby boy."

I take quick vitals and wrap him up and place him on Zaina's chest. I just delivered a baby with no assistance. Zaina and the baby appear to be doing well, and I watch on as Zaina pulls up her gown and puts the baby on her breast. She did this. I did this.

The day doesn't slow down, and by the time the last patient is seen, I feel sweaty and full of dirt. My feet hurt. I haven't eaten. Now that I think of it, I haven't used the bathroom either. I've changed scrubs three times and am officially done. I know the hospital hallways so well now that I don't even need to watch where I'm going. My hands cover my face, rubbing my forehead muscles and then moving to my temples.

When I open my eyes, Andrew has walked out of his office and is watching me.

"You should really watch where you're walking, Kate."

His voice sounds harsh, and I stop in front of him to further study his face. He looks as disheveled as me. His eyes look tired, and his one hand rubs his temple as he wrinkles his face.

"It looks like you had a rough day," I say to him.

Andrew rubs his forehead with both hands. "Editha said you delivered a baby on your own today. Tell me about it."

I smile immediately. "The patient's name was Zaina, and it was textbook. It was her second birth, and she progressed quickly. I barely needed to do anything. She pushed, and the baby was out and thriving."

"Congratulations, Kate. I'm happy it went well." He continues to look at me, expressionless.

"Are you doing okay?" I ask.

Andrew looks into his office and holds the door for me. He shuts his door and stands in front of me. He turns his head slightly.

"Not really," Andrew responds, unable to look at me. "You kissed him in front of me."

His comment surprises me. My head tries to steady my heart, which is near escaping my chest. I turn around and look at the door, before turning to Andrew again. "I don't want to hurt you. That isn't my intent."

Andrew shakes his head and lets out a laugh that is void of all joy. "So you spent the night with your fiancé? Are the two of you happily back together?" Andrew folds his arms over the chest, and his entire expression changes.

"I've been honest with you, Andrew. I told you I had a lot to figure out, and I do."

Andrew's voice gets quiet, and he closes his eyes in a long blink before looking down at me. "Did you sleep with him?"

The words sting me. I know I haven't handled everything as well as I should, but I've been honest with Andrew about where my head is at. Andrew takes a step toward me, and tears prick at the back of my eyes. Before they have a chance to fall, I quickly open the door to Andrew's office and slam it behind me and hurry down the stairs before he has a chance to catch me.

I shower and feel the dirt and grime of the day slip off me. My skin feels raw as I vigorously rub the soap all over me. I feel tense, and I'm sure this is the least relaxing shower I've ever taken. I keep replaying conversations I've had with Andrew; he told me as long as I choose myself, I'll be fine. Yet I feel pressure from Andrew the moment he thinks I'm not choosing him, and I feel pressure from Peter when he thinks I'm going to move on without him. Does anyone actually want me to choose me?

I throw on a pair of shorts and a T-shirt and stand in front of the mirror as I comb through my wet hair. My blue eyes stare back at me, and I lean closer to the mirror and look at how blue my eyes have gotten since arriving here.

Did you sleep with him?

I pace back and forth in the kitchen, walking to the front door, to the back door, and then back again. I'm worn-out and can practically see my heart beating out of my chest. I close my eyes and shake my head. What is even bothering me? I've been looking forward to my parents leaving for a few days. I've been looking forward to saying goodbye to Peter so I could process and figure things out on my own, without him being around. I wanted Peter gone so I could explore my feelings for Andrew. Andrew. I stop pacing and put my hands on my knees, almost out of breath.

I've spent so much time with Andrew the past couple of months. He's quickly become a close friend and one of my confidants. We've talked about everything. I have spent more time in the village with him than even Maria. I pull at the collar of my T-shirt, unable to catch my breath. I force myself to sit down, and I prop my elbows on the cold laminate table. I rest my head in my hands and shut my eyes, and even with my eyes shut, it's Andrew's face that I see. There is a loud knock at the door, and I stand abruptly and see that it's Andrew.

He pushes the door further open. "I'm coming in."

I take a step back and stare at Andrew. He paces in my kitchen and then leans on my counter, looking away from me. Water slowly drips from his hair. I stand against the counter, waiting to hear what he has to say. Andrew doesn't look any better than I feel. He wears glasses that I have never seen him in before and didn't realize he needed, and his eyes look tired.

"You don't get to run away from the hard questions, Kate."

I cackle. "Fine. But I get to run away from the offensive ones." I lean back on the counter and stare at Andrew as he slowly turns around.

"You're right, Kate." Andrew's voice softens. "I don't know what got into me." Andrew puts his head in his hands. Andrew leans against the counter and finally looks up at me. "I'm a thirty-three-year-old man, acting like a child."

Andrew has never seemed more human than now. He's stripped of all his accolades and accomplishments, and instead, he's just Andrew. He wears his heart on his sleeve. He walks over to me and leans against the counter, boxing me in.

"You are a grown woman, Kate." His breath causes my entire body to fill with goose bumps. "You, of course, can do what you choose. But if you slept with him, your feelings are more unresolved than you admit, and I need to fully step away."

Andrew and I are almost eye-level with each other as he continues to lean in. "I'm not saying it's not your right to know. I'm saying it's offensive you had to ask." I do everything in my power not to allow my lips to collide with his.

"But I saw the two of you kiss," he says.

"I didn't feel anything," I admit, and the words hurt for me to say out loud, even though they are the truth.

"No?" he asks, with hope.

I stare at his lips and lick my own. "I didn't sleep with him."

A flood of relief crosses over Andrew's face, and before I have a chance to register the change in his eyes, Andrew's lips crash into mine. It's a fiery explosion on contact, as we work to get closer. Andrew puts his hand on each one of my hips, and in one effortless motion, lifts me onto the counter. He wraps his arms around my waist, and I hold his head against me and kiss the top of his hair. He nips at my lips with his until I can't take it anymore, and I wrap my legs around him to make sure he isn't going anywhere. This is the time Andrew usually pulls away from me, but tonight, I won't let him.

I'm nearly breathless as Andrew moves his lips to my neck. His lips are silky and light, and I arch my back until my breasts push up against his chest. His thumbs press into my sides, right below my breasts. I grab Andrew behind his neck and turn his lips to mine. My stomach flutters as he smiles against my lips. I feel weightless as Andrew's other hand finds its way beneath me, and he carries me to my room, with my legs tightly wrapped around him.

Andrew leans into me and supports my back as he gently lays me on the bed. I reach my hands up and start at the bottom of Andrew's shirt while he unbuttons the top buttons, and our hands touch as we meet in the middle. His top is finally free, and he hurriedly takes it off and then pulls his white T-shirt over his head.

Andrew is the vision of a perfect man, all muscle and masculinity, with the face that should be on the cover of magazines. He hovers over me but moves to his elbows as he leans in and kisses me. I take my time feeling the hardness and curves of Andrew's chest, finally, I have full access to all of him. I spread my fingers and move them across where his shoulders meet his chest. His skin is smooth and warm, and I kiss him everywhere, starting at his neck and moving to every surface. His knee parts my legs, and his jeans feel rough as they rub against the bare skin of my thighs. I reach my hands around Andrew, exploring his back and keep moving my hands until I feel the sharp contrast of his butt. I forcefully pull him into me, and he loses his balance, and his entire weight falls onto me.

Andrew smiles into our kiss. "Kate, I will crush you."

I hold him against me anyway. His weight feels exhilarating, and I'd forgotten what it feels like to feel the heat of a man's skin against mine. I rub my nails along Andrew's smooth back, and he moans into my mouth.

Andrew takes his weight off me and rubs my face as he looks into my eyes.

"What do you want, Kate?"

I pull my lips into my mouth and take a deep breath. "You."

Andrew intoxicates me with his next kiss. It is deep, and it speaks to me. It says you mean something to me. This means something to me. You're important. The kiss hypnotizes me. With zero regret, Andrew and I make love, and our relationship crosses over into attraction and respect to something so much more. Every touch of his hands and glance of his eyes, I know I'm where I'm supposed to be in this moment. I've never felt the way Andrew just made me feel, and I blush at how little sleep was had.

When we finally decide to try to sleep, Andrew reaches down and pulls the sheet up over us. He kisses my forehead and then the tip of my nose, before tracing my swollen lips with his index finger. There go my insides, completely melting once again. His mouth opens like he's going to say something, but instead, he pulls me into a hug and wraps his strong arms around me. I feel sleep coming, and Andrew whispers into my hair.

"Don't go back home. Stay with me."

CHAPTER 23

When deeds speak, words are nothing.

—African Proverb

The blanket is pulled up to my chin, and I hear sizzling from a pan in my kitchen and feel an empty space next to me. For a moment, I think I'm back in Minneapolis, enjoying our Sunday morning brunch that we did weekly. I rub my eyes and slowly open them and remember that I'm not in my bungalow alone and that Andrew is with me. If I thought kissing Andrew would irrevocably change our relationship, then sleeping with him will flip it on its side. There was such relief giving in to the magnetic pull that had captivated both of us, but now there are only consequences.

I give myself a pep talk as I rub the sleep out of my eyes and pinch color into my cheeks. I look down, and I'm wearing Andrew's T-shirt, which hangs down mid-knee on my body. My clothes are in a pile over in a corner, and I refuse the urge to pull the blanket back over my head.

I jump at the sound of a phone buzzing and see mine lighting up on the chair across the room. I peek toward the kitchen and don't see Andrew, and I scurry over to check it. My heart sinks when I see it was Peter. He is the last person I've been thinking about recently, and a wave of guilt crashes into my chest.

PETER

Katherine, our safari is almost over, and it's been life-changing. I can't wait to tell you all about it and spend a couple of more days in the village with you. I love you.

I stare at the text for what feels like a few minutes. I shake my head and decide I'm not in the right frame of mind to answer it. I throw on a pair of pants and a T-shirt and walk into the kitchen. Andrew stands at the stovetop, leaning over and checking on the sunny-side up eggs on the pan. I lean against the door entrance and watch how his smooth skin shimmers in the light peeking through the kitchen window and how his shorts hang low on his hips. Every time he moves, new muscles appear on his back.

Andrew turns to grab something from the fridge and sees me. His smile doesn't just reach his eyes, it reaches my heart, and I look down, trying to hide from him. "Good morning, beautiful. I'm making you breakfast."

Andrew's smile puts me at ease, and now my only surprise is how natural this feels. "Hi."

Andrew pulls me in for a quick hug and kisses the top of my head. "I've made coffee for you." He hands me a cup and then turns toward the eggs.

"Thank you."

I walk into the bathroom to brush my teeth and am startled when I look in the mirror. I didn't need to pinch my cheeks earlier because my face is flushed. My lips are pink and swollen, and my eyes are the brightest blue this morning. I feel alive.

"Is everything okay, Kate?" Andrew calls from the kitchen.

"Yep." I've been numb for so long, but I feel like my heart has grown several sizes.

Andrew laughs. "Breakfast is ready if you would like to join me."

I slowly open the door and look at Andrew and walk to the table. He takes my breath away in every possible way. I struggle looking directly at him. It's like, he's the sun, and too bright for direct eye contact.

"You didn't need to make me breakfast." I look up shyly and try to meet his eyes.

"I wanted to make you breakfast. It's my ploy to get to spend more time with you." Andrew winks at me, and I shake my head as my face burns with heat.

Andrew leans over me and hands me my plate, and I take a seat at the table. "How long have you been up?"

"I have the inability to sleep in. Once the sun comes up, my mind races, and I can't seem to shut out my thoughts."

When I got my text from Peter, my phone said it was after nine. "You've been up for hours?"

"Yes, but don't worry. I only sat and watched you sleep for about two of those hours."

I raise my forehead and gasp and then cover my mouth. Andrew rolls his head back and laughs.

"Kate, that was a joke. I sat outside and read for a while and then made breakfast."

I dip the soft bread into my runny eggs, and everything tastes heavenly. The coffee is hot and strong, and this may be the best morning I've had in Tanzania.

Andrew reaches across the table and takes my hand in his. Andrew turns his head and smiles at me, and I'm happy I don't have to guess where I stand with him. I'm sure that comes with age and maturity, but I'm again taken aback by how easy it feels to wake up with him.

"What do you want to do today, Kate?"

Panic sets in again. "See how things are at the hospital and maybe sleep some more."

"Did you not sleep well last night?"

I look at Andrew's eyes and can't lie to him. "I slept well, just not long enough." I look down and shake my head and laugh.

Andrew smiles. "Okay, we'll go to the hospital for a while, but then I'd love to take you for a drive to see some sites. I'd like to take you on a date."

I nearly drop my fork. I finish chewing my eggs. "A date?"

Andrew's laugh makes my bungalow shine brighter. "This all feels a little backward, I know. But yes, I'd like to take you on a date. A first date."

I smile and look down at my empty plate. I bring my dish to the sink and stare out at the hospital. The building anchors the entire village. Andrew's hands wrap around me, and he rests his chin on my shoulder, and I feel his warm breath in my hair.

I turn around and rub my fingers down his arms. "Did you just smell my hair?"

Andrew once again wraps his arms around me, and my arms instinctively wrap around him, and I lay my head on his chest. His skin on mine calms my breathing, and I feel like I belong. I wonder if it's the same feeling new mothers describe when their baby is placed on them for the first time. It's a feeling of calm and belonging, and I can nearly see my heart grow.

We hold each other, not saying anything. In one swift motion, Andrew lifts me off the floor and puts me on the cold metal counter and stands between my legs. Even with me on the counter, I still have to look up to meet his eyes.

"I worry that last night wasn't a good idea." I chew on the side of my cheek, and Andrew lifts his hand to move a loose hair out of my face.

His face squints, and a small wrinkle appears on his forehead as he grimaces. "I was worried about going too fast." He sounds apologetic.

I hold my hand up to his chest and shake my head. "No, no, it's not that." I put my hand down. "It's just that things feel more complicated now."

Andrew gathers my hair and holds it behind my head, and peppers my face with small kisses until every surface has gotten the same amount of attention. "I think we are already fairly complicated."

As Andrew leans down to kiss me, there is an indescribable tenderness. His hands go underneath me, and as he carries me back to my room. I know it's going to take a lot to get sick of how it feels when Andrew touches me.

*****

The moment I reach the second floor of the hospital, Editha runs to me.

"Fatima's here. She thinks she's in labor."

I hurry my pace to the waiting room, and Fatima is doubled over, like she's in pain. Our eyes meet, and she stands up, and I take her arm and lead her to the exam room. Fatima isn't ready to have this baby, but babies don't always come when they're supposed to.

"Fatima," I say, "what's going on with you?"

She holds her belly but looks up at me. "I think the baby is ready to come. I told my father I was going to Centro Market and came here instead."

I try to reassure Fatima with my eyes. I turn away as she disrobes, and I help her lie back. I check the baby's heartbeat, and it sounds strong. I start doing an examination, and notice new bruises on her upper thighs and vaginal area. I've never had such an urge to hurt someone as I have to hurt her father. I do an internal examination, and her cervix is high and still hard, and there are no signs of her baby.

"Fatima, how often does the pain come?"

"It's constant, Ms. Kate. Like a pulling against my skin."

I examine her belly. Fatima is a petite girl, and her long traditional clothes hide her figure well, but her stomach looks stretched as far as it will go. I push gently on her side, and Fatima cries out. I do the same to the other side of her stomach, and Fatima cries out again.

"Fatima, the baby is not quite ready to arrive. I think you're having something called round ligament pain. You aren't a very large person, and your belly keeps growing for the baby, and it's causing pain and cramping. I'm glad you came in, but today is not the day for the baby."

Fatima looks at me with worry and covers herself back up with the sheet. The door swings open, and both of us look to the door, and Andrew walks in.

He walks over to Fatima and places his hand on her shoulder. "I heard you were in labor. Is everything okay?"

Anger rises to my chest, and I take slow and deep breaths to calm down. "Dr. Andrew," I say, "I did an examination, and the baby isn't ready to come. Based on her symptoms, I think she's dealing with round ligament pain."

Andrew looks at me, and then Fatima. "Did you do an exam?"

"Yes, Fatima's cervix is high and closed. She'd been here for over thirty minutes now and hasn't had a contraction. Her pain is constant and isolated to her sides."

Andrew folds his hand over his lips. "Okay. Fatima, if you feel any more symptoms, please come back."

Andrew smiles at me, and part of my heart warms at my feelings toward him, but part of me continues to feel undermined by his constant presence. He says his goodbyes to Fatima, and I finish up with her.

Women continue to flock to the waiting room, and I know this hospital will need more staff to stay sustainable. Andrew hardly ever gets time off, and I know I can take as much time as I want, but I'm here for such a short time that I rarely do. By the time the last patient is seen, my feet ache with every step, and I squeeze the back of my neck and move my head around to loosen up my muscles.

I change out of my scrubs and think to back home. What would I be doing? Would I have a job by now? I remember sitting by the fire a few weeks ago, telling Andrew that one of my greatest fears is that home will never be the same. Minneapolis is a midsized city, and even if I find a midwife position at the hospital most situated at the city center, I don't know if I'd be able to make the impact that I feel like I make here.

"Kate"—I hear, the moment I walk out of the scrub room. Andrew hurries his step to catch up with me—"I was hoping today would be a lot less busy, so let's revisit my original plan for later, but I was thinking it would be fun to go to the bar at Centro Market. They have the best *ugali* I've ever had."

"I need a quick shower," I say. "I'll pick you up at your place afterward."

Instead of a quick shower, I take my time, thinking about the day, the previous day, and the days to come. By the time I get dressed and head out the door, the sun is nearly gone, and Andrew stands in front of his bungalow.

"I was nearly going to send a search party out for you, Kate."

"Sorry about that." I point to the path. "Do you want to lead the way?"

Andrew and I walk down the dirt pathway toward Centro Market. In all the time I've been here, I've never ventured to one of the restaurants or bars in town. I've been to Centro several times, but everything social has been at someone's house. Andrew brushes up against my arm and takes my hand in his.

"You're quiet this evening, Kate."

I look up at Andrew; the white of his eyes shine down on me.

"Why did you come in while I was seeing Fatima?"

"I wanted to make sure she was okay. Editha said she was in labor."

We reach the bar, and Andrew stops and turns to me, keeping my hand in his.

"I feel like you always second-guess me, Andrew. You told me when I started that I needed confidence, and now I'm starting to feel more confident, but you're always there."

Andrew pulls up my hand to his lips and kisses it gently. "I apologize, Kate. I see you have gained so much more confidence than you've ever had before. Trust me when I say, I'm not trying to undermine you."

"Okay. Because you're always there, and, Andrew, I appreciate it, but I need to know I can do this on my own."

He takes my hand and places it against his chest. "You're right, Kate. I'm sorry." He smiles, and I can't stay mad. "Can we eat now?"

I playfully push Andrew in the arm, and he takes my hand and kisses it once again. I know Andrew means no harm, and I relax slightly as he takes my hand and leads me inside. As the door to the bar slams behind us, all eyes follow our every move. Andrew leads me to a table in the back of the bar, and as we walk by people, my face burns from all the eyes on Andrew and me.

Our table is a high-top for two, and I take a seat hesitantly as I look around at people more interested in us than of anything else. I can no longer feel the vibrations under my feet from the music. Andrew bobs his head slightly to the sound of the African drums playing from the speakers in the bar. He looks around, and the whiteness of his teeth are a contrast against the darkness of his skin, and he smiles as he catches me watching him.

"Andrew"—I lean in so he can hear me better—"everyone is staring at us."

He breaks his smile but looks at me thoughtfully. "They're staring at you, Kate. You radiate beauty."

Heat rushes to my cheeks, and I place my hand on one and then the other to cool them off. I slowly glance to the table next to us, and a young man and woman lean into each other and speak, but their eyes never leave me. At the hospital, I feel accepted, and as soon as women realize I have knowledge that will help them with their pregnancies and childbirth, the questioning and curious looks stop. But being at this bar, with Andrew, I feel like I'm the center of attention, which is never a place I purposely want to be.

I fold my hands on the table in front of me, and Andrew takes one of my hands in his. I look around again, and instinctually, I quickly pull my hand back and put my hands on my lap. A look of hurt spreads across Andrew's face, but then his lips turn up in a smile.

"I was hoping I'd be able to take you away today, but the night got too late. Can I take you away tomorrow for one evening? There's something I want to show you."

Curiosity spreads across my face, as I wonder where Andrew wants to take me. I finish my food and beer as quickly as possible because I don't feel entirely comfortable tonight with everyone's stares and attention. Andrew and I walk quietly back to his place, our path only illuminated by the moon. As we get farther from the center of the village, the sound slowly gets quieter until it's only my breathing that I hear.

Andrew takes his arm and wraps it around my shoulder and pulls me closer to him as we walk. "People will always stare, Kate."

I look straight ahead and don't slow down my pace. "Doesn't it bother you?"

"I will never be able to control how anyone sees me or sees us as a couple."

We reach Andrew's bungalow, and he opens the door. I stand for a moment, and he holds the door open for me, questioning me and my next move. I sigh and walk into his bungalow. With the door shut behind me, Andrew leans down, and his lips touch mine, and our lips move together methodically and tenderly.

I loop my fingers through Andrew's belt loop and lean my back against the door. "You didn't answer my question, Andrew. Does it bother you?"

Andrew sighs and runs his hand through my hair. "No, it doesn't bother me. I was able to spend a lovely evening with you tonight, and no one has the power to change that or how I feel about you."

Andrew reaches his hand out, and I place mine in his, and he leads me to his bedroom. He turns to me and gently strokes both my arms, and his eyes penetrate mine. "Kate, do the stares bother you?"

Andrew's low voice trails off with his question. I take a deep breath, ready to answer, but instead, I pull him to me and hold him closely, so there is no space between us.

CHAPTER 24

You have little power over what's not yours.

—Zimbabwean Proverb

The weather has turned hotter in Tanzania as their winter, Minnesota's summer, is nearing its end. I sweat as I throw clothes into an overnight bag, and I expect Andrew any minute now. Maria and Noor went backpacking for a couple of nights immediately following their wedding, and now that she's back, I feel like I have a lifetime of stories to catch her up on.

The door to my bungalow flies open, and Maria nearly skips in. She runs and hugs me, and I pull her back to look at her for a moment. Her skin glows, and her eyes shine with the newness of being a newlywed. Her hair is no longer gathered at the top of her head, instead, her long braids hang with purple beads at the end of each one.

"Where were you last night, Kate? I came over here as soon as Noor and I got home." I go to answer, but before the words come out, Maria continues, "Please tell me you weren't still at the hospital. You've been working too long of hours."

I pour Maria a cup of coffee and wait until she's had a sip to begin. "That's kind of what I want to talk to you about."

Maria puts her cup down and runs to me and takes both my hands in hers. "You're scaring me, Kate. Is everything okay? How are your parents? Did something happen to them on the safari?"

I laugh lightly and wave Maria away. "Everyone is fine, I promise. But I think you should sit down."

Maria looks at me suspiciously but walks to the table and takes a chair. She sighs and dramatically folds her legs and points to the chair across from her.

I sit down hesitantly. "It's nothing bad or anything, but I thought you should know. Andrew and I are kind of together."

Coffee shoots out of Maria's mouth and lands on the table, causing me to gasp. "I'm sorry, Kate. Did you say you and Andrew are kind of together? What do you mean by that?"

I explore ways to explain it to Maria, without having to go into the physical details of the past couple of days. "I think you know what I mean, Maria, and before you just arrived, I was packing an overnight bag because he's taking me on a surprise tonight."

Maria looks at the bag near the door, and I can tell by her expression that she didn't see it when she first got here. She stands up and grabs a towel from the counter and wipes up the coffee she spewed. I stare at her intently, and she paces a few times before sitting back down.

"I honestly don't know what to say. When did this happen? Who initiated it, and what's your plan, Kate? You leave in less than a month."

The words pour out of Maria, which is usually the way she speaks. But I was expecting her to bounce up and down, hold me in one of her famous hugs, and then ask me for the details. But her expression has remained neutral, with concern causing wrinkle marks around her eyes.

"I'm sorry to spring this on you. Honestly, feelings were building gradually, but it happened a couple of days ago, and well, now we're going somewhere today, as a couple."

"As a couple?" Maria's voice is sharp. "A couple of what?" Maria closes her eyes and wrinkles up her face. "You leave so soon, Kate," she again reminds me.

Maria stops talking and looks down at her cup. I blink back the tears that begin to form behind my eyes.

"I'm sorry, Maria. I'm surprised by your reaction."

Maria stands up and comes over to me and puts her hand on my cheek. "Kate, you know I only want what's best for you. I love you, and I don't want to see you get hurt. I also love Andrew and don't want him to be hurt either. You are both my family, and it doesn't seem like a lot of thought went into this before you both jumped."

Maria isn't wrong. Everything she says is practical, and these are all thoughts that I've purposely been avoiding.

"It just happened."

Maria moves her chair next to mine and holds my hands. "Things are so different in Tanzania, especially the rural parts. I worry about the negative attention you'll receive from being an interracial couple. I'm also worried about where your head is at."

Anxiety slowly builds up until it nearly suffocates me. "What do you mean?"

"Oh, Kate"—Maria looks at me—"I don't think you've even fully figured out if you want to get back together with Peter. But, Andrew, well, I've known him for a lifetime. He doesn't jump into things quickly or without thought. If you two are together, Andrew is committed. I worry about him getting hurt."

"I don't want to hurt him."

"I know you don't." Maria's expression looks as pained as I feel. "I also know you wouldn't jump into anything if you didn't have feelings. But with you leaving so soon, and not fully resolving your feelings for Peter, someone is bound to get hurt."

A knock interrupts us, and we both jump slightly when the door opens, and a smiling Andrew walks through. The moment he sees our faces his countenance shifts to one of concern.

"Maria, welcome back." Maria walks toward him, and they warmly greet each other. She pauses as her hand reaches the doorknob.

"Have fun tonight." Maria looks to me and then Andrew. "Andrew, we need to meet when you're back to finalize the fundraiser plans." Maria glances at me once more before walking out the door and puts her hand to her heart and smiles at me.

Andrew takes my bag, and I pull on my straw hat, and we get in his jeep. The village is small, so it doesn't take long to be on the open, albeit dirt road. The day is hot, and I pull my hat down further to protect myself. I look down at my arms, sure I've never been this shade of brown before. The sun in Tanzania never seems to sleep. It's relentless and beats down constantly as a reminder of how fragile and small we humans are.

Andrew gently squeezes my knee, sending electrical waves throughout my entire body. I've never had this sort of chemistry with anyone, even Peter. My heart and body react immensely to every touch or glance. I'm wildly attracted to this beautiful man, and I appear to have a similar effect on him.

"I'm a good listener if you want to talk about it," Andrew says, as he rubs my upper leg.

I know he's referring to what he walked into between Maria and me, but I don't know how to process it, let alone talk about it. There have been so many times since I've been here that Noor, Maria, Andrew, and me hung out. I always assumed Maria was pushing us together because she certainly wasn't pushing me toward Peter. Her reaction has left me confused. A large part of me thought she'd jump up and down from the news.

"I appreciate that, Andrew. But there is nothing to share," I lie.

"Well, I have news to share. But you have to promise me that you'll only listen and not respond." I look at Andrew curiously. "Do you promise?"

"I promise." I laugh.

"As you know, Maria is a miracle worker as the hospital's administrator. She does so many things, but one thing she focuses on heavily is fundraising and financial efforts for our hospital. The hospital runs entirely on donations. I don't take a salary, but I need to pay the other workers, and to operate a hospital is not a cheap endeavor."

I nod as Andrew looks over to me. Nothing he is sharing is new. This is so much what he and Maria talk about when we all get together, which causes Noor and I to go to the other room and drink wine.

"A while back, before you arrived here, Maria applied for a grant with Doctors Without Borders. It was always my dream to have that organization's support because not only do they provide funding for the staff that get placed here, but they also provide general funding for hospital initiatives. You know, Kate, not everyone is like you and comes to a developing nation for free." Andrew laughs.

"This is a long way to say, we were chosen for a grant, Kate!" Andrew practically yells as the words come out. "You have no idea how big of a deal it is to be accepted. We'll get two full-time positions here—one in labor and delivery and one in general medicine. These employees will get paid salaries and benefits. And the best news is, once Doctors Without Borders work with a site, they usually keep funding the sites for many years."

I take my seatbelt off for a moment and lean over to Andrew and wrap my arms around his waist and kiss him on his cheek. Both of us smile as we look at each other.

"Congratulations, Andrew. That is a really big deal. I'm so proud of you."

Andrew looks at me and smiles. "I was hoping you would be. Here's the part I don't want you to react to, at least not immediately."

We stare at each other until Andrew turns his eyes back to the road. "Kate, I want you to take the position in labor and delivery. It's a two-year position. You'd get paid, and best of all, we'd be together."

My heartbeat takes up the entire space in my chest, leaving no room for air. As I listened intently to Andrew's story, I didn't anticipate that this was where it was heading. Andrew keeps glancing at me, and I feel frozen as I stare at him. I force myself to take deep breaths to prevent myself from fainting. Andrew takes my hand in his and pulls it up to his lips and softly kisses me.

"I know I ask a lot of you, and I know I caught you off guard, which is why I don't want you to process it with me until you've had a chance to process it internally. I'm ready to talk about it whenever you are."

I glance slowly in Andrew's direction and squeeze his hand, but I take his advice and don't process this decision with him. I have too many thoughts going through my head and have never considered the option of staying here. To be honest, all I've processed is how Andrew has a magnetic pull about him that has drawn me in from the very first time he walked through the exam room while I was giving Bupe a checkup. Maria's words continue to echo in my head.

"We're here, Kate," Andrew says as he smiles in my direction.

And here, is the Ruaha National Park, according to the large wooden sign that we drive under. Andrew's smile lights up the entire jeep, and he looks like an excited boy, and I can't help but to feel joy when I look at him.

"I haven't been here since I was a boy. It was one of my favorite places."

Andrew speaks to a guide, who places a sticker on the window of the jeep. Andrew gets out of the jeep and motions me to the backseat, and another guide gets in the driver's seat, and our journey through the national park begins.

Andrew pulls me close to him, and the guide slows down every time we pass animals. The entire ground shakes beneath us as a large herd of elephants runs to the closest watering hole. My cheeks nearly hurt from smiling, and Andrew watches me more than he watches the animals. Andrew wraps both his arms around me and holds me as the guide points out a cheetah, a group of hyenas, and then a family of giraffes, reaching high into a tree to eat.

I lean back into Andrew and feel his strong chest behind me. He places kisses along my neck and smiles against my cheek. My head rises and falls with every breath he takes.

"Thank you for this, Andrew."

I turn my head and give him a kiss. He speaks into the kiss. "This is my favorite day."

After a drive through parts of the park, the guide pulls over and parks the jeep, and another jeep approaches with two more guides. One of them hands a basket to Andrew and start setting up a tent.

I point to them and whisper to Andrew, "What are they doing?"

"We're going to sleep out here. The guides are armed and take shifts through the night to scare off wildlife if they approach, and we'll eat here, and they'll set up a tent for sleeping."

My eyes go wide and cut to the men setting up a tent for two. We'll get to sleep in a tent, with blankets and covering, and these three men will stand guard.

As if Andrew reads my mind, he leans over and says. "They get paid a lot of money for this. Don't feel too sorry for them."

Andrew and I watch as the sun sets behind the trees, and soon after, every star in the galaxy seems to appear. The stars are beautiful in the village, and even though the village is small, it's never completely dark. Out here, there aren't any other lights, and the sky is lit up by a million of lights that all seem to be lit just for us.

"Come here," Andrew says as he takes my hand, "I want to show you something."

Andrew grabs a blanket from the tent, and we walk to one of the guide's closed-top jeeps. After the exchange of a few words, Andrew takes my hand and helps me to the top of the jeep. He lays the blanket down and pulls me down on top of it. We lie, side by side, looking up at the sky. Our arms touch, and Andrew intertwines his fingers in mine.

Andrew points to the sky. "Those stars there, Kate, are Altair and Vega. Vega was a celestial princess, a goddess of the sky. She was weary and thought she would forever live in eternity alone. Altair was a mere mortal and caught the eyes of Vega. But when Vega's parents found out, they became enraged and didn't think that Vega should be in love with such a commoner. Vega's parents became further enraged when they realize that she promised Altair a place next to her in the heavens. In the cruelest of acts, Vega's father grants her wish, and he places Vega and Altair in the sky as stars, yet while they were both in the heavens, they were not together. The great celestial river, what we now know as the Milky Way, separated them. Yet each year, on the seventh night of the seventh moon, a bridge forms across the celestial river, and although it's only for one night a year, the two lovers are reunited. In the dark years where Altair cannot make it to Vega, her tears cause raindrops that fall all over the region."

I further lean my head back into Andrew and look at the two bright stars, Vega and Altair. "How do you know so much about stars?"

I feel Andrew smile against my face. "The sky fascinates me. It's mystical and massive and has existed longer than my mind can comprehend. I don't know, there is something that feels comforting and uniting about it."

We turn our heads to face each other. No words need to be spoken because I feel like a lot is being said with our eyes. The whites of Andrews eyes are nearly as bright as the stars above us. In this moment, nothing that happened before, or anything that will happen after seems important. I'm in the middle of the African savanna, with the best view of the stars I've ever seen and with a man who makes my heart do funny things.

Andrew leans into me and brushes his soft lips against mine. I wrap my arms around him and pull him back to me.

Andrew's eyes beat into mine. "Please stay, Kate."

CHAPTER 25

You must attend to your business with the vendor in the market and not the noise of the market.

—Beninese Proverb

PETER

We'll be back in the village in a couple of hours. I can't wait to tell you about Ruaha National Park. It was the most incredible experience.

It's not as if I needed a reminder that Peter and my parents would be coming back to the village today. It's all I've been thinking about. Mr. and Mrs. Jacobson are most likely halfway to Dar right now, and my parents and Peter are almost here. When Andrew brought me to Ruaha, I panicked for a moment that we'd run into their tour, but Andrew reminded me that they were on the other side of the park, almost an entire day's drive away where the majority of the luxury cabins are.

I turn on my side, where Andrew lies next to me. I run my fingers along his chest muscles and then trace his perfectly chiseled abdomen. His lips turn up in a smile, but his eyes don't open, as I stare at the long eyelashes that blow with the breeze from the open window.

I've spent the night with Andrew every night since the first we were together, but now that my parent's will be back in the village, along with Peter, I'll once again have to navigate this all again. They'll only be here for three nights, but their presence makes me feel like I'm lying to everyone in my life. I don't know how to talk about this with my family and Peter though. How do I be honest with the progression of my relationship with Andrew if I don't even understand how I feel? And how do I tell Peter everything when there is part of me that doesn't know if I'm ready to give him up? If Peter knows about Andrew, any chance of a reconciliation will be over.

All I know is that I need to start being honest with everyone in my life, including myself. I continue telling myself that I have feelings for two men, but I no longer think that's the case. I press my lips into Andrew's warm cheek, and he tries to pull me back into bed when I stand up. He finally opens his eyes and smile at me as he props himself up.

"My family is almost here, so I need to go shower and clean up a bit."

I pull on my skirt and top and run my fingers through my hair. Andrew gets up and pulls on a pair of pants, and they hang low on his muscular figure.

"Remind me how long they'll be here for?"

"Only three nights. Then they'll make their drive to Dar for their flight."

Andrew sleepily yawns and pulls me into a hug. "What will you tell them about us?"

I slip into my shoes and walk toward the door, with Andrew on my heels. I pause as I reach the door and turn around.

"I don't plan to say anything. We'll need to create a bit of space from each other while they're here. But it's only for three nights, and then I'll have an entire three weeks with you before I leave."

Andrew's expression drops, and I can tell I've wounded him with my words. Instead of telling me that he's hurt, his lips turn up slightly into a smile. "I hope you're still considering my offer to sign on with Doctors Without Borders and extend your stay."

I pull Andrew into a quick hug and leave for my bungalow. Andrew has been good about not bringing it up to me, and it's most likely consuming his mind as much as it's consuming mine, but we haven't discussed it since he brought it up initially. In my head, I know there is no practical way I can say yes. Even if I wanted to stay, I'd need to go home first and gather more of my things for a two-year stay. I packed enough clothes and personal items for a few months, not for two years. And more importantly, my parents wouldn't support me staying here for so long.

Before I look at the waiting room to see how many women are waiting, I knock on Maria's office and step in.

Her smile lights up the room as she sees me, and I know instantly that there are no negative feelings on her end toward me after our last conversation. She pushes up on her desk and comes over to me and gives me a hug.

"I was hoping to see you today, Kate. How was Ruaha? Isn't it beautiful there?"

"Maria, it was gorgeous. I want to see more of the park someday. One night wasn't enough."

Maria smiles up at me knowingly and walks back behind her desk. "I have so much to prepare for before the hospital fundraiser event tomorrow evening. Today, several people arrive from the village from different foundations across Europe, and I need to make sure they are settled."

Maria stands up from her desk and walks over to me. "But I need to apologize to you. I didn't mean to react the way I did when you told me about Andrew. You know, Kate, if you're happy, I'm happy."

Relief spreads throughout my body. "Maria, you didn't say anything that I didn't need to hear. Thanks for being a good enough friend to be honest."

Maria puts her hands around my waist and speaks into my chest. "I feel like I've gotten to witness you emerging from your shell these past few months."

I play with the braids on top of Maria's head. "I feel like I've changed so much since being here."

"You have. In good ways. You've blossomed, and I trust that you're going to do what's best for you. And I'll always be on your side, Kate."

Maria lets go of me, and we look at each other. "Even if I don't trust myself?"

"Give yourself credit." Maria walks back to her desk and then turns to me. "You know what you want."

*****

I'm distracted as I see patients throughout the day. I can't believe I had almost forgotten about tomorrow night's fundraiser. It's all Andrew and Maria have been discussing since I arrived in June. A few foundations are sending members to hear about the hospital and determine if they'll provide long-term funding for a potential expansion and to hire more medical professionals. Doctors Without Borders was a huge win for the hospital, but extra funding would guarantee the hospital's sustainability for years to come.

I finish with a patient, and Editha walks into the exam room as I'm cleaning up. "Kate, Andrew would like you in exam room 2."

I look up and follow Editha out of the room and into exam room 2. A woman lies on the exam bed, sitting up slightly, and Andrew looks at me.

"Kate, this here is Zahra. I examined her, but would like you to do the same and tell me any findings you may have."

I look at Andrew curiously and smile at Zahra. She doesn't seem in pain, so it doesn't look like labor is imminent. I pull out my stethoscope and start with the baby's heartbeat, which is strong. I then listen to Zahra's, and it's a little fast, but that could be because she's anxious about me examining her. I start my measurements, and Zahra is a little over thirty-six weeks pregnant, so she has about a month to go until she should deliver.

I turn to Zahra. "How have you been feeling?"

"I've been feeling fine, but I came to the hospital because my headaches aren't getting any better."

"How long have you had a headache?"

"Two weeks."

Hormones can cause headaches in pregnant women, especially later on in the pregnancy when there is a surge of them. To be sure,

I get out the blood pressure cuff and have Zahra sit up and place her legs straight down. I put the cuff around her upper arm, and when I look at the reading, it's alarmingly high. I decide to try her other arm.

"How else have you been feeling? Have you had a change of vision or any vomiting?"

"My vision is fine, but I have vomited a few times, mostly in the morning."

Zahra's blood pressure is just as high on her other arm. I do an external exam and notice how much fluid Zahra has in her hands and ankles. I look up at Andrew as he watches me do the exam.

"We could test her urine, Dr. Andrew, but I believe Zahra has preeclampsia."

Andrew places his hand under his chin. "What do you recommend we do?"

I pause and look at Zahra and then Andrew. A few scenarios run through my head, and my chest tightens. I feel unable to get the words out of my mouth. My head and fingers go tingly, and I feel like I'm having a panic attack.

"Well, we could give her blood pressure medicine and monitor her closely here at the hospital to make sure her blood pressure doesn't spike."

"Are you asking me a question, Kate?" My eyes cut to Andrew.

"Without having time to wait for a urine test, Zahra needs at least two blood-pressure readings, four hours apart."

Andrew puts his hand under his chin and nods. "Based on her blood-pressure readings, the headaches, and vomiting, as well as her severe edema, I'm going to forego the urine test, as all clinical signs are pointing toward preeclampsia. I'm going to give her a shot of betamethasone and wait for two hours while monitoring her and then start Pitocin and deliver the baby today. Her blood pressure is too high to monitor her overnight. Hopefully, the betamethasone will help with the lung development, but I'm not too concerned as she's close to thirty-seven weeks pregnant."

"Do you need me to stay?" I ask Andrew. It's clear to me Andrew has already made up his mind about how he wants to treat this patient.

He shakes his head quickly. "No, I'll have the nurse come give her the injection and monitor her for the next two hours, and then I'll start the Pitocin."

I direct my attention to Zahra. "Good luck on your delivery, Zahra. I can't wait to meet your baby."

I smile at her and turn and walk out of the room. It's already starting to get late, so I change into my clothes, and I nearly jump as Peter stands in the hallway waiting for me. The moment he sees me he smiles and walks to me with his arms extended. He wraps his tanned arms around me and pulls me near him, and I feel him smile against my face. Peter smells like everything familiar, and I take a deep breath into him.

"I've only been away from you for a week, Kate, but I missed you so much."

I pull away from Peter, and he puts his arms around my waist. I've never seen him look so tan and relaxed. Tanzania has been good for him. Peter continues to smile at me, and I look into his blue eyes. I turn to the side because I can feel eyes burning into me. I don't know how long Andrew has been standing there, but he's watching my interaction with Peter carefully. He walks our way, expressionless, and then puts his hand out to shake Peter's.

"Welcome back to the village, Peter," Andrew says and attempts to smile. "Kate, can I have one moment with you before you leave?"

Peter releases my hips, and I follow Andrew into his office, where he closes the door. I'm tempted to glance back at Peter, but I already can imagine the expression on his face.

Andrew leans against his desk. "Thanks for examining Zahra."

I fold my arms against my chest. "You already knew what course of action you were going to take with her. Why bring me into the conversation, and then disagree with me in front her?"

"You're here to learn. I don't believe you've seen a preeclampsia patient since you've been here, and I thought it would be helpful."

The words are on the tip of my tongue, but I open my mouth and decide against saying anything.

"Kate, you were spot on with the diagnosis, but then I saw you pause when I asked you what course of action to take. You have all the tools and knowledge to be even more excellent than you already are. But don't pause. You know this stuff."

Andrew pushes off from his desk and walks toward me, and my heartbeat increases. I'm aware of Peter, waiting for me on the other side of the door. Andrew leans into me, but I raise my hand and spread my fingers across his chest.

"Not now, Andrew."

"Kate." His eyes plead with mine. Andrew looks down and then puts his hand on my cheek. "Please know, I'm only trying to make you better. I never want to make you feel like you aren't good enough. You are everything."

"I'm going to leave now." I push back on Andrew and go to open the door.

"Wait!" Andrew practically shouts, "when are you going to tell Peter about us?"

Us. Andrew sounds so confident. He's not wrong. I need to.

"The day after the fundraiser. It would be too hard to tell him now." I quickly open the door to a waiting Peter.

Peter and I walk silently back to my bungalow until he finally asks. "What was that all about?"

"A complicated patient that is still at the hospital and about to give birth."

I open the door to my bungalow and invite Peter in. My body continues to feel anxious, as I know, I need to be honest with Peter about what has transpired with Andrew, and I need to be honest with Andrew about where my head and heart is at. I pour us both a glass of wine, and Peter sits down. He goes to open his mouth, but I beat him to it.

"Peter, I want to talk to you about something."

He takes a large gulp of wine, followed by another, until his entire glass is empty. He puts his hand up toward me to stop me from talking.

"Let me go first." He slowly pours himself another glass. "I had a lot of time to do some thinking while on safari. I know my actions haven't always been consistent with what I'm about to say, but I know, without a shadow of a doubt, that you and I are supposed to be together. If you let me, I'll spend the rest of my life showing you how much you mean to me." Peter leans over, his eyes filled with hope.

I fold my hands into my lap as he tries to grab them.

"Peter, we need to talk." I hang my head low and stare at my feet beneath me. "I need to be honest with you as well. I'm not sure being together again is best for me. I'm trying to figure a few things out."

Peter pulls his chair closer to me and grabs my hands out of my lap and holds them. "I know, Kate. I can tell you're grappling with a few things. But as I sat in the jeep and looked out at the elephants and lions, it struck me. You're it for me. I love you. I've always loved you, and we have a history with each other that no one else can ever have."

"I need to tell you something." I try to interject because it doesn't feel right to delay telling Peter about Andrew.

Peter holds his finger up to my lips and presses into them. "I know you have a lot on your mind but not tonight. Think about what I said, and we can talk tomorrow."

"Peter," I say, "it's about Andrew."

"Not tonight, Kate."

Peter slowly removes his finger. I am prepared to tell him everything, but why is he stopping me? My relationship with Andrew is on the tip of my tongue. I am going to disclose it all, but Peter stands up, so I do the same.

"I love you, Kate. I'll see you tomorrow."

Peter leans into me and gives me a quick hug and then walks out into the dark night.

CHAPTER 26

When the roots of a tree begin to decay, it spreads death to the branches.

—Nigerian Proverb

It's the day of the fundraiser at the hospital, and the bungalows buzz with excited energy. I've tried to find Maria, but she's been at the hospital all day finalizing last-minute details. My parents come over in the dressiest outfits they've brought to Tanzania and watch as I slowly move around my bungalow, unsure of what to wear. I finally settle on a long black dress and wear my hair down in soft curls.

Nothing feels right around me. My stomach constricts with anxiety, and I feel unsettled. So much of my truth is being omitted, and I feel like a walking fraud. I replay my conversation with Peter and how I tried to be honest with him, and now my parents sit at the table, talking about tonight's fundraiser and all they have to catch up on when they get back to Minneapolis.

"Hey, guys," I say, and both of them look up at me, "Andrew told me about an opportunity to stay on here longer and join Doctors Without Borders—"

"Absolutely not, Kate," my mom interrupts before I have a chance to finish my sentence.

My dad lowers his eyes and shoots my mom a look. "Paula, let Kate talk before you go inserting your opinions."

My mom crosses her arms across her chest, and my dad looks to me, letting me know he's ready for me to continue. "I don't know if I'm even interested. But I thought I should tell you both that it's an option."

"What about Peter?" my mom asks.

"What about Peter? We aren't together. If I do this, it's because I think it's best for me. It's not a decision based on anyone else."

"Doctors Without Borders is an excellent organization," my dad states. "You'd be able to earn a paycheck, and no one will argue that the experience you're gaining from being here will serve you well your entire life."

My mom dramatically slams her fist into the table. "John, you cannot encourage her. Kate, you have a life back home. There is a shortage of midwives in Minneapolis, and you'll have no issues finding employment. I can't help but think your Dr. Andrew has ulterior motives."

"Paula, that's enough!" My dad raises his voice, which is out of character for him. "This is Kate's decision, and we'll support her in whatever that is. Kate, think about this, and if it's best for you, it's your decision and your decision alone."

My dad rarely stands up to my mom and takes a stance, and both my mom and I stare back as our mouths hang open, surprised by his assertiveness.

I sigh and look at the door. "Unfortunately, we don't have time to continue this conversation as we need to get to the hospital."

We walk by the bungalow Peter is staying at to pick him up, and the four of us head to the hospital. The cafeteria that has been under construction on the first floor has been transformed, and beautiful linens lay over the tables with flower centerpieces. I look around the small space and see many people I don't recognize and know they must be from the various foundations. Andrew talks to two gentlemen, and I observe how nice he looks. He has on khaki pants and a white button down tucked into them and wears a blue-and-white bowtie. We make eye contact, and he gives me a wink, letting me know he sees me. Peter's hand digs into my arm as he tightens his grip around me.

A server comes by with wine and hors d'oeuvres, and Maria and Noor approach us.

"Didn't Maria do a wonderful job on this space?" Noor looks at all of us.

I pull Maria into an embrace. "It really does look beautiful."

"I agree," Peter says. "The space looks great."

We make small talk, and then we are told to take a seat as the program is about to begin. I look around and see so many of the staff from the hospital, dressed up, smiling, and anxious.

Maria sits next to me and whispers in my ear, "Is it weird having Peter here again?"

"So weird," I respond. "I know you've always liked him, Maria."

Maria smiles into her drink and then leans into me again. "I have always liked him, but that doesn't mean that I like the two of you together."

My eyes widen with surprise, and we all turn our attention to the front of the room. Andrew starts off by thanking everyone who has traveled far and wide to be here and then goes into the history of the hospital and his vision behind it. I watch the foundation visitors, trying to read their faces. They seem engaged and nod their heads constantly.

"Recently," Andrew continues, "we received a grant from Doctors Without Borders. This will allow us to hire two full-time medical workers for two years at a time. We will be able to provide better services and expand more fully into prenatal care."

Andrew's low British accent roles off his tongue, as he pronounces each syllable with elegance.

"I'd be remiss not to give credit to the wonderful hospital staff we have from around the village. Some of the staff works here, but some have relocated here from other places in Tanzania."

Everyone claps as we look around at all the staff who sit at the tables.

"I want to give a special thank-you to Dr. Eric, who has been leading our general medicine floor for nearly nine months now. And finally, I want to thank Kate Malone, who is a nurse practitioner and certified midwife, who joined us all the way from the United States."

I smile, as everyone's eyes fixate on me. Andrew holds my gaze as he smiles at me, beaming with pride. My dad smiles at me from the other side of the table, and as I glance at my mom, her look is full of contempt.

As our food is served, Andrew continues to talk about the financial targets the hospital needs to be sustainable. My dad walks over to me and whispers in my ear, "I would like to make a financial contribution, Kate. I'll talk to Andrew after the event."

I look at my dad surprised, as I know he and my mom have the means to contribute, but I didn't think they'd be interested.

After dinner, everyone stands around and mingles, and my eyes keep following Andrew as he works the room and talks to potential donors. Maria also works the room, and I can hear her indistinguishable laugh no matter where she in the room. The crowd thins, and I notice my dad has a conversation with Andrew before he and my mom say goodbye for the evening. Peter lingers a bit longer, but at this point, the people from the foundation have left, and a few of us start to clean up the space.

"Peter, why don't you head back. I want to help clean up."

"I don't mind helping."

"I appreciate that"—I smile—"but I want to talk numbers, and I don't know if anyone will feel comfortable doing that with a non-hospital worker present."

"Ah, I get it. I know it's late, but will you stop over when you're done?"

"Yeah," I say quickly, "I want to talk."

He slowly nods his head, and I can see my words weigh on him heavily. We say goodbye, and now it's only Noor, Maria, Andrew, and me. I help pull linens off tables and put the room back together. We clear off the dishes and put them in the dishwasher.

Maria finally breaks the silence. "I can't wait any longer. How'd we do tonight, Andrew?"

Andrew stops what he's doing, and his smile extends his entire face. "According to the preliminary results, we had a good enough evening to stay sustainable for the next five years."

We all yell and clap. Maria pulls me into a hug first and bounces me up and down. Then Noor takes my hand and spins me toward Andrew. Andrew takes my face in his hands, and I stand on my tippy toes as he pulls my face to his and presses his lips to mine. I've gone a couple of days without the feeling of being held by Andrew, and it feels good.

"Come with me for a moment." Andrew takes my hand and leads me down the dark hallway. Because there are only ten beds on the labor and delivery floor, it's rarely busy in the evenings, but tonight it's dead. Zahra and her newborn went home this morning, and there are no mothers or babies here.

My high heels echo against the hospital floors, and Andrew picks up his pace until he stops in front of his office door. Andrew looks down the hallway and also realizes we're alone. Andrew leans into me as I stand against the closed door to his office. "You look beautiful tonight. I never got to tell you that."

I nibble on my bottom lip. "You look nice too. And you look very smart, Dr. Andrew."

Andrew presses into me, and our lips finally connect. I've missed the exhilarating way I feel when we kiss. My hands go to Andrew's cheekbones, and we both smile into the kiss as we explore each other.

I see the blur at my side before I understand what's happening. Peter's voice rings out into the empty hallway. "What the hell?"

Footsteps hurry down the hallway, and Maria and Noor run to us. I turn quickly as Peter's fist meets Andrew's jaw. Andrew charges quickly and pushes Peter against the wall, immobilizing him, and his arm goes up in the air like he's going to hit Peter back. I try to get between them, but before I have a chance, Noor grabs Andrew's arm and pulls him back.

"Let's calm down, guys!" Noor yells between panting breaths.

Andrew's body relaxes, but then Peter charges him again, and now Noor holds Peter back. Peter shakes his fist out, and I can tell it's already getting black and blue. Andrew holds his jaw, and Maria comes and puts her arm on my back.

"Is anyone going to tell me what's going on here?" Peter yells at me.

I wipe at my eyes as a tear starts to fall. "I don't want to do this here. Can we please leave and talk about this?"

"No," Peter responds, "I walk into him kissing you, and I feel like all of you are in on some secret and purposely hiding it from me."

Maria leaves my side and tries to wrap her arm around Peter. "It's not like that, Peter. You need to calm down though."

Peter tries to brush Maria's arm off him. "Are you in a relationship with him now?" Peter's eyes cut to mine, and I observe how much hatred is behind the word him. Peter refuses to use Andrew's name.

"I don't want to talk about this here," I practically cry. "Things are complicated, and I tried to tell you last night, and I was going to head to your place shortly to share everything."

"Did things with Andrew start before or after I spent the night in your bungalow the night of Maria and Noor's wedding?"

Andrew once again charges at Peter, but Noor and Maria both grab him first. All eyes are on me, and I'm mortified that Maria and Noor have been brought into this private situation. In this moment, I know I've handled everything wrong. I should have forced myself to tell Peter yesterday, even if he didn't want to hear it. And I should have been more forthcoming with Andrew about how confused I am about a path forward. I care about both of them, and now they both stare at me with such disdain in their eyes.

"Peter, I've been seeing Andrew," I cry, as I wipe at my eyes. "I tried to tell you, I did. I didn't plan on hurting you."

Peter stares at me but doesn't say a word. I turn to Andrew, who is still being held back by Noor and Maria.

"Andrew, I don't know what to say to you," I say, wishing I wasn't doing this in front of an audience. "Everything with you happened so fast, and I've tried to be as honest with you as possible that I'm still sorting out my feelings."

The room is entirely silent, and the only thing I hear is my heart. All eyes are on me, and I want nothing more than to turn on my heels and run out of this room. Everything is now out in the open, but I didn't want it to happen like this.

Maria takes my arm and motions toward the door. Noor puts his hand on Peter's back, and Andrew takes a step back. Maria walks as stunned as me back to my bungalow and puts the teapot on the kettle. I sit at the table, with my face in my hands.

"Here, Kate. Drink this." Maria hands me a cup.

Maria doesn't say anything for a moment, but I feel her eyes on me.

"Say it, Maria. I know you want to say something."

A sigh escapes her mouth. "Are you okay, Kate?"

"Not really. I'm mortified. I didn't want anyone to be hurt. I messed this one up."

Maria takes my hand in hers. "Let's start with Peter. He'll get over it. You're single, and you had the right. And maybe now he'll understand how you felt when you walked in on him kissing Jane. If you want to get back together with Peter, what happened tonight won't prohibit that from happening."

Maria has always had a gift of cutting through the crap and speaks with pragmatism. It's one of my favorite things about her, and she's talked me off more than one ledge in our friendship.

"Now let's talk about Andrew. I've known him for a lifetime, Kate. I've never known him to enter into a relationship casually. He thinks everything through, and if that led him to pursuing you, then I know he has deep feelings for you—"

"But, Maria," I interrupt, "no one wants me to be with him. We go around the village together, and people stare. My own mom has commented on how complicated things would be with him."

"Kate, as a Black woman, I feel like I can tell you this." Maria twists her braids in her fingers. "Being with a Black man will not make your life easier. Every day, you'll face people who don't think it's right. You'll face Black women who think you're stealing one of the good ones, and you'll face White people who think you're a traitor to your race. You'll need to intentionally choose each other every day if it will ever work between you guys."

Maria pauses and looks at me. "But no matter what, Andrew deserves your complete honesty, and he needs to know where he stands with you."

The walls close around me, and as I look at my surroundings, everything becomes blurry. My kitchen spins, and I tap the bridge of my nose and pinch away my tears. I feel like I'm suffocating, and that there is no good decision. Maria kisses my cheek and walks out, and I'm left with a million questions on what to do next.

CHAPTER 27

He who loves, loves you with your dirt.

—Ugandan Proverb

Seventeen—that's how many squares I counted and recounted on the ceiling of my bungalow bedroom instead of sleeping. I tossed and turned all night. I'd face the open window for a bit and thought the calming wind through the window would help my mind turn off, but it didn't. I'd face the white walls and feel the wind at my back, but that didn't help either. I finally laid on my back and stared up at the seventeen perfectly square panels on the ceiling.

How does one fall asleep when a million things take up space in the brain all at once? I don't know what to do, but I know when the new day begins, whether I'm ready to or not, conversations will be had and decisions will be made. It's finally when the dawn of a new day starts shining through the window that my eyes get heavy enough for sleep.

*****

"Kate, are you in there?"

There's a pounding at the door, and I hear my mom's voice. I jolt up, sure I only just fell asleep and rub my eyes and throw on a pair of yoga pants. I rush to the door, and before exchanging words, my mom barges in, followed by my dad, who only makes eye contact with me briefly, and his eyes are apologetic.

"Peter came over and told us what happened last night. You have a lot of explaining to do," my mom says through gritted teeth.

"Paula," my dad interjects, "you promised you'd be calm."

I start the coffee pot, and the emotion rumbles up through my stomach, chest, and then out through my mouth, and I cry.

"Last night was such a mess. It wasn't supposed to happen like that. I'm sorry Peter's feelings are hurt. I didn't want to hurt him."

My dad's hands rub my shoulders, and he moves my hair to the side. "Kate, are you okay?"

I cry into his shirt. "Not really."

My mom huffs as she puts her arm on me. "Peter came over last night saying that now he doesn't know if he wants to get back together with you. We find out that the hospital's doctor put his moves on you, and then a spectacle was made."

"That isn't what happened, Mom." I sit down, and they both join me.

My dad brushes his wrinkled-up forehead. "Will you share what happened?"

"Peter ended things with me." I throw my hands up in the air, unsure why that is an important distinction, just for me. "I came here because you guys thought it would be a good idea. I didn't think anything like this would happen. But Andrew and I developed feelings for each other. I was planning on telling Peter. In fact, I tried to."

My mom looks to my dad. "John, will you leave us be for a moment? I want to talk to our daughter, woman to woman."

My dad's eyes cut to mine, seeking permission. I don't want him to go, but I know if my mom wants me alone, that is what she'll get. He turns his back to us and slowly walks out the door.

"Kate, I'm only going to say this once. You're young, and I remember what that felt like. You wanted a bit of an adventure, and Andrew seems exotic, and you wanted to get it out of your system before settling down for the rest of your life. I get it, I do. But it would never work. He'll tire of you and move on to someone else, and in the meantime, Peter will move on, and you'll lose the chance to be with him. I think it's best for everyone concerned if you return home with us tomorrow."

I go to speak, but the words don't come out, and my mom continues, "I'm sure Andrew is nice enough, but it wouldn't work, and if you think about it, and I mean really think about it, you'll see that too. Now clean yourself up, as you have quite a few goodbyes to say here before we all leave tomorrow."

"Mom—" I try to stop her, and she turns to me.

"Your father and I will work on arrangements today."

My mom walks out the door before I have an opportunity to protest. I have three weeks left in Tanzania, and my mom wants me to cut that short and return home tomorrow. I stand up and look through the window. The hospital stares back at me, a permanent fixture in this village that has been my home for the past few months.

Logically, everyone is telling me what I already know. Peter is the safer choice. Everything about my relationship with Andrew would be difficult—the race issue, the cultural issue, and not to mention the geographical issues of my living in the United States and him living in Tanzania. Not only that, but how well do I really know him? I've been here for such a short time. I've known Peter my entire life and loved him for the past eight years.

*****

The entire day is a blur. I walk over to Andrew's, and he doesn't answer. Peter won't answer my texts, and my mom has called the airline and changed my flight. I don't feel ready to leave, yet now she's in my bungalow cleaning up and throwing my clothes into my bag. I don't have the energy to push back. I lie on my bed, with my arms folded behind my head, tears running down my face. No matter what happens next, someone will be hurt.

"Kate"—my mom's voice interrupts my thoughts—"finish packing and say your goodbyes. We will leave in an hour."

I hear the door slam, and I'm alone. I sit up, and my bungalow no longer looks like mine. My mom cleaned out my fridge, with Maria's help, and every surface is empty and wiped down. It looks ready for the next tenant. In a matter of time, the bungalow will have forgotten my presence entirely.

The door to my bungalow swings open, and Andrew runs in, out of breath. He puts his hands on his knees, and when he stands up, I see his discolored jaw from where Peter's fist made contact.

He looks around at the emptiness. "You're leaving?"

"I have no choice," I say, my hands limply hang at my sides.

"I thought we had three more weeks to figure things out."

A sob escapes. "Everything got too hard. No one wants me to stay here it seems."

"That's a cop-out, Kate. Everyone here wants you to stay. What do you want?"

"I don't know," I cry. "But everything got so messed up last night, and I have so many relationships to repair."

"I'm sorry last night happened the way it did, but I'm not sorry it happened. I want to be with you, and now that things are out in the open, we can be."

"Please," I plead, "don't make this harder than it needs to be."

"Harder, Kate?" Andrew flicks a tear that falls from his eye. "I'm in love with you."

His words stab my heart, and for a moment, I don't think I can breathe, and I'm at a loss of words how to respond.

Andrew's face floods with relief with the words he spoke. "I've been in love with you for so long," he continues. "I'm only sorry I didn't tell you sooner."

My heart feels like it's going to break into two. "I can't leave these relationships like this. I need to leave."

Andrew takes a step back from me, his mouth open, and his face riddled with confusion.

"I told you I'm in love with you, Kate, and you tell me you're leaving. Doesn't what I said mean anything to you?"

"Yes, it means something to me." The tears pour out of my eyes. "But things are too hard right now. There are too many obstacles in the way, and the beginning of relationships shouldn't be this difficult."

"I know things are difficult, and I'd be lying if I said we won't experience hard things in the future. But I love you, Kate, and I have for so long. I'll choose you every day, and we can navigate this together."

A sob escapes again, and I turn from Andrew and look out my kitchen window. "No one wants us to be together. No one. Even Maria said it would be hard."

Andrew spreads his fingers across my upper back. "It will be hard. We don't get to decide who we fall in love with, Kate. I fell in love with you—a White girl who lives on the other side of the world. And I know you have feelings for me too. We can do anything as long as we're together. Please don't leave."

I turn to Andrew. "I'm leaving. I have to."

His face breaks my heart. He turns his head slightly and wipes a tear with the back of his hand. I look up at Andrew just in time for him to crash into me with his lips. They are urgent and needy and suck every last breath out of me. My knees go weak, and I lean on him to support me. I kiss him back with everything in me, and just like the first time we kissed, nothing else in the world matters, and every one of my nerves is brought to life by the magnetic current that touching Andrew gives me.

Andrew pulls away from the kiss, holding both my shoulders with his hands. He studies my face. "You're actually going to leave?" His voice breaks as he says it.

"I have no choice." I wipe at my moist eyes as I continue to stare up at him.

"Don't do that. Don't say that. Choose me. Take the Doctors Without Borders position."

The sun through my windows shine off his eyes and glistens against the tears escaping his eyes and slowly fall down his golden-brown cheeks. I look down because I can't stand to see the hurt on his face. I shake my head.

"I'm sorry I hurt you. This is all my fault."

Andrew drops his hands from my shoulders, and our distance suddenly feels immense. "Don't do that." His thumb presses into my chin as he raises my head to look at him. "Be brave for once, Kate. Choose you."

I try to swallow my cry, but it's too late and comes out loud and unsteady. "I make a lot of decisions for me. You don't know even know me."

"And Peter knows you? You spent years with him, without ever letting him see you. You let me in. I see you, Kate."

I cover my wet face and try to slow down my breathing, so I don't sob. Andrew pulls my hands down, so I'm forced to look at him.

"I do know you. I know that you bite your lip when you're nervous. I see the way your face lights up every time you hear a baby's heartbeat through the stethoscope. Every time you deliver a baby, I see you cry and pray over the child. I know it's been your dream to come to a developing nation and deliver babies."

Andrew cries. "I know you wish you had a closer relationship with your mom. I know that your chest and neck turn red when you're embarrassed. You're extremely shy, and you don't let many people in. I know that you always make the safe choices because you never want to rock the boat. I know you aren't in love with Peter and haven't been in a long time. I also know that you would probably spend the rest of your life with him because that's what people in your life want. I know that isn't the best life for you."

The room once again spins, and I can't catch my breath. I'm trapped, and there is no way out. I don't even know what being in love feels like. Maybe Andrew is right, and I haven't been in love with Peter for a long time. But I don't believe in all that romantic stuff. Like Peter told me, those feelings disappear anyway. What we're left with is someone we're comfortable with and who we can coexist with in life.

"Kate, I love you more than you'll ever know. I know you're scared, and I know this is all unexpected. Please just be honest about what you want and about how you feel." Andrew pinches the bridge of his nose and looks up toward the ceiling. "I know you love me, Kate."

"I don't know how I feel."

"You're going to leave, aren't you?" Andrew turns away and leans against the counter.

"I'm going to leave." The words have a finality to them.

Andrew continues to look away, and the sun feels like a betrayal. His next breath is heavy. "I guess there isn't anything left to say."

I wrap my arms around his waist, but he stiffens and steps out of my embrace.

"Please, Andrew, you have to know I never wanted to hurt you."

He turns but doesn't look at me, instead stares at the door.

"I think you're a coward, Kate Malone."

I inch away. His words sting. Then the anger rises, making the desire to lash out too strong to resist. "Just because I didn't choose you doesn't make me a coward."

Andrew's entire face contorts, and for the first time in minutes, he looks me in the eyes. His almond brown eyes squint and pierce into mine, and the pain and vulnerability I see in them make me taste bile in my mouth from the lie I told to hurt him. He looks wounded and small, and my fear paralyzes me, and I do nothing.

"Kate, if you don't want to be with me, then don't be. But I know you've always dreamed of coming to a place like this village and making an impact. At least take the position. I promise I'll never profess my love to you again unless you welcome it. But don't give up your dream because of me. Giving up your dream for someone else is what makes you a coward."

"I'm sorry." The words are insignificant, but it's all I can think to say.

"I'm sorry too."

Andrew walks out of my bungalow, and I feel as uncertain about my future as I did when I arrived in this village more than three months ago.

CHAPTER 28

For tomorrow belongs to the people who prepare for it today.

—African Proverb

It's been a challenging and heartbreaking few months, but nothing has felt as difficult as this moment. We're only two hours into the car ride and have two more hours until we reach our hotel in Izazi, where we'll stay for the night. My parents follow Maria's parents in their rental car, and it's only Peter and me in the third car in the caravan, heading to Dar, where we have a flight in four days.

I avoid looking in Peter's direction, with his clenched jaw and his white knuckles around the steering wheel. We haven't said a word to each other, and the air in the car feels tense. The village seems like a distant memory as we continue to drive east, farther away from it. Saying goodbye to Maria was awful, but thinking of Andrew's face the last time I saw him, makes me want to curl in a ball and cry myself to sleep. But I can't mourn him while I sit so closely to Peter.

"Kate, we need to talk." Peter breaks the silence first.

I adjust the sunglasses that hide my bloodshot eyes and continue to look at the road in front of us.

"If we're going to make our relationship work, I need to know exactly what happened between you and Andrew."

"I don't think Andrew has anything to do with determining what our path forward is."

"That's where you're wrong. I won't be able to move forward until I know. I'm only going to ask you this once, Kate. Did you sleep with him?"

The way Peter says the words, cheapens the experience. I haven't fully wrapped my head around what the past few months with Andrew meant, but I know it wasn't a lust-driven moment where we ended up in bed together. I wouldn't feel so broken if that's all it was.

I wipe my eyes underneath my sunglasses. "Yes."

I look into Peter's blue eyes. His sprinkling of freckles isn't visible at the moment, but I feel like I'm looking at someone entirely familiar. I don't want to hurt Peter, but he deserves my honesty.

"Well, I guess we have nothing else to say to each other."

I let out a cry of frustration. "We haven't even said anything to each other yet. If we're going to have an honest conversation, let's talk about how things felt wrong in our relationship. Because us not working has nothing to do with Jane, and nothing to do with Andrew."

"I can't have this conversation right now." Peter's red face has now turned translucent, as he continues to shake his head. "You are something else, Kate."

We go back to silence; neither of us have anywhere to escape to. I shut my eyes, and it doesn't take me long to start dreaming. I can practically smell the embers of the fire. Andrew and I sit in his backyard with a high flame and a sky full of stars. We share a lawn chair, and I lean back into Andrew's chest as he points to the stars. He tells me again the story of the stars Altair and Vega. In my dream, every word Andrew speaks is enunciated and exaggerated. And then I have a realization about Andrew and me. We are the stars. We are Altair and Vega. We are separated by continents and oceans, by race and by parents—a forbidden love.

In my dream, I turn to Andrew after his story and place his face in my hands. "I would find you anywhere, Andrew. I love you."

"And I love you."

He pulls me into his chest and strokes my hair, and I feel like I'm safe and at home. I smile and breathe him in, knowing I have found my Altair. I look over to the chair next to me, and Bupe is with us at the fire. She grabs my hand and squeezes it.

"I told you there was a greater purpose to you coming to Tanzania."

"Bupe, what are you doing here? I've missed you!"

Bupe stands up and walks toward the fire. She glances at me over her shoulder. "I never left, Kate. I've been here the entire time."

Bupe steps closer to the fire, her white dress blows in the wind. "Come back to the village. This is where you belong." Bupe disappears and becomes the vibrant flames of the fire.

"We're here." I jerk my head off the side of the car and rub my eyes and see the Izazi hotel in my view.

Peter goes up to his room to nap, and my mom says she is going to lie down and read for a while. The other patrons of the hotel walk by us in every direction as my dad and me walk to the hotel restaurant.

"I'm glad I get some time with you, kiddo, just you and me."

I force myself to smile.

"I can imagine none of this is easy for you, especially the way you left the village."

I do my best to force a laugh. "I'm sorry to be such a downer."

"Don't apologize, Kate." My dad puts his hand on mine.

After ordering food, we sit silently for a few moments. "Is this about Andrew?"

I look down, and I am grateful the restaurant is dimly lit because tears start to fall down my face. Tanzania is having a drought, but I have enough tears to water the country. The sound of his name makes my heart rip open.

"Not entirely"—I rest my face on my fist—"I was doing good things in the village. I was learning and growing and making a difference." I continue, "But it is somewhat about Andrew. He told me he's in love with me. And I didn't tell him back."

My dad's eyebrows raise. "How do you feel about him?"

I look at my dad and finally admit to myself how I feel. Why didn't I see it before? "I love him, Dad. I'm scared though."

"Tell me about him, Kate." My dad leans into me and props his face on his hands.

"I don't know what to tell you. I mean, you met him, you know. He is smart and kind, and I guess he loves me, and he has no problem expressing his feelings toward me. He was my best friend. We would talk for hours, and it was like time stood still. He took care of me and was patient with me when I didn't deserve it. He wasn't just nice to me. He was kind to everyone he met. He was, I don't know, he was mine."

I wipe at my wet eyes. "I hurt him, Dad."

"How did you hurt him?" My dad's words are slow with concern.

"I knew how I felt. I mean, if I really think about it, I knew. But I didn't tell him. I left, letting him think that he was the only one with feelings. He looked broken."

"Why didn't you tell him?" My dad turns his stool to look at me.

"I didn't realize until right now that's how I felt. I haven't felt this in so long."

My face is hot from the dam of tears that have been opened again. "And there is no way we could be together. Could you imagine Andrew moving to Minneapolis? He couldn't even be a doctor there. He would not fit in, and he'd hate it." I start laughing through the tears. "And can you imagine me living in Tanzania? Mom would dis-own me as she's made it clear what she thinks about the relationship."

"You like Tanzania, Kate. I've never seen you happier. Ever. And I've known you for a long time." My dad winks at me.

"I can't imagine living here for the rest of my life, Dad."

My dad looks at me thoughtfully. "Did Andrew ask you to live in Tanzania for the rest of your life?"

I shake my head no, realizing that I never allowed the conver-sation to go any further than asking me to stay. I sit and pick at my food and digest everything my dad says to me.

"I was so scared. I mean, I've never felt this way, not even about Peter."

My dad looks at me, and compassion oozes from his eyes. "What's your plan with Peter?"

"I don't want to hurt him."

"Kate"—my dad looks at me—"not wanting to hurt someone isn't a reason to be in a relationship with them. Peter deserves to be with someone who loves him fully, as do you."

My dad takes the napkin out of his lap and places it on his plate. "Kate, the hardest thing about being an adult is that no one is going to tell you what to do. Only you know what's best for you, and only you know if Andrew is the one you're supposed to be with. You've had a difficult year, and I think what happened between you and Peter has scared you. If you say you love Andrew, then I imagine you also know him well, and shouldn't doubt his love for you."

My dad stands up and puts his hand on my shoulder. I don't turn around, but I grab his hand and hold it and choke back the sobs, but one escapes. My dad stands for a moment and then pats my hand and walks to the counter to pay the bill.

*****

Today is the day we drive from morning to night before staying in a hotel in Dar for our flight home. I stay silent, even though I continue to travel farther away from the village, to a world that will bring me home, which is a world I don't think I want anymore.

I turn to Peter. "I know you don't want to talk, but we have to."

Peter's sigh is heavy. "I know we do." He motions to me. "You first."

Last night, as I laid awake in bed, I realized so many truths about my current situation, truths I haven't been brave enough to consider, but that can't be denied anymore.

"I know it's hard for you to hear about my relationship with Andrew." I turn my body toward Peter and tuck my leg under my lap. "But I need you to know... I would not have slept with Andrew if I thought you and I still had a future."

Peter clenches his teeth and stares straight ahead.

"I know it's difficult to talk about, but we were drifting apart in our relationship far before what happened with Jane. I love you,

Peter, but being with you, I felt like I always had to give up parts of who I am to fit into your life—"

"What does that mean?" Peter interrupts.

With a deep breath, I continue, "You always had everything figured out for us. After we finished our degrees, you'd work at a downtown law firm, and we'd leave the city and move to a sprawling home in the suburbs. I'd work for a few years, but then stay at home once we had children."

Peter hits the steering wheel. "I don't see what's wrong with that plan. It sounds like a pretty great life to me."

"You never stopped and asked me what I wanted. I tried to tell you so many times. I even brought up working somewhere else in the world for a year to give back and gain experience. Every time I brought up my hopes and dreams, you made it seem like it didn't fit into what you had planned for our lives."

"I need to know exactly what you're saying, Kate."

"I was happy in the village. I have an opportunity to earn an income and continue to work on my craft. I don't feel ready to go home."

Peter turns to me. "You're choosing him, aren't you?"

I purse my lips. "No, I'm choosing me."

I've known Peter for a long time and never seen him cry. But now he removes his sunglasses and wipes his eyes. "Are you saying it's over?"

I take my sunglasses off and wipe my eyes too. I've been talking around everything, but there is no avoiding what are at stakes here. "Losing you scares me and breaks my heart at the same time. I don't know what the future holds, but I think our relationship has run its course."

The past eight years of my life with him flash before my eyes. Peter and I had some good times. We grew up together, and there was a time we were in love with each other. But that feels like a very long time ago. Peter isn't a bad person either. Mistakes were made, but it forced the conversation that we avoided having for years.

Peter reaches his hand across the middle console and holds my hand but doesn't say anything.

I hold my breath to avoid crying. I'm sad but not because I think I'm doing the wrong thing. In fact, having this conversation with Peter has felt like one of the most honest and necessary conversations I've ever had. Yet it's the end of something, and goodbyes are hard. But I need to make room for the new beginnings that can blossom because I had the courage to follow my heart.

After an exhausting day of driving to Dar, we arrive at our hotel. We're all exhausted, and I know I have yet to have the most difficult conversation, but I feel resolute in what I want. Now I simply need to find the courage to say it.

My mom sits on the floor, moving items out of one bag and into another, while my dad looks through our travel documents. I don't want to get on the plane tomorrow and head home. Now I need to tell them that.

"Mom, Dad, can we talk?"

My mom looks up frantically from her bags.

"I don't want to go home tomorrow. I want to stay here and take the position with Doctors Without Borders."

My mom drops what she's doing and stands up. "Absolutely not."

"I'm not asking permission. I can drive the rental car back to Izazi and see if Maria or Noor could pick me up there and return the car."

I glance at my dad, and I'm sure I see a small smirk spread across his face. My mom continues, "What about the paperwork? There are visa requirements to being here."

My dad interjects, "Paula, if you're fine traveling solo with Peter, I could stay in Dar a few days with Kate and make an appointment at the embassy."

My mom puts her hands on her hips and glares at me. "This is because of Andrew?"

I make a laughing sound, but it's actually me beginning to cry. "Why doesn't anyone have confidence in me to make my own decisions?" I fold my arms across my body. "I went from living at home to college roommates to living with Peter to living at home again. I'm twenty-four and capable of living on my own. Yes, Mom, I hate to tell you this, but I love Andrew. But I'm not stupid and wouldn't change my life just for a guy. I'm doing this because it's what I've always wanted to do."

"That settles it then." My dad smiles.

"Kate, I'll never accept him."

"Isn't that a shame, Mom?" Bias is usually based on fear and uncertainty, yet I pity my mom in this moment. "All I know is, for the first time in ages, I feel like I'm doing exactly what I'm supposed to be doing."

My mom rolls her eyes and storms out of the room. My dad pulls me in and holds his arms tightly around me.

"I'm proud of you, kiddo. And your mom will come around."

CHAPTER 29

If I have ever seen magic, it has been in Africa.

—African Proverb

Sweat drips down my face, and I wipe it with the back of my hand. Every window is open in my little bungalow, but there is no breeze to give me a reprieve. By the time Noor and Maria picked me up in Izazi and brought me back to the village, I was gone fourteen days. Everything took longer at the embassy than my dad and I expected, yet I enjoyed getting to spend time with him, especially because I don't know the next time I'll see my parents.

I'm tempted to walk around my little bungalow and kiss every surface. I've never been surer that I made the right decision. I grab the bottom of my shirt and put my face in it to further wipe away the sweat. It's almost spring in Tanzania, but the heat is relentless. Maria says it's been an unseasonably hot winter, and I hope she's right.

The shadows move in my kitchen, which means the unyielding sun is finally saying goodbye for the day. The dirt clings to my bare legs after a day spent getting settled. I take a coldish shower and watch as today's dirt swirls down the drain. The village looks the same, but it feels entirely different. Or maybe, I feel different.

I asked Maria not to say anything to Andrew. Things were so complicated at the embassy, I had moments where it didn't look like I'd be able to extend my stay here. I went to text Andrew once and then realized that we never exchanged numbers. When I arrived last night, I wanted to run to Andrew's bungalow as soon as I arrived at the village, but Noor told me he's on an overnight trip to the countryside.

"How did you sleep, Kate?" Maria grabs my hand and squeezes it.

"Good once it cooled off a bit." I pull Maria in for a hug, and she lies down in the bed next to me, just like we used to do back home.

"I keep pinching myself that you're here. I know you only were gone for a couple of weeks, but you were missed."

I intertwine my fingers in hers. "I can't tell you how happy I am to be here."

"Kate"—Maria turns to me, so we're face-to-face, knees touching—"I want you to know that I never meant you harm by what I said. I simply want you to educate yourself on what the experience will be for you if you and Andrew decide to be together."

I smile at the sound of his name. "I know that. I appreciate you always being honest with me. You know I love you, Maria."

Maria squishes her face against mine. "And I love you. Welcome home, Kate."

Home. This tiny village in Tanzania does feel like home.

There's a loud knock at the door, and Noor yells out. "Hey, Kate. Fatima just arrived at the hospital. She's in labor."

I jump up and throw on shoes and head to the hospital. One of the reasons I hated leaving is I wanted to be here to help deliver Fatima's child. The last time I saw her, she was having false labor, and if my calculation is correct, she's still a couple of weeks out from delivery, but I've learned that babies come when they're ready.

My original date to go home is in a few days, and I've been concerned throughout Fatima's pregnancy that I would miss the birth. She's become special to me. All the women I've met have been, but Fatima feels like a younger sister, and I have this great need to take care of her.

I turn the corner and see the waiting room, and Editha sitting behind the desk. She points to Fatima, who is bent down, as if she's in pain.

"Hi, Fatima. Let me take you back."

I take her arm in mine and lead her to an exam room. Fatima moans frequently and grimaces her face as she bends over and holds her belly.

"Fatima, I want you in a gown, and I'm going to check you."

Fatima looks so young and fragile in the oversized hospital gown. She adjusts her hijab over her hair and lies back on the bed. I quickly identify that Fatima is in active labor, and she's already dilated to a six.

"Fatima, it looks like you're going to have a baby today." I give her a reassuring smile and quickly go out to the hall to see if I can get support of one of the staff.

"Editha, do you know when Andrew will be back?"

"He should be back sometime today, Ms. Malone, but that's all I know." Editha shrugs her shoulders. I've asked Andrew for space so many times with patients, but now that Fatima is here, I want nothing more than his support.

I go back into the room to join Fatima's side. I check the baby, who has remained breech throughout the pregnancy. The baby's heartbeat sounds strong, but my head fills with options of how to deliver a baby when a cesarean needs to be the absolute last resort because of the nature of Fatima's pregnancy and her relationship with her dad.

I think back to my conversation with Andrew a while ago. The one we had when Peter barged in the room. He said that her father would kill her if he knew she came to the hospital because it meant that people in the village are aware of the scandal in their family. It leaves me with one option—a vaginal birth. However, I refuse to allow anything happen to Fatima.

"Fatima, does your dad know where you are?"

"No," she cries through a contraction, "I told him I had errands in the village."

I feel the baby and consider trying to manipulate it out of the breech position. I saw it back home on one of the hospital rounds I was on. But in that scenario, we had monitors, and I remember the baby's heartbeat dipping heavily, and I don't want to take that chance. So many breech manipulations end up in a cesarean section anyway. Adimu, one of the staff on the labor and delivery floor, walks in, and I instruct her to get a wet rag for Fatima.

I check her again, and she's close to being fully dilated. "Fatima, you're very close, but I don't want you to push until I say you can."

Adimu goes to Fatima's head and rubs a washcloth on her forehead. I wish Andrew were here, as he'd know what to do. I check Fatima again, and she's fully dilated.

"Ms. Malone, I feel so much pain," Fatima cries. Tears leave marks down her cheeks, and I've never wished more for the ability to take away someone else's pain.

I go to her opening, and I can see toes that peek out every time Fatima pushes. I put on my gloves and feel around, and a knee is bent, and there is no way the baby will be able to be delivered in the current position.

"Adimu," I whisper, "please find out if there is staff and an operating room available in case we need to do a cesarean."

"No," Fatima yells, "I can't be cut open. My father will kill me if he knew I was coming here."

I still motion Adimu to the door, and she exits in a hurry. If I were back in Minneapolis, Fatima would already be in an operating room, and the doctor would be prepping for her surgery. I know things are different here, and I need to weigh Fatima's concerns over her father, but I can't let her or her baby die. My mind flashes to Bupe and her final moments.

"Fatima, it's just in case. Don't worry, I'll do everything to help you have the baby vaginally."

My mind goes back to one of my courses toward the end of my program. The baby was breech and coming too quickly, and the physician had the patient get on her hands and knees which created more room at the opening for the baby to be delivered. I remember watching the video, and thinking it was similar to a horse giving birth, yet it worked.

"Fatima, I want you to switch positions, and I'm going to have you get on your hands and knees. I'll help you."

Fatima moans, and I help her maneuver positions until she's on her hands and her knees. She cries out, and I steady her on the bed. Adimu comes back into the exam room.

"Dr. Eric is in a surgery, and there is no one else who can assist with a cesarean."

The question is answered for me and takes the choice out of the equation. I motion to Adimu to bring me a good supply of rags. I try to straighten the bended knee of Fatima's baby, as she once again cries out. The knee straightens, and the baby starts sliding more into the birth canal.

"Fatima, you're making great progress. At your next contraction, I want you to push as hard as you can."

I wrap my arm around to feel Fatima's belly, and when it starts contracting, I say calmly, "Push right now, Fatima. Give it everything you have."

Fatima screams, and the baby descends further until both legs are out. I reach up and try to provide slack around the umbilical cord. The last obstacle will be the shoulders, and Fatima will have delivered the baby.

"You are doing great, Fatima. Your next contraction, I want you to bare down slightly. Not too hard this time."

Fatima pushes, and the shoulders clear her opening and then the head. I hand the newborn baby girl to Adimu and gently turn Fatima on her back. Fatima's entire petite body shakes with every cry, and I clean up the blood she's losing. I've seen more blood than this, but I want to make sure she hasn't torn in any way.

From the corner of the room, Adimu speaks in Swahili to the baby girl, as she cleans her off. The vibrations of the newborn cry echoes throughout the exam room. I call for some crushed ice and put it in a bag against Fatima to help with the pain and swelling.

"Fatima, you did great. That was a very challenging delivery having your baby feet first, but you did it."

Fatima grabs my hand and pulls me to her and wraps her small arms around me and cries. I hold onto her tight, as her cries start soft, and then reverberate through the room as her cries sound more anguished. We stay in the embrace for several minutes, and she finally releases me.

"Do you want to hold her, Fatima?"

Adimu walks toward us. Fatima nods, and Adimu places the baby in her arms. The baby looks just like Fatima. She has Fatima's round face and the same shape of her big brown eyes. The baby is so alert as she looks up at Fatima.

"Adimu and I are going to give you a minute alone with her, Fatima. I'll be right outside if you need me." Fatima doesn't look up as we walk out of the room.

I look down at my scrubs as I pace in front of Fatima's room. I'm covered in blood, yet I don't care. My heart nearly beats out of my chest from the adrenaline of the delivery. I did it. I didn't hesitate; I was decisive, and Fatima was able to deliver a healthy baby girl.

I think back to home. If this situation would have presented itself, I would have been pushed out of the room, and decisions would be made by physicians. The patient would have received first-class medical intervention, but I wouldn't have been part of it. I just delivered a breech baby, mostly by myself.

I look down the hallway, and I know there is no one I'd rather share this news with than Andrew. I may have come back to the village for me, but I'm hoping Andrew gives me another chance to be with him. He's the one I want to share the big and little things with. Yet if he were here today, I would have relied on him.

I quickly change out of my dirty scrubs and put a fresh pair on and check on Fatima. Her cheeks are soaked with tears. She looks up at me as I walk in the room.

"How are you feeling, Fatima?"

She rubs her thumb gently into the baby's chin. "I wasn't expecting to love her like this."

"You know you can change your mind. You don't have to place her for adoption."

"Yes, I do, Ms. Malone."

The conversation brings me down from my high of a successful delivery and quickly reminds me that I'm in Tanzania, and Fatima's circumstances are nearly impossible. The goal from the first time I met Fatima was to see her in private, help her have a delivery with as few complications as possible, and then help her child be placed for adoption. I hadn't let my mind go to the moment Fatima met her child, and the intricate emotions that would ensue.

"I've said my goodbyes to her. I need to get back home before my father looks for me."

I send her baby to the nursery and make sure that Fatima is well enough to leave. I want to make sure the bleeding has stopped as much as possible, and I send her home with icepacks. Before Fatima walks out of the hospital, I give her a long hug and make her promise to come back for a checkup soon.

CHAPTER 30

If you are filled with pride, you will have no room for wisdom.

—African Proverb

After I shower, I go to Andrew's bungalow, but there is no answer, and no jeep out front. He must not be back from the countryside, so I must wait another day before speaking to him. I have so much I want to say, and I'm losing patience. Where could he be?

I lie in bed, and the next time I open my eyes, all I see out my bedroom window is darkness, with the silhouette of the moon creating specks of glass on my floors. I inhale slowly and let the breath out through my mouth, and for the first time in months, I don't feel the sadness or heaviness in the pit of my stomach. Whatever happens, I'll be okay. As long as I keep choosing me, no matter how Andrew or anyone else feels, I'll be fine.

My mind goes again to Fatima. What would have happened if I didn't come back, and if Andrew was in the countryside? There was no one else at the hospital equipped to deliver the baby. Fatima and her baby could have died. Moments like this remind me of the importance for additional funding and resources for this hospital. In its current state, too much of a burden is on Andrew. I'm surprised he went to the countryside knowing Fatima was so close to delivery. He must have had a high-priority patient there as well.

First thing in the morning, I get dressed and head to the hospital. I notice Andrew's jeep is now in front of his bungalow, so he must have arrived sometime in the night. I debate heading to his place right away, but the morning is so early, and seeing that he got in late, he may not be awake yet. I have so much I want to say to him, but the first thing I want to do is check on Fatima's baby girl.

I walk to the nursery and see her right away. Her mother's eyes look into mine, and a yellow hat covers her soft black tufts of hair. I gently pick her up and hold her against me. The tiny baby puckers her lips and starts kneading against my body, so I make her a bottle and sit in a chair and rock her.

Her eyes try to stay open and look at me, but the baby's blinks continue to get longer until her eyes shut entirely. I hum her a lullaby and make wishes for what I hope her life will become. First, I hope she knows that a strong woman gave birth to her and that she has life because of Fatima's strength. I hope she gets adopted by a wonderful family who will adore her and celebrate her start to life. I hope that if adoption brings her outside of Tanzania, that her family will celebrate her roots and speak about Tanzania and maybe even someday bring her back to the village where her life began.

More than anything, I hope Fatima's baby girl knows how much she is loved. I want her to know the look on Fatima's face when she had to say goodbye. That even though the circumstances surrounding her conception are heartbreaking, that Fatima having the strength to say goodbye is because of how much she loves this child. I kiss the baby softly, right where her squishy cheek meets her ear.

"Kate?" Andrew sounds startled as he walks into the nursery and sees me feeding a baby. "What are you doing here?" Andrew stares at me like he's seen a ghost.

Andrew wears his glasses, and it looks like he hasn't slept in days.

"I came back."

He stares at me longer and then the baby. "I see that. Whose child is that?"

"Fatima had her baby yesterday." I look down, and the baby has finished, and her eyes are closed. I hold her up and get a couple of burps out of her and place her back in the bassinet.

I stand up and walk toward Andrew but pause when I think I see him back up.

"I'm hoping we can talk," I say to Andrew.

"I need to call the orphanage in Izazi and make arrangements."

I push on. "I know, Andrew, but I'm hoping we can go into your office and talk."

Andrew holds the nursery door open for me and lets me walk out first. As soon as we do, the universe speaks to me, and there are no less than ten women in the waiting room.

"It's going to have to wait, Kate." Andrew turns from me and goes into an exam room before I have a chance to respond.

The next few hours are spent seeing many patients while continuing to pass Andrew in the hallway, but barely exchanging words with each other. I know I hurt him, but I'm surprised that he isn't happier to see me. Every time we pass, he avoids looking at me. We are two strangers, walking to the waiting room, picking a patient out, and going to the exam rooms. My heart aches being this near him but feeling this far apart.

The sun is much lower in the sky by the time the last patient has been seen. The night staff starts to arrive, and the commotion of the hospital dies down. I look around the halls and don't see Andrew anymore, and there isn't a light shining from underneath his office door. I knock once, but no one answers, and when I turn the doorknob, the door is locked.

I run down the hospital stairwell, two at a time, and run toward Andrew's bungalow. I need to get everything out. I'll never find the courage again. Maria steps out of her bungalow and waves as I look like a crazy person running down the dirt path in the dark. I smell a fire, and I hope I'm right, and that Andrew will hear me out.

I knock once, and when there is no answer, I walk into his bungalow. It's mostly dark, and I go out the back door. Andrew doesn't see me at first, and for a moment, I watch him. He sits several feet back from the fire, not needing its warmth on this hot evening. His long legs are crossed at the ankle, and his hands are behind his head. He didn't change out of his scrubs, and I smile, thinking of the first time I saw him. Scrubs were made for his body.

"Andrew," I say softly.

He doesn't look away from the fire or appear startled at the sound of my voice. "You came."

I sit in the chair next to him and turn my body toward his. "I'm hoping we can talk."

Andrew swings his legs off his chair, so now we're knee to knee. "For two weeks, I didn't hear from you, Kate." His voice grows in intensity. "I thought you were on the other side of the world."

"I know." Tears fill my eyes.

Andrew's eyes widen. "You broke my heart, Kate. I put it all out there on the line. I feel so—" He doesn't finish his sentence.

"I hate how I left things with you, Andrew. But I don't regret the lessons I learned because of how things happened."

Andrew shoots up and covers his mouth as he paces. "You came back to tell me that how things ended were for a reason?"

"For so many reasons, yes." I stand too as I feel too small with Andrew standing above me. "I got to deliver Fatima's baby all by myself. That never would have happened if I would have stayed with you."

Andrew stares at me blankly. "It was a challenging delivery, especially because we couldn't do a cesarean or an episiotomy. I thought I needed you there so badly, but I did it, alone. It was exhilarating."

Andrew turns his back to me, but I continue, "You're the one who has been telling me since you met me, 'Kate, you need more confidence. You need to believe in yourself. You need to trust yourself.' I do, and it's because of you."

"Kate—"

"Let me finish, Andrew." I close the space between us, and this time, Andrew doesn't move away from me. "I'm sorry with the way I left, but if I hadn't, I never would have been sure about us. I would have always second-guessed staying and why I was staying."

Hope rises in my chest when I see the tenderness that Andrew still has for me. He holds all his emotions in his almond eyes. "The farther I drove away from here, the more my heart broke. I realized something so important on that drive. I will always love Peter, but you're right. I haven't been in love with him for a long time." With a deep breath, I speak my truth. "But I'm so in love with you that I thought my heart was going to rip into pieces the farther I got from you."

Andrew puts his hand on my heart, and I'm sure he can tell it's close to falling outside of my body; it is beating so fast. I place my hand on his, and the moon reflects off the glistening of Andrew's eyes, making them almost glow.

"I needed to stay, not because you asked me to, but because it's what's best for me." I laugh through my tears. "I'm sorry it took me longer to figure things out, but I'm here because of me."

Andrew swallows a large lump in his throat. "Are you staying?"

"Yes," I practically shout through my laugh. "I mean, if you'll have me. I want to stay, I want to do Doctors Without Borders, and most importantly, I want to be with you."

Andrew smiles at me for the first time since we saw each other this morning. I shriek as he lifts me off the ground and spins me. We both laugh, and my entire body fills with relief. Andrew sets me down and cups my cheek in his hand. Andrew's lips press into mine, and I stand on my tippy toes to reach him better. Andrew has never kissed me like this before, and I can picture small pieces of my heart being put back into place to create one whole heart. And it's not because Andrew completes me because he doesn't. I complete me, and I choose Andrew.

I pull away and hold Andrew's face in mine. "You've said so little." I grin. "Will you have me?"

Andrew sits down in the chair and pulls me on his lap. "I know I like to remind you that I'm so much older than you." Andrew kisses my chin. "But it turns out, you're the wise one in the relationship."

Andrew pulls my head to his chest, and there is so much comfort hearing his heart against my ear. "I'm happy you're here for you. I wouldn't have wanted it any other way."

"Yeah?" I look up at him.

"Yeah." Andrew kisses the top of my head. "I love you, Kate Malone."

*****

My eyes darts open the next morning the same time as the sun, which is early. The hours of light continue to get longer here, and my heart feels too full to waste it on sleeping today. But Andrew doesn't have the same idea. We both lie on our sides, facing each other, his eyes closed. I resist the urge to touch him because I want to watch him sleep a while longer.

Andrew is the only person I know who sleeps with a smile, but both corners of his mouth are turned up, and whatever he's thinking must be peaceful. His top lip meets in the center in a perfect heart, and his lips hold so much truth and beauty. His eyes though are what capture me the most. His eyelashes droopily hang over his eyes and sway with the small breeze coming from outside. If I ever want to know how Andrew feels, I only have to look in his eyes.

"Are you watching me sleep, Kate?" Andrew asks without opening his eyes.

I laugh and fill his face with kisses. "Sorry, I like looking at you."

Andrew slowly opens his eyes and stretches his arms above his head. "I need to get to the hospital, but I texted Noor last night, and tonight, we celebrate."

That evening, Maria comes to my bungalow to get ready, as we're going to one of the bars in the village to dance. I once again borrow Maria's gold belt and wear it over my black dress. We play music and stand in my bathroom, both of us putting on makeup.

"I'm still pinching myself that you'll be here for the next two years," Maria says as she sways her hips into mine.

"It all happened fast, but I'm pinching myself too."

I am exactly twenty-four years old when I realized that home isn't necessarily a location; it's who you're with, and right now, Tanzania is home.

Maria smacks her lips together, and I follow her out of the bathroom. "When I saw Andrew at the hospital today, he looked human again. I don't know why I didn't see it before, but you two have so much in common."

We walk out the door over to Maria and Noor's, where the men are having a drink. "You know, Maria, I think I underestimated how sensitive Andrew is. He's all tall and brainy and masculine, and I'm realizing he wears his emotions on his sleeve."

Maria loops her arm in mine and smiles. "That's what I've been trying to tell you."

This is my first evening out dancing in the village. Besides having food with Andrew once at one of the bars, this is the first time I'm seeing the night scene. Andrew holds my hand in his and doesn't let go, even when he orders us drinks from the bar. I look around and notice the stares but try to focus my energy on Andrew.

Andrew leans in and kisses my cheek. "Not to talk work with you, but I submitted the paperwork today for Doctors Without Borders. Hopefully, everything happens quickly so you can start earning money."

I squeeze Andrew's hand and decide not to tell him that my dad has been depositing money into my checking account weekly for all living expenses until the income comes in.

Andrew takes my hand and leads me to the dance floor, where Noor and Maria are already dancing. I again look around, and so many eyes are on us. Andrew pulls me in and takes my hand.

"Remember, Kate. It's not always going to be easy, but as long as we purposely choose each other, every single day, we can navigate anything."

I give Andrew a reassuring smile because I know he's right. Other people's problems aren't my problems.

"I love you, Kate." Andrew kisses me, and my entire body warms.

The song switches, and Maria screams out. The song Maria Salome blares through the speakers. I grab her hand and laugh, as she has made me listen to this song no less than one thousand times. The four of us join hands and sway to the music, and I'm sure this is now my favorite night in Tanzania.

EPILOGUE

ONE YEAR LATER

Maria and Noor are expecting a child, and it's due in February. I love being near her every step of the way and getting to lead her care with Andrew by my side. I can't wait to meet their child. Maria already calls me *Shangazi* Kate, which means Aunt Kate. I like the ring to it.

My parents visited for two full weeks in August. They stayed in my old bungalow because I decided to move in with Andrew. Yes, his bungalow was bigger, and yes, as the staff at the hospital had ramped up so had the need for empty bungalows. But the truth is, I moved in with Andrew because I wanted to. We spent every night together anyway, and I was proud of all we've done to make it a home.

My parents' visit went better than I expected. My dad had officially replaced me and only had eyes for Andrew, which I love. He spent nearly every moment of his time in the village at the hospital with Andrew, seeing patients and learning how things work. My dad had even held some lectures back in Minneapolis about the village hospital, which helped tremendously with additional fundraising. When my dad retires in a few years, he wants to spend a couple of months in the village annually helping out. I had to fight Andrew for time with my dad because they spent many evenings at a bar, talking about the hospital. My dad never called Andrew by name the entire time he was here; he only called him son.

My mom was the one who surprised me the most during their visit. We talked and texted almost daily when she was back home, and although I knew she'd like to see me more, she realized how happy I was here. She actually made an effort to get to know Andrew better, and my mom isn't one who readily admits when she's wrong, but I could tell she really liked him, and more than anything, she knew how happy I was. She also seemed interested in volunteering at the hospital after retirement. I don't know what the long-term vision is, but I know a cardiologist is a unique skillset that the hospital would value.

My parents bought me a plane ticket home for Christmas, and it will be my first time coming home since I arrived here nearly a year and a half ago. Andrew wishes he could come with me, but I'd be gone for two weeks, and it was too hard for him to get away that long. Additionally, his visa paperwork to travel to the States most likely won't be completed in time. I'm actually looking forward to a white Christmas and getting to spend it with my parents and relatives.

I only have a year left on my contract with Doctors Without Borders, but I already know what it meant when I signed the contract with them last October; my home is where Andrew is. So whether it means I should renew a contract with them or become an unpaid volunteer at the hospital once again, I'm not stressing about it. Andrew is my present and future, and we'll make decisions on where to live together.

Fatima stops and visits me at least two times every week. I love seeing her, and my mind is always busy thinking of ways to get her out of her current situation. There may be nothing I'll ever be able to do, but I'll be a friendly face whenever she needs one and support her in any way I can. Andrew has been giving her a birth control shot too. Hopefully, we can at least prevent her becoming pregnant again, or at least until she wants to, hopefully, from a husband whom she loves.

One of my biggest worries about deciding to stay in Tanzania and the village was that my life would feel small. Yet I managed to see more of the world than I ever did before. Last Christmas, Andrew brought me to London for a few days as he knew I was missing my family. I was able to meet many of his university friends and experience a slice of Europe for the first time.

Now we're in Paris for the week. Andrew is attending a medical conference, and I didn't hesitate when he asked me to come with him. It's a warm day in Paris, and the breeze blows my hair into my face, and I grab a rubber band and tie it back. Andrew takes me to one of his favorite cafés on Champs-Elysees, and I'm sure I've never had a better glass of wine. I pull my lips into my mouth to savor the flavor and moan.

Andrew crosses his leg and laughs. "It's good, isn't it?"

I close my eyes and look up. "It's the best."

A server comes to our table, and Andrew orders something in French. I love hearing the beautiful language roll off his tongue so effortlessly. People walk by us in a hurry; no one is taking the time to look at us. We don't look any differently from the many couples in Paris, and it feels nice to blend in for once.

Paris is as beautiful as I always imagined it would be—the cobblestone streets and the archways with the Eiffel tower that watches over the city. Everything is so diverse, and people seem to come from every country and all walks of life. Maybe when Andrew attends a seminar tomorrow, I'll sit at a café and watch people all day long.

Andrew pulls out his phone. "Kate, we don't have anywhere to be until the dinner at seven, so I'm thinking we should play tourists for the day."

I pop a piece of cheese in my mouth and smile. "That sounds great. I have a list of places I want to see this week before we go home."

Andrew reaches across the table and takes my hand. "I figured you would."

The sun beats down on us, and I close my eyes and lean back in my chair. I think to myself that today is another perfect day. I've been lucky to have many of them in the last year. I look down at the engagement ring on my finger. Andrew knows me well and know I wouldn't want a diamond, especially in my profession. Instead, he got me a thick white-gold band, and the inside is engraved with the words *I choose you, every day.*

I smile as I think of Andrew proposing. He did it in the most perfect way, in our backyard, with a fire and the stars over our heads. That backyard is a sacred place for us, and every time I look at the fire, I'm sure I can hear Bupe's happy voice, welcoming me home. We don't know when we'll get married, but I'm in no rush. Andrew and I belong together.

"Kate, did you hear me?" I jolt up, not realizing how lost in my thoughts I was.

I laugh. "I'm sorry, what did you say?"

Andrew looks at the table, and there are two bottles of Serengeti beer. I nearly snort when I see them and look up at a laughing Andrew.

"I was saying that now that our wine is gone, we should enjoy a Serengeti beer. I couldn't believe they carried it here."

I put my hand over my heart and look at Andrew. "That sounds perfect."

About the Author

Leah Omar was born and raised in Eyota, Minnesota, and as long as she could remember, has been an avid reader and writer. Her debut novel, *A Labor of Love*, lived in her mind for years before she put pen to paper. Leah is a lover of all romance novels but set out to create compelling stories that tackle the complexities of relationships.

Leah has a bachelor's of art in communications and English literature and a master's degree in business administration. She now calls Minneapolis home, which she shares with her husband and two children. In her free time, Leah enjoys traveling the world and learning about different cultures, reading and writing, and spending time with those she loves best.

As a writer, Leah is devoted to giving her readers contemporary love stories that make us remember that we have more similarities than differences, and that love can conquer all. She loves to interact with readers. You can follow her in Instagram and Facebook using the handle Leahomarbooks.

CPSIA information can be obtained
at www.ICGtesting.com
Printed in the USA
LVHW011350040521
686461LV00004B/152